MW00477845

MOOD SWINGS

MOOD SWINGS

A Novel

FRANKIE BARNET

ASTRA HOUSE
NEW YORK

Astra House
A Division of Astra Publishing House
astrahouse.com
Printed in the United States of America

Library of Congress Cataloging-in-Publication Data

Names: Barnet, Frankie, author.
Title: Mood swings : a novel / Frankie Barnet.
Description: First edition. | New York : Astra House, 2024. | Summary: "In a pre-apocalyptic world not unlike our own, a young Instagram poet starts an affair with a California billionaire who's promised a time machine that will make everything normal again—whatever that means"—Provided by publisher.
Identifiers: LCCN 2023043636 (print) | LCCN 2023043637 (ebook) | ISBN 9781662602597 (hardcover) | ISBN 9781662602580 (ebook)
Subjects: LCGFT: Apocalyptic fiction. | Novels.
Classification: LCC PR9199.4.B3667 M66 2024 (print) | LCC PR9199.4.B3667 (ebook) | DDC 813/.6—dc23/eng/20231013
LC record available at https://lccn.loc.gov/2023043636
LC ebook record available at https://lccn.loc.gov/2023043637

First edition
10 9 8 7 6 5 4 3 2 1

Design by Alissa Theodor
The text is set in Sabon MT Std.
The titles are set in Sabon MT Std Semibold.

For Jacob

I am able to take a wire line and go into the air and define the air without stealing from anyone. A line can enclose and define space while letting the air remain air.

—RUTH ASAWA

MOOD SWINGS

CHAPTER ONE

Jenlena Stays Inside

1.

It began with over a hundred rats in one long line on Sainte-Catherine Street in the middle of the afternoon. This was just about a year before the machine.

"Rats," spoke the blond-haired woman on the news. "One of our planet's most resourceful species, rats have traditionally survived in the shadows of our society. But today, along one of the city's busiest streets, they have chosen to make themselves known."

"Look at her," sneered Jenlena's roommate Daphne. "It's like she's getting wet for the rats. She doesn't even try to hide it."

"She's trying to ingratiate herself," Jenlena figured. "She wants to be a rat bride."

Ultimately, such an allegiance would prove to be a miscalculation.

2.

Who could believe the mood swings they'd been having? It was in the way they felt but also people's general demeanor, the nuances in their collective frown lines. It was in rivers and streams too, all water, as well as the moonlight, and animals frothing at the mouth.

They held their feelings in their bodies and when they died, where did the feelings go? They buried one another and flowers sprouted from hopes and petty jealousies. Other times they burned one another in contained fires and their loved ones read poetry. They claimed to see one another in dreams. But that too was, perhaps, just the way they felt. It was a wily adversary, this mood, seared into their skin and the food they ate and the things they were afraid of. *Click to see the CRAZY things Muslims BELIEVE in! What the government doesn't WANT you to know! How this peaceful Native American tribe learned to embrace their SORROW. Arkansas man kills wife and three others, explains, "I just felt like it."*

3.

A month later, nobody was allowed to go outside. Jenlena wasn't staying at her own place then—she stayed over at her not-boyfriend Adam's. They were very happy, at least in the beginning. At least during that first week or so. They had sex and watched television and ate junk food. Sometimes it didn't even seem like he was her not-boyfriend; sometimes it seemed like they were really in love. Once, for example, they stayed up all night laughing, and when the morning came it was like the first time it had ever happened.

Her own roommates had only recently taken in a kitten from a box full of his dead brothers and sisters in the alley. Rolex, they'd called him. Sometimes they threw toy birds, sometimes they dangled a string. Then, the day of the rats, the animal tore up the couch, sprayed all over the wall, and snuck out through the fire escape. No one had seen him since.

Other animals, though. Such robust hostility: wasps targeted small children and the elderly; dogs bit off toes; a woman in

Longueuil had her eyes torn out by a rabbit, the same Holland Lop who'd slept in her bed for three and a half years. A man's parakeet pecked apart his grandson's cheek. It was like one day all the animals just got together and decided. Moths went after hand-me-down sweaters and then fucked in the dry goods, a whole generation of their babies writhing among basmati.

Some reports had it that the Moon Bethlehems were helping the animals. They must have given them certain tactical advice, at the very least turning keys for them and opening doors. How else would the raccoons have gotten inside the power plant and switched off all the lights? They'd stormed supermarkets and pooped in all the water.

One of Adam's classmates disappeared on the eve of the first day of the siege, leaving only a cryptic email to the listserv: *To whom it may concern: I've fallen in love. I know you won't approve but I can't help it anymore and he says if he cloaks me in his scent I'll be protected.*

And though the animals' methods were a bit extreme, most people Adam and Jenlena's age were on their side. You couldn't not be; so many of their earliest memories were of an animal's smell and texture. One species or another had chosen their lap to sit in, out of all the other laps available at a party. It was the beloved family chinchilla who first taught them about death. Adam had grown up with animals in the house and knew all the names for their gatherings: a murder, a flock, a shadow. They'd slept in his bed and shared secrets.

Jenlena too; she'd have been an animal if she could. Really, she'd have grown a tail. Adam wouldn't have minded eating from a trough. He'd always found cutlery bourgeois. See? They were not even asking to fly.

4.

They survived on what he had in the pantry: peanut butter, instant ramen, graham crackers, and marshmallows, all in various combinations. Adam did French lessons on his phone in the mornings, and in the afternoons read literary theory for his master's degree. This was how they knew each other: he was the TA for one of her classes at school.

Jenlena felt certain she'd always remember the moment she first saw him. "Adam, from England," was how Professor Hudson had introduced him to the class, and he'd stood up in his denim shirt with the top three buttons undone. He was studying in Canada because he was obsessed with America, but America was too frightening, so Quebec would have to be the compromise.

Everyone loved him. You could feel it in the room when he gave his minilecture using examples from *The Office*. Everybody laughed and laughed. They would have laughed at anything, probably; it was simply a pleasure to make noises in his presence. "It might not make sense to you at first," he said of postmodernism, "but just think about it. Be open-minded. Then one day you'll be sitting on a bus and it's like a light bulb goes off. It'll all click into place. You'll be experts at it then. I'll be out of a stipend."

Everyone loved him, but it was Jenlena who ran into him one night at a loft party on Beaubien. She was the one who got to talk to him alone in a dark corner. "Jim Halpert is a fucking loser!" he slurred. "An allegory for the mediocrity of the American white man. No wonder we're in the shape we're in now, when he was a leading man of the aughts." He slid his hand down the small of her back like he could have been using her for balance.

Jenlena agreed with him but said the real problem with their society was that more people knew Hunter Biden's rising sign than who the mayor of their own city was.

He shrugged. "Well, it's different here when you're Anglo. I reckon it's better for everyone if we're not really a part of things."

She supposed she saw his point. "Sun in Aquarius, Moon in Capricorn, Scorpio rising. Year of the rooster, five foot eight." Being pithy about American politics was the love language of their generation. She had wanted to sleep with a professor all her life, but most grown men were too frightening, so a TA would have to be the compromise.

The morning after, he'd pulled out a stack of exams from his backpack and started to grade. "You don't mind, do you? I'm right swamped."

Then, when hers appeared at the top of the pile, he'd asked, "What did you mean here? Your handwriting's so messy."

"That's Edward *Said*," she said, pronouncing it with much sophistication.

In time she would have done anything. A usual story. He was four years older than she was and she liked the way he talked about "the telly." A person has to like some things, she figured; they've got to give it a shot. She would have jumped off a bridge, shaved off her pubes, grown out her pubes, let him into her asshole. He said it "grossed him out."

What Adam liked was to come inside what he called her "wet hot tectonic pussy." She had an app on her phone to tell her when it was safe to tell him yes or the five days a month it became necessary to politely redirect him to her mouth.

Her own desire was somewhat less reliable. "What do you want?" he'd ask in the heat of the moment.

"You," she'd say.

"Your hard cock," she'd say.

But that wasn't it, not exactly.

Her orgasm could be fickle, hidden among layers of childhood memories, scenes from Hollywood movies, and tips she'd heard on podcasts. Adam grew frustrated when a trick he used Wednesday did not work again on Saturday. "It always works on other girls," he said. And now his wrist was sore.

5.

Adam wanted to finish his master's degree, then get a PhD, followed by a postdoc position, a full-time teaching job, and finally tenure. It was not so complicated when you laid out all the steps like that, and he always got his assignments in on time. He also had a brother who had died of brain cancer when Adam was only fifteen, and this, he was convinced, granted him a certain immunity when it came to life's difficulties. So far, he'd never received lower than an A- in school and was rarely rebuked by the girls he wanted to sleep with.

He had a trendy bowl cut and wore black pants that made his skinny legs look like a cartoon drawing. His skin was so pale that sometimes when he was about to come, Jenlena could see the blue blood rushing down his body. She'd reach up and chase it with her fingertips.

She wasn't foreign, just named after three dead grandmothers at the same time, a mélange of cancers and bad luck. Mostly, she liked to write poems in a coil notebook that had daisies on the cover. Every so often, she typed them up to share on Instagram. During the siege, her feed was made up mostly of the people she went to university with, those who loved the animals so much more than anyone else. They posted selfies crying about it and shared infographics: 5 *Signs Your Dog Was Faking It When You Came Home from Work.*

Sometimes, someone conservative from her high school popped up, those who respected the government because of how the animals were breaking into people's homes. "*They're going to undermine our whole infrastructure!*" Jenlena read aloud to Adam for a laugh.

"No!" he said. "*Really?*" He leaned over to see for himself, regarding the post as if it were a cultural artifact.

They were in his bed, both dressed in his clothes, but this, the grotesque horror of other people, brought them even closer. "Boys with that haircut always go on like that," Adam said. "I reckon they get the idea from that program about Vikings."

She asked him if he thought there would ever be an all-out war. By now, already, the animals had lasted longer than anyone had expected. "Would you fight?"

Adam said he was more inclined to fight *with* the animals because they saw more eye to eye on environmental issues. The government, on the other hand, would poison anyone as long as it came with a profit.

"No," Jenlena meant. "If they made you."

"Then they'd make you too," he said.

She said no because she was a girl.

"Doesn't matter." He shook his head with his lips tight. "Not in this day and age. Girls are the same as boys now."

"Then I'd run away," she said. "That'd be exciting. Go to an island somewhere. Swim if I had to, live out the rest of my life wearing really comfy clothes with nothing in particular ever happening again."

The one story she was proud of was that as a kid she'd been very good at swimming. "I passed six levels in a single summer," she'd told him. "It set a record at the pool. There was me, this tiny little girl, swimming with all the teenagers." She said she could still remember the way the boys' chiseled arms had splashed through the water. "No one has ever been as big to me as the boys from high school when I was small," she said, then added wistfully, "I wonder what they're doing now, if they ever think about swimming too."

Gun to his head, if there was one thing wrong with Jenlena, it was that she could be a little insecure. She was always asking questions about her weight and how her body compared to the women on the reality TV shows where British people had sex with each other on an island. "They don't have pretty faces, though," he'd say.

Jenlena, he thought, looked like a girl from a movie who you don't necessarily notice at first. She was petite in both mind and body, but he was often impressed by her sexual enthusiasm. Even if he didn't always quite believe her, he knew that in this day and age it was considered violence to not take people at their word when it came to sexual matters.

6.

Historically, Jenlena had always been horny for boys. Thin boys, tall ones, but also thick boys with strong arms and shoulders. She liked funny boys. Boys from upstate New York, the Maritimes, and Nelson, B.C. Boys with mustaches or lip rings. Boys who had totally given up: once, a group of boys who identified as Moon Bethlehems had stood up at the front of the lecture hall in the middle of class and ripped through their textbooks page by page, because how could knowledge be meaningful when all it had ever done was get them to this point in history? The rest of the class watched until it bored them, scrolled through their phones. Jenlena swiped through more and more boys. They were endlessly renewable, like the sun.

She loved the way a boy's posture shifted when he tried to get you into bed. There was a gentleness there. Even if it was put on and an element of his coercion, no internet think piece could keep her from loving the softness in their faces and the way their voices changed when they'd chosen you. She'd think, *None of your friends ever get to see you like this.*

Sex was a miracle. For one moment she became the most important person in the world to one other person who was also the most important person to her. She was addicted to believing this. Even with Adam, who never made her come a single time. She would only be twenty-one during the siege once, and she wasn't interested in wasting the whole time contemplating the deluge of mediocrity that surrounded nearly everything she had ever known, at least when she could help it. "Your hard cock," she'd say. "Baby."

Sometimes she thought of his dead brother while he was inside her, the photograph Adam had shown her from their yearbook where the boy's bald head was glowing like a moon. Jenlena hadn't known many people who died and so the concept fascinated her. Where did they go? She thought that the worst part about being dead was that you would never again be three drinks deep listening to a song you really liked. Apart from that, it did not seem unreasonable.

7.

The wolves did it because their homeland had been plowed and subdivided into gated communities, places called Meadowbrook, Ocean Terrace, River Blossom. The cats did it because they were tired of all the complaining. The dogs felt taken advantage of. For centuries, the horses' bodies had been used for violence; then you had canaries who had sacrificed their bodies—for what? The rabbits did it in solidarity with the polar bears. The cows did it because how else were they supposed to look their children in the face? White mice across the Ivy Leagues played dead en masse, sabotaging clinical trials. The toads did it because too many of them had been born with too many eyes. The hyenas did it because sometimes there was nothing left to joke about.

After a couple of weeks, Adam stopped sleeping. Staying up in the light made him feel like a squirrel; staying up in the dark made him feel like a rat. He felt there was much to learn from each species, though he could never quite articulate what these lessons might be exactly.

Everything Jenlena did bothered him. He despised the way she sat hunched over, scrolling through her phone with her eyes glazed. He hated how she was so sad all the time. It wasn't like *her* brother had died. Sometimes she'd try to coax his sympathies with how her father had run away when she was a baby, but it wasn't the same because she'd hardly even known him. It wasn't like they'd ever done things together (played Lego, for example), and she hadn't had to watch the whole thing happen, slowly at first, then very quickly, when he was only in the tenth grade. Plus, he knew she had a new father, a man in Calgary who worked in the oil industry and paid for everything she did.

She often talked with her mouth open and had no ambitions. She said that when she graduated she would "just probably well like, I dunno." Twice in the last year she had sold her panties on the internet to buy new panties designed, allegedly, by Rihanna. Her roommate Daphne was dating a canceled man. They were not serious people.

But worse was when Jenlena did try, when she said things like, "Yeah, actually, I've been googling grad schools in the States," which insulted him because he was in grad school and worked very hard, whereas her poetry mostly went like this:

<u>*once i stuck a beer-soaked tampon up my pussy*</u>
because i wanted to get fucked up
and tell you everything I was feeling
because ever since we fucked
at the biodome i've been so confused
you came looking at the monkeys and i pretended
to come looking for the sloth
but never saw it and never came
didn't a girl die somewhere in america
from sticking a beer-soaked tampon up her pussy?

sometimes i stand in the corner of a party
wondering, am i drunk yet?
am i drunk now?
then the next thing i know i'm passed out on the floor

if i died, would you come to my funeral?
and be like, yeah i fucked that dead girl
how sexy you would be
awash in that weird glow that surrounds us all
when we know someone who has died.

8.

That winter was short but fierce, which seemed to represent many things to many different people. They may all have been living in the same weather, but were nonetheless free to interpret it in their own unique ways. When the siege first began, Jenlena had chapped lips and chilblains on her toes. Now the sun was out and the snow was melting. The animals had lasted longer than anyone could have imagined. It wasn't healthy to be kept inside like this. Nobody could believe the government had so little power. Where had all their tax dollars gone?

Though the animals may also have been to blame. It was ill-advised to be paternalistic about these things, Jenlena thought, because the animals had agency too. They weren't all puppies and butterflies, for example. Plus, it was getting boring, staying inside, which more and more people felt emboldened to say out loud.

Even people Jenlena went to university with had begun to concede this. They shared new kinds of articles: a chimpanzee in Japan who ripped off a little girl's face, and two dolphins in Spain who raped a woman. The Moon Bethlehems, too, were to blame. A new report out of Ireland claimed that a faction had filled their pockets with ground beef and sacrificed themselves to the country's last Bengal tiger in solidarity. People like that, it was said in op-ed after op-ed, only fueled the flames. Why not grow up and get a job?

Adam and Jenlena began to fight over small things. He wasn't sleeping and she slept all the time. She knew he stayed up, watching her. He said he could see her pupils move under her eyelids and he always wanted to know what she was dreaming about. She found herself unwilling to tell him.

"Really?" he pressed. "What's the big deal?"

"It's my *one* place," she said, then locked herself in the bathroom for the next three hours, scrolling, texting, scrolling. She took pictures of herself until her eyes ached and her wrists began to spasm, and then she stretched out her fingers wide and made fists over and over again, the one useful thing she remembered from gym class. Taught as a warm-up stretch for volleyball, now it was the only way she knew how to help her body get along better with her phone.

The boy from her high school with the Viking haircut had posted a video of how he drowned mice caught in his live traps, dropping one animal into a blue plastic bucket at a time. They clasped on to the lifeless bodies of those who came before them until they too succumbed to the water. Jenlena remembered the time she'd given him a hand job under a tree in the cemetery by school and hated herself.

"What are you doing in there?" Adam knocked on the door.

"Nothing," she said. It was literally true.

Other people were lonely: *Is anyone up? I will come to you and pay cash. Just cuddles if you want. Very discreet.*

"What's wrong?"

"I don't know."

She knew he knew how often she pretended during sex, and he knew she knew he knew, so it became just a question of how deep they were willing to let it go.

9.

But sometimes, still, it seemed like they were really in love. On her birthday, he managed a big surprise, lighting a match at midnight and telling her to make a wish. She closed her eyes. "You're going swimming," he told her.

"What?"

"Yes, I've arranged everything. We'll leave in a few hours when it's safe. I've found a pool and you'll have it all to yourself. Not far from here."

It was clear she was excited. Little things: she bobbed from side to side when she brushed her teeth and she took extra care washing her face. "I wonder if I'll remember," she said, then started to act out all the strokes with her arms: front crawl, back crawl, butterfly.

"I'm sure it'll be like riding a bike," he said. She kissed him on the tip of his nose.

The pool was in the basement of a big brick building they'd passed a hundred times, back in their lives before the animals took over the city. They waited until three in the morning. It was so strange for both of them to see the streets empty like that, the exact same places where they had shopped for groceries and been high on drugs and even fucked once or twice in the vestibules. Now they could hear their own footsteps. "Relax," Adam said. "We're almost there. Besides, they're only animals, remember?"

"I just don't understand what they want," Jenlena replied.

"Respect," he answered.

Adam performed a special knock on the wide iron door and a stout man in cargo pants led them inside. It smelled like so many birthday parties. Jenlena stripped down to her bra and panties and approached the pool, shivering with excitement. She had always loved the idea of her body under water.

Adam stayed on the deck.

"You could get in too," the man told him in a heavy accent as he settled into a torn lawn chair. "It's yours for the hour. Pretend I'm not here."

But Adam had never been much of a swimmer. Besides, he enjoyed watching Jenlena move like that, loose and unselfconscious, so unlike sex he almost couldn't recognize her. She was like an animal, like deep down they were all the same.

"Wild about these critters," the man said, drinking from a thermos the length of his forearm.

Adam nodded.

"I've seen it coming since my ex—old lady's Yorkie used to shit on my pillow. You'd think with such strange ideas about what belongs to them they woulda tried harder to develop thumbs." The man talked as if he were chewing. "But nobody ever wants to listen to ol' Ri*chahr*."

Once the hour was up, Jenlena dried off and they were on their way. She grabbed Adam's hand and said that she could not have imagined turning twenty-two with anyone else. He squeezed her palm and kissed her forehead.

It was just after four and the sun had begun to rise at the end of the long avenue. As the darkness softened, Adam said he couldn't believe that morning was happening so early. It must have been later in the year than he'd thought.

"I always feel that way about my birthday," Jenlena said.

The animal first began as a shadow. A flicker out of the corners of their eyes. Just a trick of the light because they were so close to home, it couldn't be. Adam jumped; Jenlena held her breath. The creature revealed itself from beneath the grocer's fruit stand and stopped them in front of the pharmacy.

Adam knew what to do: tilt his head and give that look he'd been practicing so it'd know they weren't like other humans. "We'll be fine," Adam whispered over and over. "Don't worry, we'll be fine."

Jenlena relaxed. "Oh, he's a little one. Look, I think he's just a baby really."

The animal came closer.

"We're almost home." Adam's voice trembled as he spoke to it. "Not far. Right over there, just needed some air."

"We can help you," Jenlena added. "Come over for a bath and a warm meal, whatever you want."

The animal said nothing. Patches of fur were missing around its eyes, and its ribs were showing. It sniffed up Jenlena's skirt, then stood on its hind legs and bit a hole in her tights. Jenlena flinched but held her spine straight. She could smell it, even over the chlorine, a rich scent that evoked life and death at the same time.

"Please," Adam tried, but the word was stuck in his throat. The animal turned to regard him, looking up with its beady eyes. "Don't make me," he pleaded. Then the animal lunged forward with its teeth out. Adam took a sharp inhale and kicked it. He kicked it again harder, harder still, and when the animal hit the ground several feet away, it wasn't moving.

"Run!" Adam grabbed Jenlena and pulled her along with him. They made it home and he locked the door behind them.

For the rest of the day they kept to themselves. Adam watched Moon Bethlehem videos on his phone, Jenlena stayed in the bathroom.

"What?" he finally asked when she was still pouting as the evening settled in around them. "I did it for you. I had to or it would have hurt you."

Her eyes were red. "No." She didn't feel like talking. "It's only from the pool."

10.

Two days later, the animals were dead. The California billionaire Roderick Maeve had funded the manufacture of a sonic signal that killed them all. Every last one. Adam and Jenlena watched from the window. It was a sound only animals could hear, so piercing it ruptured their eardrums and flooded their lungs. Birds fell from the sky and mice died in the walls. They rotted for weeks but at least the people did not need to be afraid anymore.

The government used snowplows to gather the bodies and then dumped them in a big pit north of the overpass, where the old bus depot had been. Jenlena went with Daphne and her canceled boyfriend Jordan to watch. They had candles and a pixelated photograph of their cat Rolex taped to a piece of cardboard and they stood in the thick crowd of other people who white-knuckled their own photographs of animals: a rat named Pickle, a dog named Boo, a ferret named Noam Chomsky.

In the following days, the government sent patrols all across the city. They went to people's houses, confirming that no animals had been left alive inside. The waste agents wore olive-green uniforms and parked at the curb in front of Adam's building with a truck that had legs sticking out the back, the paws of a big white dog. "All dead in here?" they asked.

"Yes, all dead."

"And any flesh you need taken care of?"

"No, sir. No flesh."

Jenlena was there picking up some books for school, and asked Adam if he'd like to take a walk with her. "Daphne and Jordan are checking out the grocery stores, you know, while supplies last."

But he was too busy reading something on his phone, so she went alone and stopped in at the corner store down the block. All that was left on the shelves was a pepperoni stick for ten dollars. She bought it with some money her mom had sent for her birthday and ate the dense meat unceremoniously on her way back to Adam's. It was spring, there was no denying it now. A young woman she knew vaguely from campus was plastering a lamppost with posters of her dead dog. "Stolen by corporate America," it said above the mastiff's portrait in big black letters. "Reward: common decency."

"I can't kiss you while you smell like that," Adam said when she got back. "It's safe for you to go home now anyways."

They had sex one last time and she was so fixated on dislodging a piece of meat from between her back teeth that she forgot to tell him no, no you cannot come inside me. It's said that the brain unraveled is about twenty feet long, or is that the large intestines? It would not have surprised her to one day turn down a wrong corner while exploring her feelings and never find her way back.

"Oh, my god," he squealed like a pig.

11.

There were a million ways to start something. Starting was the best part. There were more than a thousand kits to help you, a thousand symbols representing *etc.*, and all the opinions were each more neon than the next. Jenlena had had an opinion once, about animals. It lasted an entire menstrual cycle. Other thoughts and feelings too—they came and went, postured and shrunk. Some she was still quite fond of; for example, the six o'clock light in winter, like a shade of blue only a computer could have come up with. Yesterday she thought she saw a bird pierce right through it, but no, all the birds were gone. Remember how they moved through the air as if it were slick. Big groups of them in unison like that, not an individual among them.

The middle was difficult, tedious and excruciating. They tore out their hair and called each other names. *Tomorrow!* they swore. *It'll all get better, just you wait until tomorrow.*

Endings seemed to come without consent, but perhaps had instead been embarked upon before one could even remember.

Something sparked without thinking, then chiseled away communally with neighbors and parents and the British people on TV and cows looking their children in the face.

12.

Once upon a time, she wrote in a coiled notebook with daisies on the cover, *there was a modern girl who lived in filth and her name was me. One year ago we couldn't leave our houses, then all the animals died. Now I'm having sex with a California billionaire but I guess that's just what your twenties are for.*

CHAPTER TWO

Jenlena, *d'habitude*

1.

She would like to state for the record that she was not blood-related to the oil and petroleum industry. In fact, Jenlena was never even supposed to be Albertan. Her mother met her *real* father on the set of a movie made in British Columbia that went straight to video, the only role she'd landed in her whole four years of trying to make it as an actress in the burgeoning Vancouver movie scene, which locals were desperate to term "Hollywood North."

Her mother was the female lead, playing a woman who drove through the Rockies in an old convertible to meet her widowed lover in the Prairies. Her biological father had been the animal trainer, handling rattlesnakes and chipmunks he captured illegally and kept in his apartment. This was his thing, trying to make a living selling animals in the movie business. For their first date, he took her mother to an IGA. They walked up and down the aisles, talking about what products they knew and which ones they wanted to try. Stores to him were like museums. After they left he pulled all kinds of candy from his pockets. It was September 10, 2001. The next day they woke up in his twin bed in a rancid basement suite and the new world was all around them.

Together her parents were poor but happy. Picture her mother and father like children, rolling around on the bed then onto the floor, this ache between them that condenses into liquid, squirts from dad to mom, and begins to form vertebrae, fingernails.

Is it normal for a girl to visualize her own conception?

Her parents had a real love story, the kind that is only possible when you don't really know each other and you're twenty-one in a strange city with dreams so big they physically hurt. He turns your head into fireworks when you come, then leaves you with his baby and his absence fills in the rest.

All fantasies were laced with sex. Even when she was a child and had wanted to marry the dog next door, she'd fantasized about sleeping next to him in a red bed. Dogs were better than boys, she thought. They were soft and it tickled when they licked you. At times she was so ecstatic to be alive she thought she'd burst. But later, within the same week or even minute, it felt cruel that a girl named Jenlena was ever made. A sick joke to make other people feel better about their lives.

2.

They lived on the top floor of a three-story white brick building in Mile End, a fashionable neighborhood just north of the mountain. Inside, they had mostly ordinary things: candles and their dirty underwear in strange places. A dog-eared Sally Rooney novel and a hundred doodles of stick-and-poke tattoos they were thinking of giving and receiving. Daphne had been out of school for a year and Jordan had never gone, but that spring after the animals, Jenlena still had a handful of papers to finish. She read a lot of summaries online and wrote poems like:

<u>to the boy who took me swimming on my birthday</u>
i still don't get most lit.
theory maybe
all i ever really learned
are your favorite wars
to talk about when you're drunk
iraq and vietnam
sometimes it's like you
really believe in america
so much it killed you
and this is some just dream life
where nothing's
really real
and nothing
really touches
when we
touch.

me, version of heaven
ha!

Daphne was tall and had dark hair she bleached blond. Jenlena was shorter, with a curvier frame, and she usually kept her uncolored brown hair in a topknot. This too could have been their feelings.

More specifically, Jenlena was the kind of pretty who'd make another girl feel like they could be pretty too because she was laid-back and made it look so easy, whereas Daphne was the kind of pretty that made you feel like you'd never be pretty because her bone structure had such artfulness to it, a genetic grace. She had long legs almost entirely without cellulite, save for a couple hours in the mid to late afternoon when the light was just so, though

Jenlena knew for a fact that even this, from certain angles, was worth over a hundred likes on Instagram. It was a true story. Similar to Daphne's mustache, which appeared at twilight and glittered like gold. But it was normal to mythologize your best friend. Sometimes, mythology was all they had.

They knew each other from school, where they first met in a class called Cults and Religious Controversies, held in the basement of an old mall the university had converted into lecture halls. It was Daphne's second year and Jenlena's first, so although they'd seen each other around the English department, they weren't personally acquainted. But in Cults, Tuesdays and Thursdays from 1:15 to 3, they bonded over a fascination with their professor, a woman who kept her silver hair in two French braids and wore a uniform of long skirts and crocheted vests. Dr. Sabina, as she preferred to be called, didn't even like to use the term *cult*, and told everyone on the first day that the department had named the course for her just to attract students.

The politically correct term was *New Religious Movements*, and the groups weren't anything to be afraid of. No more so than the old, decrepit religions most people took for granted. "I think of them like baby religions," Dr. Sabina said. "They're cute, not quite sure of themselves. They do a lot of stumbling around and sometimes take things too far."

"No late papers, no plagiarism, no Kool-Aid jokes" were her ground rules, her philosophy being that there was something to be respected about a person who had turned their back on society in search of a new way of life. "Whereas most people I know my age just watch television," she said. "There's no greater threat to our culture than people who've truly found a way around it."

By the grace of something, Daphne and Jenlena were seated beside each other in the sprawling lecture hall. A look of unadulterated thrill passed over both their faces as the professor described her close ties to one of the biggest Moon Bethlehem factions in the city. She knew all the big names: Rael, J.Z. Knight, Keith Raniere. She'd even had lunch with Tom Cruise, though he wasn't very interesting to her. "Really," she said of Scientology, "if I'm going to devote my studies to an NRM, it has to have some heart."

It may have been the first time in history that a tall girl and a short girl had bonded so quickly. All of Jenlena's other friends were from the dorms and they were all within her milieu, give or take an inch or two. She knew what they were saying behind her back: "What does she think she's doing with that tall girl?" "So she thinks she can just get along with tall girls all of a sudden?" "They'll never be able to wear the same clothes."

But she didn't care. Daphne and Jenlena had plans to write a movie together, they had plans to produce a two-person show, they had plans to start a band, they had plans to run away and live in a caravan, they had plans to buy male and female Angora rabbits and populate the prairies with their offspring, they were really very close to self-publishing a chapbook of poetry.

That semester a man who called himself a Hedo-Buddhist came to the lecture hall to talk about what reincarnation had come to mean in a world with a growing number of right-wing authoritarian governments. Fascism was hot that semester. Everyone was talking about it, telling each other what to think.

"You have to seriously consider that you might not want to be human in the next life," he said. "We've always believed that to have a human body is the ultimate privilege, but with the current political climate, we're starting to pursue other options, and behaving in this life accordingly."

What if in our past lives, Jenlena wrote to Daphne on a sheet of paper torn from her notebook, *you were the short one and I was the tall one?*

No, Daphne wrote back in her unwieldy cursive. *We were probably just normal, perfectly happy.*

3.

Or maybe the main difference between them was that Daphne believed in excelling at all costs. To do well had, for her, always been a matter of efficiency. At school she won prizes and used all kinds of big words, every last one pronounced correctly. She even got a full-time job after graduation, practically unheard of with an English degree. The office was on Kahnawake, a First Nations reserve across the river. The job was writing clickbait for online gambling websites, mostly made-up stories about ordinary people whose whole lives changed after winning $25,000. It had dental but not vision, which wasn't bad.

Jenlena believed in mediocrity. Yes, it was a choice, but it also came naturally to her and it felt good. Every day an Instagram post told her to think more highly of herself, but the idea was so often repugnant, perhaps because it was a recurring theme of her mother's pedantic lectures growing up.

"Serious people focus on the positive," her mother liked to say. "When you have better things to do, you don't zone in on all your little flaws. Look at Christopher. He's nothing special. He doesn't know all the cool bands or read books or have a great body, but do you know how much money he makes? When you put people at ease, they'll want to give you business opportunities."

"Sure," Jenlena had probably responded. "Whatever."

"You know one day the wind will blow and your face'll be stuck like that."

Hygge, a word she learned from Daphne. Also: *hegemony*, and *la santé mentale*, which was a French term for mental health, the feelings they all lived inside of but were also their greatest adversary. Much like their bodies, really, which gave them touch, taste, et cetera, but inside that same cocoon was where they would die.

Yes, her life was quiet but this was by design, monastically arranged. She owned two pairs of pants, both cut high in the waist and cuffed three times over at the hem, five or so shirts depending on what she spilled on them. She'd had the same toothbrush for over a year and a half and sometimes even reused floss—you just rinsed it off and laid it out on the sink for tomorrow.

For Jenlena, life, before the siege at least, didn't make any sense. It was like anal sex. You had to really relax to enjoy it, but if you relaxed too much, then your bowels released all over the bed. This had literally happened to a friend of hers, and no, the guy never called her back. Every rule that ever existed had an evil stepsister that told you to do the opposite. Her grandmother Jennifer ran marathons and still got cancer of the gut, her grandmother Eileen ate a vegetarian diet and still got cancer of the brain, her grandmother Anna smoked a pack a day and still got run over by a drunk truck driver delivering cereal. So it made sense, didn't it, to do absolutely nothing. You could not fail. Jenlena, by age twenty-one and some change, had finally cracked the code. Hallelujah!

Which isn't to say that she didn't have, despite her mousy demeanor, her own unique brand of exceptionalism. After all, were not mice, despite their economy, daring creatures? They took what was not theirs, they ventured into foreign habitats and procreated so brazenly it could only be taken as an affirmation of the future.

By seemingly making no choices, she was clearing the path for one big choice down the line, when opportunity would allow for a great shift in circumstance that would change her life forever. The only reasonable goal in the life of any modern girl was to be prepared to leave at a moment's notice. To be swept off one's feet, exhilarated, plucked from her measly surroundings. Jenlena was ready and willing.

In contrast was her mother, a woman who had wanted many things earnestly in her youth: beauty, glamour, fame, love, and had followed each desire as it led her down an ever-narrowing tunnel until her only way out had been to marry Christopher, a dull fat man who once ordered a steak tartare well-done.

4.

Every last person is either more or less beautiful than their mother. You either represent the ascendency of your familial lines or the decline. These were her earliest memories: on the kitchen floor, poring over her mother's headshots. Their whole lives hung in the balance of details: a little to the left here, her chin tilted there, whether her hair was pulled back or parted down the center. Then, when Jenlena was five, a man pulled over his rental car outside of the restaurant where Tina waited tables. He wanted to know how to get downtown and then he wanted to know if he could have her phone number and then he wanted to know if he could kiss her. Christopher was twelve years her mother's senior and had a good job in the oil industry, facilitating the extraction of fossil fuels from deep inside the earth. At dinner that night, he told Tina that she had the most beautiful wrists he'd ever seen. "I'm not the type to talk to women this way," he said bashfully. "It must be a sign from God."

She had a little girl named Jenlena and he wanted both of them to come live with him in Calgary, where he bought a three-story house with vinyl siding in a row of identical three-story houses with vinyl siding in a development with an artificial pond. When they first moved in, it had been on the eastern edge of town, with nothing but prairies out Jenlena's bedroom window, though in the years to come more and more identical houses with vinyl siding were built, sprinkled between them more artificial ponds and punctuated every so often by a preteen cutting themself.

Sometimes, during the summer thunderstorms, the winds got so intense that the bedroom doors on the second floor would slam closed as if by their own volition. Jenlena liked to pretend it was ghosts. Women who had been violently murdered by either their husbands in a jealous rage or their own children entering this world. When she was very young they talked to her. They told her how lonely it was to be dead. She said, "I am lonely too."

"Never trust a man who keeps his fingernails too neat."

"Who are you talking to?" her mother would ask. Her mother was always "Mother" in her head, and though she called her "Mom" in spoken life, this had never made it more true.

"Nobody," she would respond. But that was a lie. She was talking to the weather.

Later, in Montreal, her friend Daphne said of the national ennui: "I'm so sick of how people here are so polite all the time. In America people are rude but it gets things done. Take Roderick Maeve, for example. Do you think a Canadian could invent a time machine like that?"

Jenlena said that she thought that was the point. "Yes, we're mediocre, but that comes in handy when you see what's going on in other places. I mean, some kid in Florida shooting up his school just because he feels lonely. I'm not sure a Canadian is even capable of having such an intense emotion. That's the trade-off."

"Oh, they've been telling me about school shootings since I was a kid. I want to be free," said Jordan.

"Besides," it felt necessary for Jenlena to add, "a Canadian invented basketball. Also, insulin."

"Exactly!" Daphne said. "Taking everything so literally!" Her opinion at that time was that a person's feelings were something to be kept at a distance and never looked at too closely, much like the sun. Like the sun, their feelings touched them all over.

5.

It was because of Christopher that Jenlena had grown up with Moon Bethlehems in her periphery. From as far back as she could remember, they'd harassed her stepfather. Jenlena knew better than to use the word *cult*. It was derogatory; she'd learned that in university. But in her teen years, she and her family had used that word all the time to describe the small but persistent group of people who hung outside her stepfather's work and sometimes followed him home.

Moon Bethlehems existed all over the world, with specific concentrations popping up near energy centers because they blamed companies like Christopher's for causing all this weather. Anyone who joined had to give up their first name, which represented individualism, but keep their last, which represented history—as much their fault as anyone's. Moon Bethlehems were people who claimed to have looked directly into their collective potential and become intoxicated with it. Separate they may be worthless, but together their power was a living thing that grew and morphed in accordance to its own prerogative. They dressed in beige and never smiled.

She remembered one Christmas when Christopher had run out into the snow in his bathrobe and screamed, "What are you doing?"

"Reminding you," said the half dozen of them gathered on the lawn.

"Of what?" he cried.

"The weather," they said. "Making the weather as uncomfortable for you as you've made it for other people."

So the Moon Bethlehems weren't new to her, which was perhaps why they didn't hold the same appeal as they did to so many of her contemporaries, who increasingly seemed to be identifying with the group and used it as an excuse to justify whatever manner of pessimism they felt like. To Jenlena, *Moon Bethlehem* was becoming one of those terms so swallowed up by the discourse that it didn't mean anything anymore, like *feminism* or *representation*. Besides, though cynicism might have been in her repertoire, she didn't hate the world. Hell, she hoped one day to be a part of it. Late at night as she lulled herself to sleep, images of its skin creams and high fashion danced in her head.

CHAPTER THREE

The Dizzying Rush of Enterprise

1.

TWINS RELEASE JOINT STATEMENT

"We are fighting for the rights of the unborn." These were the opening words spoken by Nate and Brandon Richardson at a press conference in Melbourne earlier this week. The brothers, age sixteen, have created a media storm in their native Australia after filing a lawsuit against their own parents, Luke and Kristen Richardson, for bringing them into this world. "They never asked us," the brothers, sullen in appearance and dressed in knee-length black trench coats, continued reading from their statement. "We just don't think that's fair, given everything we're being asked to endure."

In their public filing with the lower court of Victoria last week, the twins' attorney cited loneliness, grief over their gerbil Landsdale, and scientific projections for global food shortages in the next five years as grounds for the $500,000 they seek in retribution for their lives. Mr. and Mrs. Richardson, of South Yarra, could not be reached for comment.

2.

Off the coast of Argentina, a team of over two hundred marine biologists fished out the corpse of a blue whale. A man in northern Ontario was found living inside of the bones of a moose. In France, there was a general strike over the rising costs of chickpeas. In Russia, a political dissident who claimed to have seen a horde of hamsters running out of the Kremlin was disappeared. "We have not harmed him," said the government to his friends and family. "That's just the way you feel about it."

On Daphne and Jenlena's block, a neighbor played a recording of dogs howling at sundown, and the next night another neighbor did the same, and on the third yet another, and so on. There was a rumor that a ghost flock of pigeons haunted the roof of the gas station at the end of Parc Avenue. If you were lucky they would ghost shit on you, which foretold certain glory. The girls went themselves to check it out, and there was already a large crowd. Some people were taking pictures. An old woman in a sari wept openly. "What are they doing?" Jenlena asked Daphne. "It's obviously just a cloud."

A girl Jenlena knew from university began selling coats made from black cats, and another from Instagram kept a mouse's skeleton in her jewelry box. Daphne's canceled boyfriend made her a scrapbook of pressed insects, with some strands of their cat's fur he'd collected from a lint roller taped to the last page.

Jenlena still had live photos of her parents' dog Trevor, a Scottish terrier. She pressed them with her thumb and the sound turned up loud. Every so often, without solicitation or comment, her mother airdropped more, and she could hear Christopher's voice in the background: "Down, boy! Down!"

But none of that mattered now, all of that was null. Sometimes they saw cats out of the corners of their eyes but the cats were gone. It was only plastic bags biding their time in the wind. Some people marked the anniversary of when the animals took over, others marked the anniversary of when they died. This was considered politics. It said everything you needed to know about a person.

3.

"After we sold the last chuck roast, the boss's wife put up framed photos of all the cuts of meat where we used to keep 'em in the fridge. Customers brought fake flowers and sometimes wrote little cards. We spent our lives living off their flesh and never quite knew how to say thank you. Now it's too late."

—VICTOR MAROTTI, QUEENS, NEW YORK

"Am I the only one who's a little tired of all this performative grief? If you ask me, good riddance! You know it was a kangaroo collision that killed my father. Feels good to win one, even after all these years."

—DARCY JURKEVICH-MOSTOWSKI,

BRISBANE, AUSTRALIA

"I'm keeping her body in the freezer. Don't use that. You can use it, but don't put my name. When the patrols came around I said I'd never even had an iguana. She didn't get violent like the others; she was too sick. Even when she tried to bite me, she could barely lift her head. She died in my

arms. I take out her body every night after dark just to hold her, just to remember."

—ANONYMOUS, CHICAGO, ILLINOIS

4.

After he defeated the animals, the California billionaire Roderick Maeve was congratulated on all the morning shows. With a wardrobe prone to sportswear, he was disheveled in the handsome way only accessible to tall men and had a repertoire of five jokes. Each he told with measured timing. Websites wanted to know who he was dating, and though he repeated many times that he was choosing to focus on work, the internet knew he mostly dated supermodels. Rumor had it that his next project was a time machine.

Many people Jenlena's age held such intense contempt for rich people it was tantamount to sexual obsession, but she personally had never really cared all that much. Yes, wealth was often garish—the cartoonish facelifts on so many tabloid women—but then again so was poverty. Mostly, she found money a crude inconvenience, like going to the bathroom number two. Often, she skipped meals just to avoid thinking about it.

Jordan told her he'd read that Roderick Maeve owned a factory in China where the working conditions were so horrible that the company installed safety nets at the base of dormitories to catch all the people who were so stuck in their feelings that they jumped out the window. He was wearing one of Daphne's bathrobes and eating rigatoni with a lime wedge and sriracha sauce. The spice flushed his face. "I think it's sick," he said. "It's the twenty-first century. Even pedophiles have rights! If someone wants to kill themselves, they should be allowed to do it in peace!"

"At least their job gives them a place to live," she said.

He scoffed. Once upon a time, he'd been one of those fabled Montreal characters who washed dishes by day and played synth shows by night. He made music under the moniker KoolNUsual and rose to modest fame when one of his songs was in a Target commercial and everyone in the neighborhood only loved him more because he belonged to them. He was beautiful, with dark wavy hair and a body Daphne had learned the word *turgor* for, just to describe it in a poem. Then, about a year before the animals, it came out that he'd punched his teenage girlfriend in the face, and that was it. Firmly and irrevocably: canceled.

Though Jenlena had been nervous when he first came to live with them, so far he mostly stayed in Daphne's room, listening to music or drawing. It had happened to Jenlena only once with someone she hadn't wanted, the summer after first year when she went with her parents to one of her stepfather's work retreats in Florida. A man from the office invited her to take a walk with him to see the full moon on the beach. He kissed her with his scratchy face and put her hand on his penis, which could have been a miscommunication, except that even when she pulled away he reached for her again and clutched her tightly as he began to moan, softly at first, then so loudly she could no longer hear the waves. You had to leave your body sometimes. It was a skill developed through time, generations even, and could not be underestimated.

After he finished, she took off all her clothes and walked into the water, then underneath it. Later on Instagram, when the man messaged her to ask how she had liked Florida, she said specifically that she had a nice time. She didn't write any posts about it on the internet, she never even told a single person.

Even after the animals died, when Jordan had been living with them for six months and was by no means a novelty, Jenlena sure got a kick out of looking at him: his curly dark hair pressing up against the thin fabric stretched over his chest and how his eyebrows joined in the middle. Did canceled people even care about animals? Did they hope and fear the way people like her did? When they slept, were they still canceled in their dreams?

"What if I bought Daphne a succulent?" he asked one morning over coffee. "Do you think that would cheer her up?"

5.

Daphne wept for days. She wrote a list of every animal she had known personally, beginning with the seventeen cats her mom's cousin lived with in a trailer outside of Winnipeg. Then there was her first-grade class's guinea pig, Checkers. He'd died on her watch after Daphne won the draw to look after him over spring break, an albatross she carried with her until she left for university. In total there had been twelve dogs. She read out their names and when her voice broke into a sob, Jordan took her notebook and recited the rest of the list for her. "Patch, Mable, Reina, Tennyson." The next page was reptiles.

Most people figured they had a year, two tops without the animals. It was hard to deny their importance: each species had been engineered over hundreds of generations to perform its specific role in the earth's ecology, a collaboration between sex and time that had produced such classics as "the bumblebee," "bighorn sheep," and even "the rat," a cult favorite.

But Jenlena found herself surprisingly calm. It started with a sort of numbness, a passage into a land beyond feeling. She saw sadness from a distance now, its shortsightedness, vapidity. Like a high school bully in the movies, pathologically small-town.

Five, six days postfauna, people began to love plants to strange degrees. They took them on walks and gave them little names. It was necessary to have something to love, and loving just each other was unthinkable. *Okay*, Jenlena thought. *I have a couple of ideas here.* Two weeks postfauna, she snuck inside the Home Depot Garden Center in the middle of the night and found the sweetest little bonsai tree on one of the shelves. She held it in her arms, ceramic pot and all. The tiny leaves were not fur, but for somebody out there, Jenlena imagined, they'd do the job. They'd have to. She went home and posted a picture on her Instagram: #greenfriend #minime #fallinlove. Fifteen minutes later, a deal was struck with a friend of a friend for over a hundred dollars. Thus it began, the hustle.

All spring, she dug things up. She didn't know that much about plants but, like anyone raised on advertisements descended from oil paintings, had an eye for color and detail that came naturally. She lifted an orchid from the university greenhouse on one of the last days before it closed for security concerns, then sold it to a wealth management consultant for $200. Next a bushel of hyacinths for which a neighbor offered $175. One house she stole from had put a plush tabby cat in a tree, another plastic mice in the grass. At night, she saw inside of whole apartment buildings: a woman stroking her taxidermied German shepherd, a man in the unit above her talking to a photograph of his cat. On the ground floor, a little girl held goldfish crackers above a fish tank and kissed each of them softly before dropping them into the water.

Sad and lonely people, they'd buy anything. Daffodils and crocuses right on the verge, quite ready to bloom. Chives, cherry tomatoes, mint, and sage. Some were mischievous, others good listeners, some put things in perspective and made you laugh with their silly little habits. They reminded you of your mother but only in the best ways. The spring passed in a blur of stems and petals, e-transfers for which the password was always *piston*. Jenlena was happy, and not at all neurotic.

6.

On the weekends, she pretended to be a dog in hotel rooms. The most important thing to remember was that it wasn't about the costume. It wasn't even about sniffing their pant legs or picking up their shoes in your mouth—this was very important to understand. That was the mistake most girls made, assuming it was simply the act of getting on one's knees that clients so craved, but this too was false. And it wasn't sexual, though yes, a hand job here and there had been known to occur. Jenlena saw all kinds of people. A Guyanese orchestra conductor who provided the terrier costume himself. An administrator from Laval was the one who wanted to be the poodle. She had her hair in curls and wore a nose and tail. All she'd wanted from Jenlena was to lick her hand.

Real bitches knew that pretending to be a dog was actually quite spiritual. People wanted to feel like they were truly necessary to another living being. They wanted to feel special, even if it was just for that fleeting hour once a week or however often they could afford. It didn't matter what you looked like or how work was going, an animal was a creature who loved you outside of culture. Jenlena rested her head on their laps with wide eyes. A master was the whole world. All they had to do to make her happy was come home, throw the ball, fill the dish. A master could kill her if they wanted, but they wouldn't. Not today.

Jenlena knew she wasn't the first person to come up with the idea. She never claimed to be. One local influencer met clients in a custom-made costume of a Shar-Pei and posted that she'd even seen the billionaire Roderick Maeve drinking martinis at one of the hotels where she'd gone to pretend. *I'm not saying he's a furryphile but if that were true it's proof of how mainstream our practice is becoming, soon we will even be forming unions.*

———

Are you lonely? I am lonely too. Life is just not the same anymore. You know, I was always the kind of guy more comfortable with animals than the other kids at school. I understood them and they me. So where does that leave a guy like me in the new world order?

Well, that's where you come in.

If I can't have my dog Rosie anymore, then I am willing to pay top dollar for the next best thing. Yes, an impersonator. If this sounds like something you'd be interested in, respond to this message with your rates, personal information (stats, etc.), and emotional history with dogs.

Some info on Rosie to keep in mind:

Weighed 75 lbs
Loved running
White with black spots
Mild case of colitis, very manageable

The first time, sure, Jenlena had been nervous. It was a rainy Saturday and the hotel was downtown, two blocks from where she was still going to school, submitting half-finished papers, each titled after some variation of "Sex, Lies, and Videotape."

Jenlena paced the sidewalk. The Dalmatian costume she'd bought for $150 online was in her backpack. (This was called *an investment*. It was also known as *financial literacy*.) Normally, she only ever went to hotels with her parents. This one had a strange architecture: the second floor was round and much wider than the first—it jutted out like the cap of a mushroom. All she could do was notice small things. The curtains were red, the windows were dirty, she was cold, sweating too much. A woman standing on the corner said that the Jews had done it. She wore a wooden board that said "Ask me about Jesus" on the front. "He was an animal too," it said on the back.

"Emily?" A man approached Jenlena. He was broad in the chest and shoulders, with his hair shaved close on the sides. He wore leather shoes, no discernable socks.

"Emily?" The man took another step forward, holding up his phone to show her the messages they'd exchanged.

She'd forgotten that Emily was, allegedly, her name. "Yes," she said.

"Shall we?"

The room was nothing special. There was a view of where they'd just been standing, then the dip in the road leading south toward the hockey stadium. Settling in, Jenlena set up the timer on her cellphone and confirmed the rate.

He nodded, then proceeded with directions: "Change into your suit and I'll wait in the hall. What do you need, three, four minutes to get ready? But listen. When you hear me coming for the door, get excited. I mean, jump and everything, okay? Do you understand?"

"Yes."

"You knew dogs, right? You're familiar?"

"Oh, totally."

In the bathroom, Jenlena slipped the hotel toiletries into her bag before stripping down. Not bad: Pantene. She climbed into the suit. It was white with uniform black spots. Too identical, she thought, consuming her own reflection. Perfect circles. Nature would never have been that anal. It was wild and undisciplined and that's why it was losing.

She'd tried on the costume the night before for Daphne. It was a little long in the legs, and the snout strained her neck, but she was able to crawl from one end of the apartment to the other reasonably enough.

"You're really going to do this?" Daphne asked from the couch.

"Why not?" Jenlena said through the mouth's mesh opening. The only part of her body that wasn't covered was her eyes. *For optimal emotional connection*, read the packaging. "I'm providing a service. It's called being a part of society."

"Some society," Daphne replied. She'd been like this postfauna, contemptuous and unhygienic. "Did you hear about the last Big Mac? They gave it to some girl in China with cerebral palsy."

"Woof," Jenlena said to herself in the hotel mirror, baring her teeth and starting to growl. Dalmatians, she remembered vaguely, had had skulls too small for their brains and it made them hostile. Well, now they were dead. As the French said, *tant mieux*. Then the footsteps began in the hall and she dropped into position. She took a big breath and goddamn committed.

"Whoa, down girl, down!"

He led her by the scruff to the bed and asked how her day was. She looked up at him, making her eyes as wide as she could. He scratched behind her ears and asked, "You like that, you like that, girl, don't you?"

She panted and lapped up the air with her tongue. *Am I not a modern girl?*

The man seemed to like it, he seemed to be satisfied. He told her to roll on her back and she wondered if he'd rape her. She thought about it and felt proud for having figured it out before it happened. So in this case, she wouldn't be caught by surprise. She could leave her body and watch it all unfold as if it were happening to someone else.

Was it happening?

Has it started happening now?

The man took a long sigh and looked off into the distance. "Clara's not doing too well." His voice broke. "But she's strong. She's been very strong since we were kids."

His lips trembled and the cries began slowly, fragile, like something delicate to be protected: a sapling or family heirloom. "Rosie," he said, rubbing behind Jenlena's ears. "Oh Rosie, where did you go? Will you take care of Clara when she goes there too?"

As he cried the sorrow grew stronger until the weight of it against the synthetic fur was stifling. Sweat dripped down Jenlena's stomach, down her legs, pooling in all four feet.

He was the animal now, contorting himself on the bed and whining indecipherably until the alarm went off on her cellphone.

The man stood up, wiped his forehead, and handed Jenlena the money. She looked down at the bills in her hand: seven green twenties, two blue fives, slick with lamentation, like live things that could wriggle free.

It wasn't hard, she decided, dressing back into her human clothes. It was pretty easy. So what had the dogs been on about, then? Why did they all have to run away like that and cause so much trouble? She left the hotel and walked down to Sainte-Catherine Street, the same path those rats had taken when the siege first began. She wasn't a rat, though. She was a girl and she was alive.

"I've never seen you like this before," Daphne said when Jenlena got home. But she wasn't impressed, she was horrified. Since the animals, Daphne wasn't sleeping and she didn't brush her hair. Her face was all puffy.

Is this what I used to look like to her? Jenlena started to wonder, though she maintained the positive attitude that now came naturally. "It's not so complicated, really," she said. "I've seen a hole and I'm filling it."

"How masculine," Daphne responded blankly. Jordan leaned over to show her something on his phone: in Tennessee, a group of evangelicals had occupied the walk-in freezer at a Walmart, pilfered the state's last remaining ground beef, and distributed it to members of their church.

"Huh," Daphne said.

Jenlena went into her room. She wanted to count her money again and laid out the bills in a circle around her on the bed like a protective ritual. She closed her eyes and listened to her breath until the sound of her roommates kissing filled the apartment. That was the only time the two of them came alive lately, through the wet sounds of their bodies. It was enough to make Jenlena puke. Literally she did most days (despite her positive attitude).

7.

You couldn't help but hate your best friend. Either just a little, most of the time, or with a burning passion, every now and then. You didn't like what your best friend was wearing, you didn't like her yellow eye shadow or how she said that thing about the Hasidic neighbors. You yourself were pretty much beyond jokes like that. And moreover: her T-shirt! When she parted her hair that way, was it meant to be ironic? Okay, this is bad but . . . have you heard her try to pronounce *hegemony*? It wasn't mean when you only said it inside your head, and besides, you're only speaking from a place of concern. Her dad makes *how* much in the oil and petroleum industry? Yes, once she'd gotten drunk and let it slip. Who gave a shit about those prizes? Half of her poems weren't even good, they were just the kind that teachers liked. That was worse than being bad, really, being good at such a midtier school. And she's always like that, always has to be the smartest in the room. Always, always.

Lets you know how tall she is. Without her fake blond hair she wouldn't even be so pretty. You've seen her in the middle of the night without her makeup. You've seen her naked at 4 a.m. sneaking into the outdoor pool. It's easy to have a nice body when you're tall. How could she not have noticed how bloated her belly was getting? Not to be nasty, but spiritually, one had to question a person whose crop tops stretched tighter and tighter around her swelling abdomen. Did she really not realize? But then again she was the one who was dating a canceled man, but then again she was the one whose best friend was dating a canceled man. Did it mean she hated women? Did it mean she hated her own body and was fundamentally unequipped to live inside of it? You could stop if you wanted to. You would stop after this one last, burning detail. It made you feel like a shark: if you couldn't come up with any more mean things to say about your best friend, then you would die.

8.

M●●N_cicero_666 @Moon.Cicero 5m

To be moon bethlehem

M●●N_cicero_666 @Moon.Cicero 4m

Is to have grown tired of excess

M●●N_cicero_666 @Moon.Cicero 4m

To have the forest tattooed in our memory

M●●N_cicero_666 @Moon.Cicero 4m

Is to atone for our ancestors who knew better but not birdsong

M●◑N_cicero_666 @Moon.Cicero 4m

Is to be guided through darkness by sense beyond what has
been intended

M●◑N_cicero_666 @Moon.Cicero 4m

Is to break through beyond imagination into what has always
been true

M●◑N_cicero_666 @Moon.Cicero 1m

What do you call 1000 albertans at the bottom of a tar sands
tailing pond?

9.

Just after the end of the school year, Adam texted out of nowhere,
the first time Jenlena had heard from him in months. He wanted
to meet, he said. She agreed.

When she arrived at the café in between their apartments, Adam
was already sitting at a table and he looked terrible. "I've quit," he
said before even a hello. "I've given up."

"Are you all right?" she asked. "What's happened?"

He laughed out loud.

"I mean specifically."

He said that he simply could not abide. "You must have been
wondering, haven't you, where I was?"

"I figured you'd been busy with school."

He shook his head. "I'm afraid that school and I have parted
ways." His eyes filled with tears. "This world we're living in, it's
not just what happened to the animals but the profiteers. Is nothing sacred? Is there no loss they won't take advantage of?"

"But what are we supposed to do?" she asked. "Just roll over? That's life. Things go wrong. We adapt."

"Not me. I'm done participating." He started to sputter. "I'm sick of it all! Grading papers, going to parties, watching telly and eating candy with you!" His saliva caught the light. Then he leaned in close, poised to share privileged information: "What I've realized is that nothing matters. All the things I wanted, I realized that they're not even mine, it's just the things society has told me to want, and everything I think is only what society has told me to think."

The barista dropped off Jenlena's coffee, though she couldn't imagine drinking it. Her stomach felt leaded. And to think, she'd been prepared to have sex with him too. It was their culture. Young people often had sex with each other to work out complex emotional problems. Old people too. It was happening in houses and apartments all around Adam and Jenlena as they fiddled with their napkins.

Adam said he would be leaving that weekend to join a Moon Bethlehem group in the Eastern Townships where there wasn't any internet and everyone had to throw their phones into the river. It appealed to him because he'd come to understand that mental pollution from all the listicles and hot takes online was just as dangerous as whatever oil and gas were doing. "No offense."

"Why would I take offense to that?"

"Because of your father."

"My stepfather," she said, and was perplexed by herself as she added, "His company donates to a number of charitable causes."

Adam looked at her for a long time with marked pity. He reached across the table and held her hand. "You don't like society either," he said. "You were never very good at it."

Jenlena pulled away. "That was before," she said. "And you never knew me very well." This was true. They both it realized from the sudden gravity of her tone.

"No." He looked into his lap, then sheepishly up at her like all men when they've been caught and haven't yet decided on an angle to pursue.

But she wasn't angry. She wasn't feeling very much, actually. "It's okay," Jenlena said. "It was a different time, back then." They spoke like grandparents. "I didn't know myself very well either." *I didn't know myself very well uphill both ways.*

"I wish you the best," she continued. "I know it doesn't sound like I mean it, but I think I genuinely might. I guess I just, well, I just have one question."

"Yes?" The way he raised his eyebrows made it look like a real act of physical exertion.

"W-well," she began tentatively, then hit her stride. "If you say it doesn't matter, all those times with me. You know what I mean, if you really never cared, then what were you thinking taking me swimming for my birthday?"

He bit down on his lip to keep his mouth from twitching. "I guess I just wanted one last burst of humanity."

When she got home, she posted a picture of herself with a palm-sized aloe vera framing her chin. She'd bought it at the market for cheap and was sure she could turn it around fast for a profit. The isosceles shape really had something yonic about it, which was great because everybody loved a lesbian or at least a cheeky image that drew subtle references to one. *Wanna take this baby home with you? DM with best offer.* Likes rolled in but ten minutes passed and no solid responses. She double-checked to see if it had been posted correctly. She went into her messages to make sure they were loading properly. She googled *instagram shortage.* She turned her phone off, plugged it in, turned it back on. Ten likes but no offers. She checked her pulse, she pinched her wrist, she puked.

10.

One day in late May, there was a massive brawl over wild violets in a park in the north end of the city. Jenlena borrowed Daphne's bike even though she had a yeast infection. You just had to lean into it at a certain angle and it didn't itch anymore. It felt all tingly when she leaned into it like that. She was finished with school now and confident in her future.

The park was crowded when she arrived, though because she was small and dressed plainly, she could slip by the larger groups without notice. She made her way to the entrance of the park, where a long line of protestors blocked anyone from getting through. "We won't let you take them," a young man said into a megaphone. "These flowers have lived here for over a decade, blooming every spring. They belong to the park, it's their *home*."

"Oh, give me a break," said an older woman beside Jenlena, clutching a spade.

It was the first time she was truly aware of how many others there were like her in the city, those who traded in plants. All kinds of people, young and old, English and French, so many genders. But it didn't frighten her, not like how anxious she got thinking about all the other poets in the world, the hundreds of thousands of people who only ever felt truly free putting pen to paper to articulate whatever random feeling had gripped them. She knew in her heart there were more than enough plants to go around. And after the plants? Following that one final bloom? Well, the sad and lonely people were certain to need something. It was part of what made them so sad and lonely in the first place.

There, in the fields, the thin green stems reached up to God. "You don't own this land," one of the other scavengers said to the protestors. "You can't tell us what to do!"

"We're taking care of the park," replied a protestor, an older man flushed from the heat.

"They're going to die anyways. Why can't you just let us make a little money?"

"We're actually in talks!" said the first young man. "We've had some promising updates on a hand-pollination project."

Someone behind her threw a rock. Then came the mayhem. The scavengers rushed forward, pushing the protestors to the ground. Jenlena herself felt the crunch of someone's eyeglasses under her feet. And it felt amazing to use her body like that, to move without analyzing anything and feel the innate strength at the core of whatever was inside her. A soul? For a girl like her? Why not? She wrapped her hands around the delicate stems. The secret was to really get your fingers in there, dig deep under the root. The root was the whole point. By now she'd come to believe all people had one, a gnarled and tangled underside they'd die without.

In total, the violets earned her $65, minus $4.50 for the oatmeal cream she bought to soothe a rash on her left calf. She must have fallen against some poison ivy or another weed that had left her skin so itchy. Jenlena couldn't remember exactly, such was the dizzying rush of enterprise.

11.

Over the next few weeks, the rash took on an odor. "You can smell that, can't you?" Jenlena asked Daphne, holding up her calf to where Daphne lay on the couch.

"Um, no," Daphne replied. "But maybe try some cream for that?"

"I've tried creams," she snapped. "Oils too, you name it! But I can't stop smelling like rotten eggs!" She scrunched up her nose, inhaled several times, "or at least something around here does."

"Stressed over the Middle East, are you, my dear?" the jaunty doctor assumed when he waltzed in after she'd waited over two hours at the walk-in clinic.

"No," she said. "I've got this rash on my leg."

He continued nonetheless. "I know that it's difficult. The media makes us all prone to hysteria. But what I always find remarkable is how much the mind fears uncertainty. Even the worst possible scenario is preferable to the unknown. That's why all these apocalypse scenarios have taken over."

He was her stepfather's age, with wiry hair growing out of his nose and ears. He looked her over, asked about her period, and shone a bright light into both her eyes. "When in reality there's still a lot we don't know. I heard on NPR this morning that diplomacy is shifting things rapidly."

She reminded him she had a rash, but he didn't even put his glasses on to look at it. Like most people, Jenlena had always hated doctors, their coldness and superiority.

"It's nothing serious," he said flippantly. "I'll give you a cream."

"Which one?" she asked, rattling off the multisyllabic formulas she'd already bought over the counter. He needed to understand that hers was no ordinary rash, she was special.

Again, he brought up menstruation.

"I've been really busy," Jenlena admitted. A lot of girls hadn't been menstruating since the animals; she'd read about it online. She counted in her head, three, four months?

He nodded, then asked her to lie down on the leather medical bed. It was covered in a thin sheet of paper, which like all things contributed to the mounting catastrophe around them in its own specific way. He began to take great interest in her as he pressed down on her belly. Now she was mesmerizing. She fascinated him. "Are you sexually active?"

Jenlena laughed.

"And what forms of birth control do you use?"

"Pull out." *The rhythm of the night*, as she and Daphne called it.

"And does this hurt?" he pressed down on her belly.

"Yes," Jenlena winced.

He had her pee in a cup then took the cup down the hall and came back and told her she was pregnant. "My grave apologies," he said.

"No," she tried to explain. "You don't understand. I'm not, like, fertile. That's never been my personality."

12.

It was not a matter to think twice about. Maybe if Jenlena had less going on she'd have had time to entertain a baby, call it little names. Babies were famous for their smells and the clothes they wore. But this was postfauna. Jenlena had shit to do.

A procedure that far along was a three-step process. The night before the first day, the girls lit candles. It happened to be a full moon too, which Daphne said was very special. It seemed that Jenlena's abortion had breathed new life into Daphne. She rubbed Jenlena's back and said that whatever she wanted to feel, that was okay. "If you're happy, that's okay. If you're relieved that's totally fine too, or if you're sad. And I was really scared when I had mine. If you're nervous or you feel like you might be getting cold feet, that's normal too. If you decide even just tomorrow morning that you've changed your mind and you don't want to do it anymore, that's totally fine and you could just say so. Especially because, well, you know, usually people find out so much earlier. You know, usually people just have to take a pill."

"What?" Jenlena nearly choked. "Like *have* it? I'd have it and we'd all raise it here like one big, modern family?" She looked at her friend. It sounded like one of their old plans.

"Well, you'd probably have to move back with your parents," Daphne said. "But if that's what you want, your stepdad could probably set you up with a pretty good job."

Jenlena stood up to get herself another beer from the fridge.

In the morning, she took the Metro and listened to a playlist Daphne and Jordan had made for her on Spotify called "ABOR-TION," mostly Moby songs. The clinic felt very luxurious; the walls were lavender and it smelled like eucalyptus. The ultrasound was just like in the movies. She lay back with her feet up in stirrups while they inserted a thin wooden stick into her cervix, meant to stimulate dilation. One nurse had braids, the other had a green pixie cut. They told her that if she wanted to change her mind, she could, but they made her sign a form acknowledging the increased chance of miscarriage after the stick was inserted.

"Sure," she said, writing out her ridiculous name. She knew what they were thinking. *How could she be so clueless? Do you even live inside your body or is your head off in the clouds three-quarters of the time? I'll bet she only comes back into her body to take a shit.* The clouds, she tried to rationalize, if only in her own head. It's much nicer in the clouds.

On the second day, she met the doctor for the first time. He wore acetate glasses and was very young. He couldn't have been much older than she was, Jenlena thought. He even had one of those Viking haircuts. But he never looked at her directly, just right into her pussy, like he too knew it was wet hot tectonic. The nurse with green hair handed the doctor a needle that injected poison into the fetus's heart. She couldn't change her mind now. She signed a form, officially understood.

Jordan made dinner that night: fresh pasta with stolen herbs and made a big show of grating the soy-based Parmesan on everyone's behalf. Daphne asked if the doctor had been attractive.

"In theory," Jenlena said.

"Ever since I had my first abortion in high school, I've had this idea to write a movie about a woman who falls in love with her abortion doctor. Or what about a road trip comedy where a woman and her friends travel across America to get an abortion? Or they come to Canada, like an Underground Railroad type thing. You could probably get funding for that. You could get twenty-five grand from the Canada Council."

"Right."

Jordan told Jenlena that only in a capitalist country would a woman be forced to have an abortion out of poverty.

"But she's not being forced," Daphne said. "And she doesn't live in poverty. No offense." She turned to Jenlena. "But, like, your dad, you know."

"Capitalism's not even so bad," Jenlena said, "the way I see it now. You can't really have a valid opinion unless you've seen it from both sides: successful and not."

"And you don't think I have?" Jordan reminded the girls that he'd once had a song featured in a Target commercial. He pulled his phone out and showed it to them. Below, in the comments, strangers wished him a slow and painful death.

"No," said Daphne, playing with the food on her plate. "There's not much point to making movies anymore, anyways. There's not much point to anything."

13.

On the third day of her abortion, there was an unexpected delay. In the waiting room, Jenlena scrolled through her phone and saw that one of the models she followed was supposedly involved with the California billionaire Roderick Maeve. He was the one who killed all the animals. People said it had been the only way. And it hadn't hurt. The animals had died instantly—she'd watched from Adam's window. It was said they drowned in that sound. She wondered if it was true that Roderick Maeve was really building a time machine. She wondered how something like that would make people feel.

They looked comfortable, these two wealthy people on her phone. Jenlena scrolled through pictures of them walking the streets of New York City, leaving a club in Spain. She zoomed in on the billionaire's face. He had eyes, lips, et cetera. There was a sadness there, like with most famous people, at least the ones who did it best, the ones who understood the exchange. She zoomed right into his eyes.

"Julia?" the nurse with braids called what she could only assume was meant to be her name.

That was it, she'd completed her abortion.

Across the street from the clinic, a group of homeless people had set up the roof of an old bus stop against the chain-link fence of a parking lot. They had blankets and drank PBR from the dark blue cans, but it didn't seem like such an unhappy scene. Two of the men were laughing and the young girl with them had a big smile. Now they were kissing. We all make choices—Jenlena understood that very clearly now. She'd figured it out. Even in the depths of the thickest emotion, there would always be things they decide for themselves.

Her Uber was a Tesla. She remembered when she'd first begun riding in cars alone, she'd text a screenshot of the driver to her mother or a friend under the unspoken condition that all men were liable to rape and murder her. Some girls wouldn't even accept the ride if they didn't like the look of the man, if he gave them a feeling. Anyone could rape them at any time. The danger was feared but also hotly anticipated as a rite of passage.

"Jelina?" The driver rolled down the window.

She got inside. When they hit traffic on a busy street downtown, he offered a basket of Halloween candy.

"No, thank you."

"Diet." He nodded. "Me too."

Outside, people were shopping and moving in and out of restaurants. They had whole histories, complex desires. She saw women in hijabs, boys in glossy tracksuits, young girls in shorts that showed the crease of their buttocks, men pretending not to look. Lacoste, Victoria's Secret, Foot Locker, Brandy Melville, Forever 21: she tried to put it all together in some bold conclusion.

In front of the Apple store, some Moon Bethlehems were putting on a demonstration. They walked back and forth in their drab clothes with huge posters that had photographs of bad weather. Adam was among them, he was right there. He had no expression on his face, even when he turned to face the car window directly. If he made out Jenlena from behind the glass he made no show of it. He stayed still, his gaze steady and hers too, like perfect strangers. It was hard to believe how flat her stomach was. She checked her phone to stop thinking about it.

Daphne had sent a series of photographs with no text. Each showed her standing in front of a big bright fire. The light of the flames caught her cheekbones. The car was moving now, but slowly.

JENLENA: **WHERE ARE YOU?**

SO FUCKED, SAID DAPHNE. **SRSLY HAPPENED SO FAST**

DAPHNE: **WE TOOK OUT WHAT WE COULD.**

DAPHNE: **BUT NOT EVERYTHING**

DAPHNE: **:(**

It took Jenlena a moment to absorb exactly what Daphne was saying. She zoomed in on the photo and recognized the white bricks of their building peeking through the flames.

JENLENA: **WTF!?!?**

DAPHNE: **IM SOOOO SORRY**

DAPHNE: **SUCH A CRAPPY DAY FOR YOU :/**

Then, past Laurier, she saw the fire herself, great plumes just a few blocks east. "It's my building," she told the driver.

"Same thing with my brother's restaurant," he said, shaking his head. "*Poof.* Landlord does it himself to build condos."

There was great vitality in the flames, beautiful shades of orange and yellow that stretched up into the sky, eventually dissipating and joining as one. The entire street was out watching. The old Greeks, the Hasids, the boys who smoked pot in the basement.

Jenlena found her friends, each with arms full of whatever they were able to bring with them: an array of blankets and clothing and makeup bags and her coiled notebook with daisies on the cover. Jordan was covered in soot and sat panting on the curb.

"He ran back inside five times," said Daphne. "He really tried to save everything he could." Clutched in his blackened hands was her book of pressed insects.

"What happened?" Jenlena asked.

Daphne shrugged. "Nobody knows. Jordan smelled it first. Thank god. Nobody's hurt. It's just our things."

The firefighters wielded heavy streams of water from their hoses until the flames surrendered. It was just past five and the sunlight through clouds made velvet of the ash floating down among them. Soot covered the top two floors. "That's it," said the landlord, a heavyset man who paced the block. "It's gone. That's it." He ran his fleshy palm down his sweaty face and moaned.

"How did it go, by the way?" Daphne turned from the spectacle to ask her. "Are you feeling alright?"

Daphne had had two.

"Sure," Jenlena said. "It was fine."

CHAPTER FOUR

Jordan Meets a Girl

1.

Jordan met Lisa Cicero at one of his KoolNUsual shows in London, Ontario. She was seventeen but looked twelve and hardly weighed ninety pounds. That first night, back at his friend's house, she'd taken off her clothes and said his name again and again. He specifically asked if it was her first time and she laughed in his face. Soon, it was obvious from the way she moved her hips. She had wide eyes and the kind of gap between her teeth that he thought had been banned by the orthodontic community. It was about a year and a half before the siege and there was something about her.

Yes, she wore mesh-illusion leggings with racerback tank tops, but when they looked at each other he could feel it in his toes. She had this very slow way of talking, like each phrase was something decided long before and she was now having difficulty remembering, even when all she was doing was ordering a strawberry milkshake. He took her out for breakfast the next morning and was so dizzy from the previous twelve hours that he found himself telling his whole life story.

"You know my dad was basically one of these all-time, classic pieces of shit."

"Really?" she said, her auburn eyebrows furrowed as if the admission was uniquely true, just for him.

"We lived in the woods, in a town way up north, you wouldn't have heard of it. Or actually, there's a CBC podcast about a girl who was murdered there. But we didn't even have sushi."

Lisa touched his hand then stroked it gently, like it was the most sensitive part of his body. For a moment, it really was. "I don't like my parents either," she said. "My family, they don't understand me."

"You're a complicated girl?"

"No," she said. "I think I'm really quite simple."

Afterward, she took him on a walk through the woods near her parents' house, where they came across a baby bird that had fallen from its nest. Without hesitation, Lisa smashed the animal with the heel of her shoe.

Jordan squealed.

She looked at him with ire. No girl had ever done that before; they usually let him do whatever he wanted. "Kindness doesn't exist just so you can feel good about yourself," she said, tucking a lock of her dark red hair behind her ear.

2.

They texted all summer. Lisa studied the songs he sent her and watched all of *Berlin Alexanderplatz* at his recommendation. She knew so little about music and art, it was like dating a foreign exchange student. As if it hadn't been hardly five years since he himself had been on a plane for the first time or even traveled west of Sault Ste. Marie and east of Scarborough. He had an aunt who'd run away from home at seventeen after meeting an American on a class trip to Niagara Falls, the most exotic of his family's lore until he left home at seventeen after meeting a girl from Montreal who'd had a threesome with Grimes.

Thinking about u, he texted Lisa late at night. She sent pictures of herself, thinking about him. He described what it felt like and she sent him videos from her bedroom. She had hedgehog wallpaper and once he heard her mom in the background, knocking on the door to tell her dinner was ready. "Alright! Just a sec!" Lisa said. Then she got to it, looking right into the camera for him, arching her back.

Other times, she told him about whatever drama was going on with her friends: "And then Cara said this and Eva was like no, and then Blossom—"

"Oh, crazy." He did his honest best. "And this is Eva whose dad just bought the boat?"

"No, that's Marlee. You don't care, do you? It's okay. I don't think I care either. I don't think I've cared since I was twelve."

He visited her in London (Ontario) that summer at the height of an August heatwave and she took him as her date to a laser tag party. They got to third base in the corner and he gave her ketamine for the first time. Her eyes flickering open after the second bump, Lisa stood up and commenced a frenzied rampage through the course, lighting the place neon. A new high score.

Afterwards, they went to Dairy Queen and when his debit got declined for insufficient funds the other girls were more than happy to cover his KitKat Blizzard.

"Oh, let me."

"But I just got, like, twenty dollars from my grandma!"

Lisa put her arm around his waist, beaming, to let the other girls know he belonged to her. She looked up at him like he was the ice cream, he was the one who'd stay put when you flipped him upside down, chock full of chemicals.

3.

"Isn't she, like, a little *prepubescent*?"

In the fall, Lisa moved to Montreal to study meteorology on a partial scholarship at McGill. Jordan's friends took one look at her and asked him what he was doing.

"Oh, no way," he assured them. "She's way older than I was at that age."

"Still, though?" This was a sometimes-bandmate. "She sorta creeps me out? I mean like at the party last night? She just sat there, staring at everyone? Then she goes on her phone and it's like she's taking notes?"

"She's intimidated," Jordan said. "And who wouldn't be? We're artists in one of the coolest cities in the world and she's from London, Ontario. It's practically Saskatchewan."

But it was true that Lisa's presence in his most familiar contexts was bizarre. She was the wrong genre, like Anne Hathaway going full frontal or a dog on a bicycle.

"Why are all your friends so cynical?" she asked him once after a loft party.

"I think it's physical?" he said. "It's, like, this thing that happens in people's necks when you spend all your time sleeping on a mattress on the floor. The migraines."

So they tried to spend more time in her world: he went to beer pong parties and snuck into her dorm room after her roommate fell asleep, but that was strange too. At a toga party, she introduced him to a group of undeclareds as her boyfriend when he couldn't remember them ever having that conversation. "No, no, no," he couldn't resist the urge to clarify, "aren't we still just talking?"

But everyone knew girls matured faster than guys did. That was practically feminism. Jordan's first grasp of the concept was back in middle school when his classmates started putting tissue paper in their bras and loitering by the high school. Besides, Lisa's age meant that she wasn't jaded about things, she wasn't cynical. Not like the rest of the people he knew, broke artists who had not truly aspired in years. They stewed in their apathy, practically begging for the end of the world. As long as the world failed, they didn't have to feel so bad about themselves for doing the same thing.

Still, it was best between the two of them when they kept to themselves, in his sliver of a room in an apartment on Parc Avenue with six roommates. They hardly left, except to use the bathroom or to make spaghetti.

One time after sex, she asked after the dumb smile on his face.

"Just thinking about the time you massacred everyone at laser tag," he said. "It was so hot."

"You look like you've had a lobotomy."

"I dunno. Maybe I have." It felt incredible.

4.

For her eighteenth birthday, Lisa invited two girls from her dorm to see Jordan play a show at a dive bar on Saint-Denis, and once again, he was introduced as her boyfriend. The word from her lips gave him a feeling like he couldn't quite fit in his skin. Like it had shrunk in the wash. Lately, he'd been noticing the strangest thing about her posture, how she always stood as if she was right underneath something. She was just grazing the top, surrounded.

It was a Tuesday night and there was a small, passive crowd, though Lisa stood in the center with her eyes closed, mouthing all the words. Even the tracks that didn't have words, she made shapes with her mouth. When he asked her later she said they were Emily Dickinson poems.

Her friends stayed in the back, scrolling through their phones until one stepped on a sticky trap for rats and couldn't get it off her shoe. She started crying and the Québécois bartender laughed at her. "It's because you're crying in English," Lisa said.

After his set, Jordan was using the gender-neutral bathroom when a strange woman called his name from in front of the mirror.

"Yes?" he said, turning with a smile. It wasn't unusual for him to talk to girls in bathrooms.

"So you're the musician I've been hearing so much about." She wore a low-cut dress with a rhinestone peace symbol bedazzled on the bare skin between her breasts.

He was bashful, shrugging. "I've written some songs."

"Oh?" she deadpanned, eyebrows jumping for joy. "Like Bono?"

Jordan smirked, poised to take a step toward her, until she said, "You know she's seventeen, right?"

He swallowed, stumbled backwards, and nearly landed in the urinal trough.

"My sister," she clarified. "Lisa."

"Sh-sh-she's eighteen," Jordan only just managed.

She shook her head. "Not until 2 a.m. today, actually."

Just then, Lisa burst through the door and draped herself against his shoulder. "So you met Bonnie?" she asked.

"Right," Jordan replied, off balance. He looked back and forth between the two girls until a resemblance revealed itself. "So, anyone wanna do some K?"

Later, after they had sex in the alley, Lisa asked him what was wrong.

"I don't know," he said, watching a rat traverse the pavement from one dumpster to another. "Your sister was a trip."

"Oh, she's so dramatic. She thinks, like, you aren't serious about me and this isn't going anywhere. I told you my family doesn't understand anything."

He heard the battle cries of young people in the distance: laughter and exclamations. "Oh," he said. "Pretty wild."

5.

In November, one of his rivals had a song featured on an HBO show, and Jordan decided he needed to focus more on his music.

Lisa said she wanted to help. "Next summer take me with you to Europe. I can organize everything. I'll be like your new manager." By now she had started dressing in the oversized denim and platform sneakers of the girls in his scene, though on her everything looked like a costume. She bleached two orange streaks in the front sections of her auburn hair.

"Don't you have school?" He didn't understand why everyone talked about McGill like it was such a big deal when here was a girl who went there half price and the only thing she seemed interested in was chewing on his earlobes.

She waved her hand, dismissing the institution. "You're more important than anything they teach me there. We just sit in circles describing stuff, then, like, offer individual solutions."

He scratched his head to find the problem in this.

"All the while," she continued, "the weather's getting stronger every day and we're just hypothesizing."

"The weather," he repeated, then leaned in toward her. "Can I tell you a secret? You know, I've never really fallen for that hysteria."

She laughed. "I like you. What you do at least makes people happy. Let me come to Europe with you. You can put my boobs on a T-shirt."

Was she psychotic? He began, honestly, to wonder. In bed, she sure moved her hips like a psychotic girl. It was a telltale sign but also irresistible.

She was so earnest. He started to hate the way she looked at him with those big saucer eyes, so unabashedly. Everything was so unabashed with her, actually. Why couldn't she be normal, all-consumed with her own worthlessness the way he was? She was so stupid she didn't even notice that all his songs used the same three chords and he hadn't written a new one in almost six months.

Didn't she know he washed dishes at a fried chicken restaurant for a living? The only real money he'd ever made was from a fifteen-second commercial that aired across the southern United States. Eight thousand dollars that came from a corporation whose board of directors made literal billions paying poor people in Asia literal pennies to make plastic crap for demographically different poor people in America. It was just like his father had slurred when Jordan first announced he was becoming a musician: "What makes you think you're so special? You think you're some big somebody but you'll always be my son."

I could tell you stories that would make your hair curl, he thought as she rested her head on his chest and talked about Paris in the summer. *If you really wanna know the real me.*

She was like an animal, like one of those tiny dogs bounding down Parc Avenue. By the time they had been dating for six months, he was making up excuses not to see her and ignoring her calls, but it only made her want him more. Thus they began the ancient dance. She'd wait outside his apartment building. She'd tempt him with the drugs she bought herself.

Stories that would keep you up at night. He mocked her teeth and everything he liked about her. "What's wrong with you?" he screamed in her face. "Seriously, what don't you get? I need some time alone!"

"I don't believe you," she responded.

For example: I once dated a teenager who didn't even know she wasn't my girlfriend.

6.

The first time he pushed her, it just happened. He cornered her against the brick wall of his building because she wouldn't stop following him. No girl had ever made him act like that before, but when he looked into her eyes and saw how scared she was something came alive inside of him. Power didn't come out of nowhere; it was something you took from other people. Maybe he had known this all his life but was only ready to admit it then, towering over the little, crying girl. Who didn't want to be powerful? The alternative was that someone would do it to you.

"Can we please just go upstairs?" Lisa said. "If you just let me come upstairs we could be alone again and it'll be good."

Upstairs, he punched a hole in the wall and told her he was sorry. "Okay?" He kicked the baseboard with his sock foot. "I'm sorry."

He thought she'd cry again but she didn't. She just stood there, staring at him.

"I'm sorry, okay? I lost my temper."

He started to kiss her, but her expression didn't change. All her features were motionless on her face. He kissed down her neck and onto her belly and took off her clothes, just kissing and kissing until he was the one who was crying and she held him.

The next morning after she left for school, he wrote three of his best songs to date: "Petrified (Would You?)," "Usual Afternoon #4," and "Lisa."

7.

Okay, so yes, in high school he'd slapped a girl at a party but it had mostly been a joke. She'd laughed at his friend Max, so he'd slapped her, and the funny part was that he didn't mean it, not really. It was mostly ironic. Besides, he hadn't hit her hard. They were drunk in some mildewed basement and she stumbled backwards. "Oh," she said. "You're gonna be like your dad now?"

The remark stunned him. Then she started to laugh and a song began in the main room. She wanted to dance, she said. Later, she gave him a blow job. But for days, Jordan's clothes from that night smelled like mold and every time he caught a whiff of it he was haunted because how did she know about his dad? They lived up a hidden driveway. Who had been spying on them? And what else? Could they see into his room at night?

Not that then was related to today. What Jordan was going through now was all about Lisa. There was something uniquely about *her*; he couldn't resist it. The arguments fired him up. When she wanted to see him but he was busy, they fought, and when he wanted to see her but she was busy, they fought, and when they both wanted to see each other they usually got around to fighting after the first half hour or so. Each time they fought he said it would be the last time, and each time it was the most clichéd he had ever felt since he wrote all those songs about the dead girl from his town. He used metaphors to describe her hair in the creek.

"You make me so mad, you won't leave me alone," he said.

"You're pathetic," she said. "You think you're so big."

He was hot all over.

"One day you'll be even smaller than me."

He hated her because it was a faster feeling than liking her. Hating her was something he felt all over his skin, whereas liking her was generally sequestered to his dick, and occasionally his belly when she told him a funny story or some dumb joke. Most of the time he didn't even remember why they were laughing, but they couldn't stop. Love did not occur to him. And this warm, strange feeling between them—no matter how complete strangers would later describe it—he was certain that she was just as addicted to it as he was. Lisa must have liked it on some level because she kept coming back. People liked all kinds of things. Who was he to judge? Years ago, after learning he was lactose intolerant, a girl had put Cadbury Mini Eggs inside of herself and asked him to fish them out with his tongue.

The morning of one of Lisa's exams, Jordan took a long, hot shower until the water went cold. He stood there, facing the water with his eyes open thinking about how it wasn't him, not really. Yelling at a little girl like that. Everyone messed up sometimes. People slipped out of who they really were and into their shadow selves. But it wasn't real. When the shadow self did something, it didn't touch who you really were, not at the root of you.

The next weekend, when she was mad he didn't put her on the guest list. Thursday, when she started crying because she saw him talking to another girl by the VLTs. Friday, when she did all the drugs herself. He screamed at her until his voice went hoarse and she spit in his face and he grabbed her wrists, pulling her down onto the bed saying "Sorry, sorry, I'm so sorry" while kissing her all over as she moved her hips. Then he cried about the time his dad went broke trying to build a resort for people to see the northern lights, or when the CBC podcast accused his favorite uncle of being an accessory to murder.

"I never *asked* to be a man," he told her. "They just gave it to me."

Soon, he had a whole new album.

8.

In January, he went to Lisa's dorm to end things for good. *It isn't fair.* He practiced all manner of platitudes on his way there. *You can do so much better than me, trust me, there's literally thousands of fish in the sea.* But the thing was, he really meant it. She had a bright future. *I can feel that*, he would say. *Since we first met. Your future is like this vibrant, ferocious entity and I definitely wouldn't want to be face-to-face with it in a dark alley.*

Then they'd have sex one last time; they had to. As far as his experience was concerned, you were never really broken up until you did.

He felt ridiculously old, sneaking into the building after two girls in candy-cane pajama pants. He rode the elevator to Lisa's floor, where there were girls in towels and flyers for a march against daylight saving time. He knew the cold had distorted his skin, made him patchy and swollen. All the better to break the news, he thought. Lisa would see him and agree that he was old and strange, she young and beautiful. But then he would want her again, he would beg her, *please*, and promise to be different.

So maybe it was better that her roommate shook her head and said, "Sorry, she's gone."

"What do you mean, *gone*?" Jordan didn't understand.

"Like, I don't know," said the girl. "I haven't seen her since yesterday morning. She left her phone and everything."

"But *where*?"

"Umm, I really don't know and we're not allowed to have guys in our rooms." She lowered her voice. "I could get expelled."

Panicked, Jordan ran all over the neighborhood trying to find her. The weather was thick. It coated his eyelashes and twice he slipped into snowbanks. He went to all her usual places, the café where she liked to study, the library on the hill. Where else? Where else besides his room did she like to go? What else besides being with him did she like to do? He thought about finding her parents, and for a moment couldn't even remember her last name.

"Lisa!" So it was his place then. He decided to go home and check for her there. He walked up the long avenue from her dorm along the mountain, then into his neighborhood. The snow fell in sheets, obscuring the view just ten feet in front of him. "Lisa!" He kept calling her name, as if she could have been just beyond the precipitation. "Lisa!" But when he finally arrived at his apartment his roommates said they hadn't seen her. Searching his room, she was nowhere to be found. He even checked under the bed.

It makes me sick to participate in a society that sits back and enjoys itself as our planet is dying, she posted three days later on her Facebook. *I don't ask you to understand my decision, but you can respect it. I have joined the Moon Bethlehems.*

Those hippies who were always going on about the weather? Jordan didn't think it made any sense. She hadn't even been a vegetarian. She always ordered chicken fingers and sometimes didn't even save the leftovers. Sometimes she only ate the breading.

9.

TW: *abuse (verbal, emotional, physical, MTL), cult activity, mental health, family separation, long post*

The sad truth is that this man showed my sister a version of society not worth participating in. A place where manipulation and violence were the norm. He had made that her world. No wonder she's run away.

Now I live with an internet where hardly a day goes by when I don't see people post about how "genius" his new album is. People who call themselves feminists. People who call themselves allies.

Is it genius to fuck a seventeen-year-old? "Genius" to force hard drugs on her? "Genius" to scream in her face that she's a "psycho"? Punch a hole in her bedroom wall and grab her by the wrists? Is this genius to you? The saddest part is that even I can admit that the logical answer is yes. We have more than enough examples: Picasso. Woody Allen. Bill Clinton. So, let me rephrase the question: Is it original?

We can put a man on the moon but we can't expect better from the ones we have here on earth?

CRUEL and Usual, more like it.

It's been five months since I last saw my sister. I wake up every day checking all my accounts to see if she's messaged. That's 194 days since I've heard a word from her. But I can say also, from the bottom of this broken heart, that not even this pain is enough to convince me that darkness like that of Jordan Bellechasse is the true nature of the world. I refuse to ever believe that.

It's not who we are.

Lisa, if you ever read this, please hear me. I'm not going to tell you our society is great, okay? I'm not going to bullshit you. Do we have problems? You bet. But there's good stuff here. Remember how we used to get ice cream on the pier? Staying up all night watching Battlestar Galactica? It's worth sticking around for the good stuff. Please, stick around with me.

Lisa, please come home.

#mileend #believewomen #moonbethlehem #family #loveyousis #yesallmen #societalcorruption #fightingforjustice #triggerwarning #mtlmusicscene

10.

His album came out that spring, a smash success on the indie circuit. In May, he played a festival outside of Mexico City. On nights like that he felt the music flow through him. He understood the world very clearly and believed he'd been put on earth just to play these chords. Not even the weather could touch that feeling. No matter how hot it was that night, no matter how much it stung when his own sweat dripped into his eyes.

But it was then that it all began, the text messages and the missed calls that greeted him as soon as he got off the stage.

Hey did you see this?

Is this true?

Piece of shit

Fucking pedo

The label canceled his remaining tour dates, and when he played a show in Montreal, a crowd stood outside the bar with glitter tears painted down their faces. Everywhere he went, people looked away.

Then the label dropped him and three coworkers organized a petition to strip him of his dishwashing shifts. Two girls he didn't even know held a fundraiser for a women's shelter during which they burned his concert T-shirts in the field behind Casgrain, and he himself donated fifty dollars because he was so frightened that everything they were saying was true.

Not the literal things (that he had dated a seventeen-year-old, that he had shown her party drugs, that yes, he'd let his temper get the best of him on some occasions). He had no qualms with admitting the literal things. Yes, he was a man who hurt a girl, and he didn't even need the euphemisms. What scared him was the narrative emerging: that he, Jordan, was fundamentally no more than a man who hurt girls. Even the best things about him merely

existed in service of his proclivity for hurting girls. Hurting girls
was the reason he was put here on earth.

The internet said that it was because of people like him that
the world was such an awful place. Taken literally, that kind of
hyperbole was easy to laugh off. Literally, sure, he wasn't Pol Pot,
for example. Not even close. He did his recycling. But figuratively,
and especially on the days he made a show of patting his pockets
for change as he passed a homeless person, or when he took forty
minutes deciding on porn, or even shoplifting women's moisturizer
for the bags underneath his eyes, figuratively, he had to admit it
had some pull.

Lisa was making a name for herself by posting provocative
things online. While she'd first run away to join a commune in the
woods, he heard she'd since left. *Some of my comrades would
have you believe sitting in the forest all day is meaningful action*,
he read on her Twitter. *But I am out for retribution.* Jordan remembered her at laser tag. It gave him chills.

He wrote her long letters, admitting to his cruelty and apologizing. I want to be held accountable, he said. I'm trying to figure
out what that means. But he didn't have her address, so he wrote to
her family in Ontario, and her sister read them aloud on the internet just to mock him. He thought about Lisa's tiny hands against
his skin and wanted to be held accountable so tightly he couldn't
breathe.

11.

M●●N_cicero_666 @Moon.Cicero 3h

Tonight, thousands of children will starve to death in yemen, thousands
will die in africa from diarrhea, thousands will become victims of the
refugee crisis in south america

M●●N_cicero_666 @Moon.Cicero 3h

But paper straws! Vegan hot dogs! Biodegradable shopping bags!

M●●N_cicero_666 @Moon.Cicero 1h

We are all losers. It isn't (just) a value judgment.

M●●N_cicero_666 @Moon.Cicero 1h

We have lost. That's the definition.

M●●N_cicero_666 @Moon.Cicero 1h

Today marks 1 yr since my trip to AB

M●●N_cicero_666 @Moon.Cicero 1h

Bearing witness to the crimes against humanity

M●●N_cicero_666 @Moon.Cicero 20m

Here's a picture of a tailing pond, toxic runoff from tar sands production

M●●N_cicero_666 @Moon.Cicero 16m

I'll never forget the smell of burned tires and how I couldn't wash it out of my hair for weeks

M●●N_cicero_666 @Moon.Cicero 16m

Alberta is a cult.

M●●N_cicero_666 @Moon.Cicero 4m

They literally named their hockey team after 1 of the biggest weather contributors on the planet

M●●N_cicero_666 @Moon.Cicero 4m

Its like if germany had a team called the munich nazis.

12.

For a while, he stayed with his friend Gabe, another canceled man. They had to stick together; there was no alternative. So they smoked weed in the dank one-bedroom apartment Gabe's parents subsidized and watched old movies about the end of the world.

"They can't cancel us if we're dead," Jordan would laugh just as the aliens flew over New York City in their warships. But in the end, humanity always prevailed. Thanks to a few brave specimens, Planet Earth would be okay.

"I mean," said Gabe one day during the credits, pressing his head into the back of the torn velvet sofa. "I mean sometimes, though. Sometimes, do you ever just *think*?"

"About what?" Jordan asked as he held in the smoke. Lately, when he got stoned, he had this strange sensation that he could comprehend precisely how trapped he was in his body. Were there no escape routes? A toe, his left nostril.

"I mean, because," said Gabe with his long, stringy hair slick against his pale neck. "You know, like, how bad used to be good? Like, remember when people wore leather jackets and shaved off random parts of their hair?"

"But what we did was a bit too far, I think?" Jordan said.

"I'm talking about the absolutism of it all," Gabe said. "Nobody's supposed to be good all the time."

"Sure," said Jordan. The place smelled like cheap beer and socks. It was summer and you could see ants crawling across the floor. There was a crack in the baseboard in the kitchen where they flowed through like water.

"It's bad for art too. If you don't provoke people, then nothing changes. Maybe *that's* why music's gotten so bad nowadays. You ever thinka that?"

"I don't really think about things too much," said Jordan. "Gives me anxiety."

13.

Later, he'd wonder if the animals had really meant it. Just a couple of weeks before the siege, he and Daphne had taken in a stray kitten from the alley. Rolex, an orange tabby with white stripes and a pink nose. On his belly, a patch of fur grew in a very distinct tuft, though not once had he allowed anyone to touch him there. Daphne was certain she was getting close. She fed him Meow Mix from her palm every morning so that he'd trust her. She sang him little songs.

"No," said Jordan. "He likes weed. Today while you were at work he ran right over when he heard me pack the bowl. He likes it when I blow smoke right into his face. Really, he lay on his back. I got to see the tuft from an aerial view."

"No," said Daphne in disbelief. "Did you touch it?"

He shook his head. "Nah, wanted to wait for you."

She packed a bowl then, just to see if the kitten would come to her, though he did not. Eventually, they fell asleep. The next afternoon, the whole place smelled like piss. The walls were wet and Rolex had torn up the couch. He was nowhere to be found.

As an artist, Jordan was familiar with hyperbole, along with other necessary devices to prove one's point. He understood the horses all pooping in the canal and those dolphins in Spain who gang-raped a woman and the spread of eagles who flew into New York City skyscrapers in unison just to smash the glass. But could this one little kitten truly have had all that anger in his heart? This was the tiny thing Jordan had nursed to health himself after finding him in a cardboard box full of his dead brothers and sisters. He had held him against his bare skin unmindful of the fleas. So could this same kitten really, not two weeks later, have been so angry that he wanted to take over the world?

Or had he merely been pressured into participating by his friends? Perhaps the birds told the bees who told the mice who told their cousins who told more birds and then the spiders. You went along and you went along and you went along and then you went too far. It was not exactly an original story, at least in certain regards.

14.

She had come into his life like a dream. Daphne was smart and she was funny and they liked all the same movies. For the first time in his life, he was turned on by how hairy a girl was. The cherry on top was that he did not believe she was psychotic, either. She had none of the telltale signs, the neediness and sexual abandon. They hadn't even had sex at first, not until a couple months before the siege. Their abstinence, while it lasted, had been one of the shining achievements of his life. It meant he respected her. No one could argue with that.

He wrote a song about her, his first postcancellation, and the first ever about a girl's personality. "X-Ray Vision," it was called, because this was what he thought about the way her mind worked, her laser focus and keen ability to separate the things that mattered from the things that did not.

He played it for her in her room on Clarke, fingers shaking as he made the chords on the guitar. It wasn't a great song, but it came from the heart, which he figured either made it better or worse.

"You're sweet," she said.

After they'd been talking for a couple of weeks and she suggested a weekend away together, he felt compelled to interrupt the witty banter of their chat just to ask **u know I'm canceled, right?**

DAPHNE: **YEAH . . . WHAT? U THINK I LIVE UNDER A ROCK?**

JORDAN: **NO**

JORDAN: **NO**

JORDAN: **NOT AT ALL, I JUST WONDERED AND WANTED TO MAKE SURE BEFORE THIS WENT ANY FURTHER, OR MAYBE IF YOU HAD AN QUESTIONS**

JORDAN: ***ANY**

DAPHNE: **UM, YEAH, PRETTY SURE EVERYONE KNOWS THAT**

JORDAN: **OK**

JORDAN: **JUST WASN'T SURE. CAUSE YOU ALWAYS TREATED ME LIKE NORMAL.**

15.

If it went well with the cat, in three to five years they could have a baby. But then again, at their age three to five years was practically Mars. Anyway, then the siege happened. The cat turned on them and ran away. His body must have been in one of those pits north of the overpass but they'd never know for sure.

16.

The one time he'd let his anger consume him since Lisa had not been *at* Daphne but on her behalf. They'd just started seeing each other, that magical autumn when life seemed for the first time in months like something he could fathom being a part of. It was after she'd told him about a professor who took her home with him when she was so drunk she didn't even remember what happened next.

Jordan saw the man once, outside the Dollarama on Parc Avenue. The professor was small but round in the belly, with the same checkered Kangol hat Jordan had seen in his author photo online. Jordan felt his jaw tense and his toes go hot. The feeling went up both legs as he began to follow him.

Glancing over his shoulder, the professor quickened his pace, but Jordan did the same. This continued for five blocks until the professor walked up the stairs to his second-floor apartment off of Villeneuve.

All the lights went on in the apartment. He must have done the same with Daphne, Jordan thought, the sicko turning on the lights all the better to see her with. He was grinding his teeth, then picked up a rock and threw it through the fuck's window, not even running after the glass shattered because he was proud of what he'd done.

"Call the police, you fuckhead!" he called up to the second floor. "Or come down here and face me yourself!"

He wanted to touch the other man all over, press the menace's jaw into the pavement and make him cry out for God. It felt good just to think about; his fingers started to burn. And he wasn't scared because he knew if the police did come, he'd be able to explain himself calmly: *See there's this girl and she's agreed to see me separate from the mistakes of my past. If I don't do right by her now, how can I look myself in the face?*

Here, here, son, the officers would respond. *We too have made errors, but all is made right by the support of a good woman who loves you in spite of the past.*

Except, in the end, the only thing that happened was that Jordan waited outside for over an hour. The professor never came downstairs; sirens never appeared. Eventually, a neighbor walked by with a broom to sweep away the glass for his dog.

"You see what happened?" he asked. "This neighborhood's going to shit."

Jordan shook his head and made his way home. When he told Daphne what he'd done, she said he was crazy, then she started to cry. He cried too. They held each other and said that they had never felt this way before. "I think I thought I did once," he said. "But now I know it's only been true with you."

17.

So why then, that lazy morning in late May after the animals had died, did she tell him she wasn't sure if she loved him or not?

"It's just that half of me really misses my old life," she said. They were in bed and she couldn't stop crying. "My old friends and when everyone used to like me."

"Those girls who ditched you?" Her sheets had pink stripes and he could feel one of her socks at his feet, the green ones, he guessed by the way they curled against his toes, the ones with the little ruffle.

The sky through their window was clear and she spoke simply. "But they had a point. You and I have always agreed they had a point."

Jordan took a long inhale. He leaned back on the bed and told Daphne he understood. With his history, he was prepared to accept how difficult it was for a woman to be serious about him. He respected that. Respecting that was part of his accountability journey, but he also knew that what was always going to be more important was *her* journey. What *she* wanted and needed. He was committed to that, he said.

Then he swallowed. Now that he had made it through everything he was supposed to say, he told her how he really felt. "You're crazy," he said. "How can you say those things when we have so much fun together? I love you. And all that stuff with Lisa, there were still animals when that happened. You know I've changed."

He hadn't intended to make her cry more, but she sobbed and he didn't know what it meant. What was he to do with his relentless stinking life?

"The other half of me loves you very much," she said. "And I know that part of it is because it pisses other people off and part of it is because I don't care what people think and part of it is because of how you look and part of it is because of how it feels when we're together, and all it amounts to is that I love you four times over."

There was a poster of Joan Didion on one wall and a poster of Sade on the other. It always smelled like flowers and he never knew why; she didn't wear perfume or even use scented lotion, it was just one of her mysteries. He felt guilty for liking the way she looked with her nose red and her eyes all puffy. Not because he was happy she was sad, but simply because it was a new version of her. He wanted to know everything her face could do.

She took a gulp of air, then steadied herself, tucking her hair behind her ears. "But the fact of the matter is that we don't have enough money."

"I know," she continued, looking up at him, "with your *situation*, I know it's hard on you, but I'm tired of all the looks I get at parties. Meanwhile you don't even pitch in for groceries."

He got an idea then, a grand idea that occurred to him as turnkey as his best songs did: fully realized, not a detail to think twice about. Life worked best when it was easy like that. He felt good about himself, he felt powerful.

CHAPTER FIVE

Daphne Meets a Boy

1.

The night of the fire, they stayed over at Jordan's friend Gabe's place. Yes, he was canceled too, but he lived right down the street and by then everyone was exhausted. Daphne, Jordan, and Jenlena carried their things and Gabe buzzed them inside the dark, smoky apartment.

Gabe had yellow track pants sitting so low on his torso that his hip bones showed; they made little shadows in the shape of crescent moons. "Tough luck," he said to the girls. "And is it true one of you was having an abortion?"

"That'd be me," said Jenlena, dropping herself down on the couch. "A fire and an abortion in one day. I guess this is what they call scorched earth."

The living room was covered in ashtrays, sound equipment, and computer monitors. When Jordan asked, Gabe explained that he was working on a new project inspired by the California billionaire Roderick Maeve. "You know how he killed all of the animals just with sound? I think it ought to make people realize they should be paying more respect to what we do. My big comeback."

For dinner, they ordered pizza that tasted like paste.

Later, while they brushed their teeth with their fingers in the bathroom, Jenlena asked Daphne what Gabe had been canceled for, but Daphne couldn't remember. Only that several years ago she'd seen him play music at a loft on Bélanger and one of the actors from *Game of Thrones* had shown up and he'd kissed her friend in the bathroom. "But there are only so many things," she said. "Use your imagination."

Jordan had lent them two T-shirts: one with a picture of Florence Griffith Joyner and one with a coffee stain in the shape of a gun. They'd taken off their shorts so that they were wearing only their panties underneath, and Jenlena wasn't shy about changing her maxi pad in front of Daphne. "I just want to go to bed," she said, groaning. Her stomach was so flat; it didn't hurt a bit.

Daphne nodded. "You'll get the couch, don't worry. I already talked it over with Jordan. The two of us will sleep on the floor, okay?"

"Thank you."

"You know," she said, sitting on the edge of the tub so that Jenlena would do the same and they'd be closer to the same size. "Sometimes I have a feeling like there's a secret club made up of girls who've had abortions. Like, at work, I watch the women walk by on the street and try to guess if they're, like, members or not, and sometimes I can't tell, but sometimes I feel like I really actually can. In the beginning, you talk about it all the time. You, like, take up all the space at the club meetings. Then, gradually, you talk about it less and less, but you're still always going to be a part of that club."

Jenlena remained standing. "Do you ever think? Like with all this weird time machine stuff everyone's talking about?"

"Oh, no. Oh, god, no."

2.

Since before she could remember, Daphne had always been a good girl. She'd studied hard and associated with the right people. After high school, she moved to Montreal to perfect her French, choosing the English department at a university that was less renowned but, according to her research, had more professors doing innovative work. The smaller program could give her an edge among her classmates. She was sure she would go to graduate school, perhaps even in America, where rumor had it the stipends could be upward of $20,000 a year.

She'd get a master's degree, get a PhD, have a baby after her coursework—perhaps with a classmate or even one of her professors—get a postdoc, a full-time teaching position, and finally tenure. Then she'd be happy.

She knew what she wanted, but something held Daphne back. In her most bitter moments she blamed Jenlena. *If I'd gone to grad school*, Daphne often thought, *somewhere like California or New York, who'd be left to tell her when she had toothpaste on her shirt?* But that wasn't it, not exactly. She'd never even sent a single application to any of the programs she'd researched. Even when her friend Livvie lent her the money for the application fees, Daphne had spent it on collagen powder and a single afternoon at the thermal spa.

So after graduation she decided to take a year off and got a full-time office job in Kahnawake, which she felt was impressive in its own right because most people she knew in the city lived off of their parents or worked seven hours a week doing various forms of other people's domestic work.

The office was on the seventeenth floor of a high-rise with a view of Montreal's South Shore. Because it was Mohawk territory, certain things were allowed that would not have been in Montreal, which was also Mohawk territory, but not legally. Her company had the whole floor divided into cubicles with a round desk in the center where Daphne's manager sat on a swivel chair that was always sinking. Every morning, he debriefed everyone on how well their clickbait articles directed traffic to their online gambling sites. Most of the team took notes, so Daphne did too: *click rates, anti-spam laws, SEO*. But it was never long before she lost her concentration and took to doodling pictures of her coworkers: the young man who always wore a starched white shirt, the white woman with dreads, the older man who was always feeding everyone french fries he made in the air fryer he kept at his desk. Legend was that he'd won it last quarter for having the highest click rates.

On a good day, Daphne started actually working around lunchtime, concocting five to ten stories about locals who had won big in online poker: Therese the single mom, Ali the new immigrant. The chair hurt her back. Around three, she took a long break to use her phone in the bathroom, mostly googling Moon Cicero, the girl the boy she was currently falling in love with had ruined his life over. Sometimes she felt like she was daring her superiors to reprimand her, but no one ever seemed to notice how little work she did.

"Fresh batch! And these are with truffle oil!"

If she heard one more person chewing she'd scream. Daphne wanted to feel the way she did when she was younger, that the world was something that belonged to her, and not the other way around. She could reach out with her arms and bend it to her will. Out the window, the sky was clear save for one long chemtrail, dead center, and she swore it had just winked at her. It said, "You've been a good girl all your life, haven't you?"

That was when Daphne pulled the air fryer out from the wall and threw it against the glass. Down below, it fell on a woman's toe. She sued the office for $50,000 and Daphne was let go without severance. Since then, she'd been working in a coffee shop fifteen hours a week.

A few years earlier, her outburst might have been a big news story, but to be alive today was to hear things like this all the time. Perfectly normal people losing their minds. A woman who drove her car straight into a brick wall just to post it on Instagram, a group of students in China who hadn't spoken in six months. One of the horse girls who Jenlena went to high school with showed up naked one day at a supermarket. "As far as I'm concerned," she explained to reporters, "my body is now property of the weather."

3.

The only thing Daphne missed about her job in Kahnawake was the commute: two buses and a train. Days that began at 6 a.m., but it was worth it to feel like she was a part of the city's ecosystem, picking sleep out of her eyes with the rest of the populace on those raised velour seats with the funky print. Then there was this stretch of downtown where the bus turned west and she could see the sun coming up between skyscrapers, lighting the boulevard pink. Say what you want about society, but she really had it all figured out on mornings like that.

Now she worked at a coffee shop, and her commute consisted of a five-minute walk down Avenue Fairmount, a street flooded with Torontonians Airbnbing for the weekend for a final sojourn before the end of time. Despite the proximity, however, Daphne was usually at least a half hour late. But she'd been trying to show up more often than she called in sick. Of late, she'd at least been trying to try. She needed the money.

One day, after the animals but before the fire, Daphne's coworker, Patricia, wore a succulent in a tiny glass orb around her neck and said it was for emotional support. People were like this now with their plants; they called them their babies and constructed whole personalities for them. Caitlin, her cousin's monstera, for example, tended to shrivel when men were around because of past trauma.

"We have to show the plants we love and appreciate them," Patricia said. "It's our responsibility. We can't let it happen again, like with the animals."

Daphne stifled a laugh. It was beyond her why anyone was trying to make it work in a world without animals. It was psychotic. Jenlena, especially, had been driving her crazy. How could she be so happy, prancing around in her plush costumes, barking. Was it normal to hate your best friend this much?

"I talked to Troy about it and he's totally supportive," Patricia said. "But it means I can't use the steamer anymore, because it could burn the leaves."

"Only as much as it could burn our skin," Daphne said.

"Yes, but this is for my *mental* health." She stroked the leaves of the tiny jade plant softly as she spoke. "Believe me, I talked to Troy."

This didn't surprise Daphne because their boss, Troy, was a total pushover. She thought Troy was handsome, but only in the most boring way. He dressed well and was impeccably neat. Even his fingernails were manicured. Daphne had noticed this when he first showed her how to work the steamer, and was embarrassed that she still thought about it.

Before the animals, he used to keep live traps in the kitchen and drive out of the city every Sunday night to release the mice in the country. She had gone with him once when she needed the hours, and he told her about how he'd opened the shop using money from his grandfather, who'd been somehow involved with the Habs. "And my dad died pretty young, so . . ."

Daphne was used to the way rich people talked about money, always as if the particular circumstances of how they'd come to have so much of it were too mind-numbing to get into.

Upper middle class, she was used to correcting. Yada yada yada. One of her old friends was even second cousins with the prime minister. The kind of people who had beautiful haircuts and cared about society in all the respectable ways: owned bamboo forks, ran 5k for women in Afghanistan.

Her old friends: Livvie, Tobbie, Mellie, and Bryce-Ève. Most of the time they seemed like any other girls, but when you looked closely their earrings had real diamonds or their chokers were 14 karat gold. The little black backpack they carried instead of a purse was genuine Prada. They didn't "get" her friend Jenlena. "She's always staring into space. Is it a learning disability?" Daphne knew them mostly through extracurriculars.

Troy drove a nice car. It had leather seats and a little screen on the dash to help you park and change lanes. Twice, she caught herself wondering what would happen if anyone saw her like this, with a handsome, respectable man.

I guess she's come to her senses, her old friends might say. *Maybe we shouldn't have been so rash. After all, she'd been our friend for so many years. Daphne! Who was so smart and whom we admired in many ways both vague and specific, of course we should have trusted her to make the right decision!*

The mice spoke to each other in the plastic cage in the back seat. There was a rhythm to the way they squeaked, highs and lows in the frequency.

"Do you think they're scared?" Daphne asked as they crossed the river. "Or do they know this is good for them?"

"I'd be scared," he said. "But that's the thing. It *is* scary. They're trapped, they're being taken away from their home. No more almond croissants to nibble on. So it's harrowing, all stuck together in the dark. And even though we're actually helping them, there's no way for them to comprehend that. Though harrowing now, it's precisely what makes it so harrowing that's going to actually improve their standard of life."

The next week the plastic cage was full of mice again, half a dozen who looked and sounded exactly the same, who didn't even know their whole lives were about to change.

Nobody texted her. Nobody ever called to say they saw things from her perspective.

4.

In the beginning, dating a canceled man had been a rush like no other. They'd met at a party in a warehouse building where lamps were sold on the first floor. Daphne had been with her old friends sharing a liter of natural wine by the stove. Jordan was with his creepy friend Gabe, rolling a joint on the washing machine across the room.

"Come on," her friends said when they saw him. They wanted to leave. "We can't condone this."

"No," Daphne said. "I think I'll stay."

She didn't know what had possessed her. She'd been like this lately, reading about how much money corporations funneled into politics and contemplating the meaning of futility.

They got to talking and it turned out they liked a lot of the same movies and had the exact same birthday. Of her whole life, there had only been two hours without him on this earth, Daphne crowning in the late morning in Mississauga, Jordan arriving via C-section in the midafternoon four hundred thirty-five miles north, just outside of Timmins.

In the days and weeks to come, they texted. Jordan asked Daphne how she was doing at work and sent songs he thought she might like. None of her friends knew, not even Jenlena. She could hardly even admit to herself how often she was checking her phone. On YouTube, she watched all of his videos, especially the one song about releasing his pet turtle into the wild. In the comments, everyone said he was disgusting and deserved to die a hundred times, but his lyrics were so beautiful that the song made Daphne cry.

It was the autumn before the siege and so many of her other relationships had started to feel perfunctory. Jenlena was obsessing over one of her TAs, and Daphne's other friends inundated their text thread with hot takes on the latest banking scandal in America. Livvie and Tobbie had started their law degrees, Bryce-Ève and Mellie were already putting out feelers among family friends for reference letters.

But with Jordan, life began to glitter. They talked about the birds they saw on the way home from the corner store and the bass line of a song he showed her from Peru. As a boy he had promised himself never to be cold again; he had simply decided. It was a matter of attitude, he said, and tried to teach Daphne to do the same by standing with her in a cold shower and touching the places on her body he wanted her to breathe from. Sometimes they didn't talk about anything at all. This was her favorite, just lying in the bed with nothing to do.

5.

Jenlena had to check if she was hearing her correctly. "Jordan from KoolNUsual? Like, the guy who punched Moon Cicero?"

They sat facing each other on the couch in their old apartment. Both had competing scented candles lit in their rooms: cherry blossom something and vanilla freshly cut lawn. Daphne lowered her voice. "She wasn't Moon Cicero then, she was just some girl from London, Ontario. But yes, I have fallen in love with a canceled man."

Everyone knew the details: how she was underage when they first met, the bruises on her wrist; he'd been so mean to her that ketamine was the only thing that made her feel better, but then she did so much she started having visions where everything around her was on fire; her friends had taken her to the hospital because she kept trying to peel off her own skin and Jordan didn't even visit her while she was there.

"It's why Livvie and Tobbie stopped coming around. Bryce-Ève won't even text me back." Tears rimmed Daphne's lower lashes.

"In love?" Jenlena verified, her eyes wide.

"It's the craziest feeling. Every morning I wake up and I feel right on the verge of either barfing or having an orgasm."

6.

Rest assured, she put him through all kinds of hoops. Jordan read every book she told him to and they didn't even have sex. Daphne didn't forget the stories she'd heard about Moon Cicero, who was just that autumn beginning to give provocative interviews on podcasts. Daphne listened to them all: she was 100 percent on board with *bearing witness*. She followed her on Twitter and scrolled through the statuses, eyes peeled for photographs of the beautiful young girl. She read every profile, thinking all the while about what it must have been like between them, this beautiful young girl and her boyfriend.

"Do you think she's pretty?" Daphne always asked Jenlena.

"Well, sure, but only in the most obvious way."

"What does that mean?"

"Like anyone would think so."

"Oh great, so you agree she's insanely gorgeous. And she's clinically insane, which means empirically she's bonkers in bed."

Jenlena shook her head. "But sometimes people prefer something flawed so they can really feel it belongs to them rather than the obvious choice they'd share with the rest of the world. Besides, don't they say that pretty girls are bad in bed? They say that fat girls are more grateful. I had a boyfriend who told me that. I think he meant it as a compliment."

Once and only once had Daphne asked Jordan if he ever still thought about her. "Who?" He must have been lying because she'd never seen him make that shape with his nose. "Oh, Lisa? Oh, no. Never."

"What happened, exactly?"

He told her it was all his fault. "I take responsibility." He furrowed his brow, but said no more.

What had it looked and felt and tasted like? Because true cruelty must have been its own intimacy, and when it came to Jordan she wanted everything.

7.

For almost three months, all he did was eat out her pussy. "Now that's what French food *should* taste like," he told her once, his lips all buttery. For her final project at school, she wrote a poem for which she learned the word *turgor* just to describe his body.

It won a big prize, $500, but he laughed at her. "Don't you know?" he said. "If it's real art, people aren't supposed to like it for five to ten years, at least."

"But I like your songs," she said. "So what about that?"

He closed his eyes and put his palm to his chest in mock sincerity. "I suppose I can bear it."

Already people had begun to look at her sideways. Mellie asked who she was texting so much. "What's that song?" Tobbie wanted to know.

"What?"

"You were just humming."

"Oh, nothing."

Daphne didn't fuck Jordan until the day she threw the air fryer at work. She went right over to his place and told him she couldn't believe what had happened. "I got fired, I don't know what I'll do."

He took her in his arms and said that sometimes our mistakes could be the best things about us. At least that was what happened to him, he felt, because if he'd never been canceled he would have been on tour and never gone to that party where they first met. He would never have seen her standing so perfect by the stove. "Really, I know I'm supposed to regret everything, but I can't." He had a way of clenching his jaw when he really meant what he was saying, and he was doing it now; she could feel it from how she lay on his shoulder.

Then they fucked and when she came she felt her pulse envelop the room, the city, the province, she swore she could feel her heart beating from space. Yes, she understood he had made mistakes. But she'd come to believe she knew him deeper than that.

They all had this, a place inside untouched by the things they said and did. At least in theory, she thought.

He moved into her apartment and they rescued a kitten. When the animals took over the city, they watched a parade of them move through the streets: there were dogs and cats and ferrets and all the mosquitoes and black bears in from the country, a bull moose holding up the rear. The day the California billionaire released his deadly signal, Daphne and Jordan held hands as they watched the bodies fall. He wiped her cheeks and she held him when he started to shake. The next morning, she woke up and he'd drawn over a hundred pictures of all the species he could think of.

"So we don't forget," he said. He was good at everything to do with art and could see music in shapes and colors.

8.

For example:

9.

"The craziest thing about pets," Jordan said on a Monday morning before the siege as they watched their kitten sleep, the tuft of fur on his belly pointing toward the sunbeams spilling across the kitchen, "is that one year for us is like five years for them. One day he'll be older than us. Soon, he'll be the old guy, teaching us about life." They stayed like this, watching him sleep on the counter with a bag of spring greens as a pillow.

He'd saved the animal from the alley, and in the beginning, they'd been doubtful the kitten would make it through the night. Jordan fed him milk from a syringe. As she watched, Daphne had decided she wanted to know everything about Jordan. She wanted to crawl inside his body and poke around from the inside. Snuggle up, take a nap.

When the kitten made it to three pounds, Jordan suggested the name Rolex. "Because I've always wanted one," he said. "Is that bad?"

"I don't know," she said. "I'll have to check the internet."

10.

Massive droughts, a military coup, multiple suicides on the world stage. Sometimes, Daphne thought, with all the problems in the world, people might do better to care a little less about women. It all felt so stupid now, juvenile. *I'd let a hundred men rape me on st catherines street just to hear a cat purring*, she posted on her Instagram story, but it was removed for violating community standards. Besides, how come no one ever wanted to hear Jordan's side, how his dad was such a bad drunk that Jordan had practically learned how to be a man from television. That, to her, was just as much society.

11.

Other times, she cared about women very much. She herself knew from experience what it felt like be told your body wasn't really yours. For a man to do what he wanted and treat your feelings as if they were tertiary.

It meant something that in most places it was now illegal for men to rape their wives and that women no longer died from sticking coat hangers inside of themselves. Her own grandmother had gotten an abortion in a dingy hotel room in downtown Vancouver. She felt in her bones a responsibility to live up to the sacrifices others had made on her behalf. It would have been impolite not to.

She cared about her old friends too. Those bright, ambitious young women she'd spent the last four years with in university, who'd called her a rape accomplice, though not even in the most vicious corners of the comments section had Jordan ever been accused of raping anyone.

And it wasn't like the girl was complaining about it. She was pretty much the most famous Moon Bethlehem there was. Daphne saw her on *CBC Prime Time* saying, "You wanna know what I think about the world right now?" Moon Cicero had wide-set eyes and pressed the tip of her tongue through the gap in her teeth. "I think as a population, we've all become like someone on their deathbed, calling up our old transgressions and making apologies. It's pretty easy, really, when you've got no real intention of changing. You know you don't have to because you haven't got the time.

I think there's a lot more we know collectively than most of us are willing to admit individually."

Then there were the days Jordan didn't get out of bed till dinner time. He didn't get dressed or even brush his teeth and his eyes were bloodshot from scrolling through his phone. He did drugs alone while she was at work even after she expressly asked him not to. "Hey baby," he'd say. "Look at this thing I found on Reddit," and it'd be a meme of Obama farting Chernobyl.

Could people really change? People, sure. But men? Perhaps it was too soon to tell. She posted a picture of herself at the window, the sunbeams glittering across the hair on her upper lip in a way that made her feel like Frida Kahlo, though it may or may not have been racist to think so.

12.

At Gabe's, Daphne had a view underneath the couch from where she settled onto the floor with Jordan's denim jacket for a pillow. He was in the bedroom with his friend, talking about music. There was nothing she liked less than listening to that type of conversation. Not that she didn't enjoy what Jordan did. She had only three times in her life slept with someone who she did not respect artistically, and once had been with a professor who'd forced her. But music, to her, was like sex, or perhaps even more intimate, like masturbation. Best felt and not explained. Why did boys always need to go on about riffs all the time?

Now she was in one of those moods where quiet noises were made louder by noticing them. Just a friendly talk between two canceled men in the next room. What was muffled became clear simply by how much it annoyed her. She could make out whole phrases: "But the J Mascis version?" "Or *Live in Santa Fe*!"

Her hair smelled like smoke. It was hard to believe that the fire had been today, just a few hours ago. Daphne had been lying in her bed reading Moon Cicero tweets, imagining Jordan having sex with someone so explosive, when she began to smell something burning. Jordan rushed through the back door from down the fire escape and called her name. They grabbed what they could but the heat was already rising. Outside, she saw the flames, writhing and wild, the closest thing to an animal that now existed on earth. Jordan held her from behind, whispering in her ear that everything would be okay. She could feel him through his jeans and pushed backwards.

Now, lying on the floor at Gabe's, she was convinced she could hear a mouse in the walls and had to remind herself that the apartment was just dirty. She did what she always did when she found herself worked up: listed off every prize she had ever won in her head. *Emerging Poet, Promising Artist Raised by a Single Mother, Quebec Writers' Federation Rising Star.* The syllables calmed her down. She could relax, drift away to that special place. She would be alright.

Winning was not so difficult, at least for her. In general, the demands of the prizes were quite straightforward. *Best Poem by an Undergraduate. The Mile Ex Review Biannual Metaphor of the Year.* Many people believed that "best" was nebulous, but that was only true in the most general sense and generalities bored her. Real winners homed in on specifics. A term paper, a writing prize, a fuck buddy. You had to look at a situation carefully and it would tell you what it wanted.

She'd described this philosophy to that one professor. He'd invited her out for drinks to talk about some of her poems and said he couldn't remember the last time he'd met a student so ambitious.

"It's not ambition," she said. "I'm just focused. Most people are addicted to making things complicated."

"Most girls," he said, signaling to the bartender for another round, Daphne's last that she would remember. He was eleven years her senior and liked to recite "A Supermarket in California" with his eyes closed.

Daphne shook her head. "I'm serious," she said. "We pollute our own mentalities."

The Morgentaler Prize for Feminist Prose Poems, Concordia University One to Watch.

But what did it matter?

She woke up the next morning naked in his apartment with no recollection of what had happened. She groaned and he laughed. "Wild night," he said. He already had his clothes on, even his belt. He gave her a warm glass of water in an old Tostitos salsa jar, and sometimes she thought she'd spend the rest of her life trying to decide if she was lucky to not know what had really happened. *Maybe you had a nice time.*

Bryce-Ève, a psychology major, wrote her a long message theorizing that Daphne was choosing Jordan because of the professor. Victims seek out relationships with other abusers because abusers offer the illusion of safety within their familiarity. **You**, she said of Daphne, **are a textbook example.**

She went on to describe several graphic details of Daphne's intimate history that Daphne couldn't remember ever telling her, ever telling anyone, except, when she wracked her brain about it, maybe once when she was really drunk after the night in question. She'd been drinking a lot during that time; sometimes she drew on herself with permanent marker. **You didn't even shower afterwards for 3 days because you were so afraid of seeing yourself naked. That is TRAUMA and you CANT outrun it.**

Daphne never replied.

A hundred migrants drowned off the coast of Spain, children starved to death in Yemen, the animals were dead. One day she threw the air fryer out the window and fucked her canceled boyfriend and now she was sleeping on the floor. So what good was a prize, anyway? What if all along they meant nothing?

Above her, on the torn velvet couch, Jenlena mumbled in her sleep, then rolled over onto her side. It was hot and she'd slipped her left arm out of her T-shirt, revealing the lower half of her breast. Daphne looked at it—her eyes were adjusted to the dark. Not that they even needed to be: she'd seen her friend naked a million times and could easily conjure the little pink circles, smaller and lighter than her own. Her mother's were like this too, Irish ancestry.

As a teenager, Daphne had seen her mother change out of her bathing suit and was horrified to see those bright pink, delicate orbs on a woman nearly fifty, while Daphne herself, at just seventeen and following her first abortion, had dark nipples already nearly twice the size. Hers must have come from her father then, she thought, a man she'd barely seen since he'd left three years earlier to chase tornadoes in the prairies.

She tried to remember if his nipples were like hers, but couldn't picture him without his shirt. It was crazy. He was her father, surely they must have been to the pool together. Did he ever take her swimming, at least in the summer? Or on a hot day, just around the house without a shirt on. Would it have been so unusual for a father to do that and his daughter to remember it? She wanted to know where her body came from. Finally, she remembered an old photograph, him in high school with his older brother in Prince Edward Island, but by then she was already asleep.

13.

Jordan woke up the girls with fresh bagels and Ultramar mocha slushies, and said he had a great idea.

"I went back to the apartment building," he said. He jumped from side to side as though his own body were made up of hot coals and could somehow be avoided.

"Babe," said Daphne, yawning as she stretched the word into two syllables. "What's going on? Are you okay?"

A smile broke out across his face. "Aren't you *listening*? I went back to the building. Our home. I went all the way inside. It's not as bad as you think. The lower unit. I went all the way inside and it hardly even smells. I swear, baby. You'll get used to the smell." He had ash on his fingertips, a streak across his forehead.

"Jordan," she told him. "I don't understand."

"*Daphne*, it's exciting. It's what you wanted, isn't it? Just what we were talking about. How you said we couldn't afford the rent anymore. Baby, I think it's a miracle."

He was right, it was an incredible feeling to sneak into the basement of the building through a back window. Was this how fire moved? Slinky and without manners? They could pretend to be that free if they wanted to.

"So what do you think?" Jordan grinned, holding his arms out to gesture at the room around them: the kitchen of the basement unit where the three young men had lived. Dishes had been left in the sink and there was a half-eaten piece of toast on the counter. The layout was the same as the girls' apartment upstairs; there was even a maroon futon in the exact same corner where the girls had kept the IKEA pullout couch Jenlena's stepfather had bought for them when their lease first began.

"I told you," Jordan said. He stood with the posture of a beloved man, the same shoulders that had stood in front of crowds and performed his deepest feelings set to music. "Isn't it a miracle? We could live here! We could stay here for free, and you won't have to worry about money anymore."

Daphne looked at him blankly, as if the decision in front of her was a math equation whose method was just out of reach. She'd been sick from school that day and forgotten to get the notes from a friend.

"I mean it's not a *bad* idea," Jenlena ventured from behind her, already sprawled out on the futon. "But you really don't think these guys'll come back for their stuff?"

"No way," said Jordan. "Look around." There were unopened textbooks on an otherwise empty shelf and a sweat-stained Lacoste polo hanging in the bathroom. Later, Jenlena would fish out of a pair of jizz-crusted Ben Sherman briefs from between the cushions.

"Guys like this," Jordan continued, "they don't give a shit about their stuff. I heard them yesterday practically crying on the phone, begging their parents to come pick them up."

"The landlord did send an email this morning," Jenlena said, pulling out her phone. "The whole building's been condemned. All our leases are void."

Yes, it was a miracle. Daphne ran her hands through her hair and sighed. "Alright," she said, looking around. "Home it is."

"I'll always take care of you," Jordan told her that night in the dark. "I'm going to give you everything."

"Yes, baby," she said.

"Tell me you know I can do it. Tell me I can do anything for you." She licked the sweat down his neck, she bit his fingers.

14.

M●●N_cicero_666 @Moon.Cicero 6m

Baby's first spread in @chatelaine magazine. Definitely not a natural covergirl but kudos to @sheilaheti for letting me drone on

M●●N_cicero_666 @Moon.Cicero 5m

about how much i've come to believe in pessimism as a radical act of self care

M●●N_cicero_666 @Moon.Cicero 5m

+ kudos to my glam squad for dressing me in all recycled denim

M●●N_cicero_666 @Moon.Cicero 5m

Really cute looks!

M●●N_cicero_666 @Moon.Cicero 4m

Basically the point i'm tryna make is that rt now capitalism + so many of the forces creating the most weather rely on your optimism

M●●N_cicero_666 @Moon.Cicero 4m

think about when u buy things and it makes u feel better and ur life easier, but once u accept that we've reached a point

M●●N_cicero_666 @Moon.Cicero 3m

in the life of this planet where feeling good isn't a viable option, u'r rly just kidding yrself

M●●N_cicero_666 @Moon.Cicero 2m

u'd do better just accepting the inevitable

M●●N_cicero_666 @Moon.Cicero 2m

really the peace and serenity i see in ppl after just 2 weeks with us is incredible.

M●●N_cicero_666 @Moon.Cicero 2m

I drive by malls and it makes me more sad than heroin addicts

M●●N_cicero_666 @Moon.Cicero 1m

Ppl buy things becos they think it'll make them happy but rly u have 2 accept

M●●N_cicero_666 @Moon.Cicero 0m

u'll never be happy so you buy nada and the factories in china go quiet

15.

The day after they snuck back into the building, Daphne, Jordan, and Jenlena slept in and hardly grunted good morning. Daphne lay across Jordan's lap on the futon, Jenlena sat cross-legged on the floor. She was bleeding. She could smell it from her crotch, though the ash and lingering smokiness was stronger.

On Twitter, everyone was talking about Roderick Maeve, who had just confirmed that the rumors were true. Live from California, he announced that he was, indeed, building a time machine. Jordan found a stream of the press conference and propped up his phone on a near-empty bowl of cereal left behind on the coffee table.

Daphne sat up and leaned forward. The moment would never leave her. Even as it was happening, she knew that would be true.

Jordan in his Nike shorts and with toothpaste caked in the corners of his lips. Jenlena in her nightgown with chipped nail polish, the dust glittering in the light. All those weeks of drudgery released themselves in an instant. She was who she had always been. There were so many years ahead of her, calling her name: *Come on in, the water's warm!*

"They'll bring the animals back with this," she said. "I'm sure of it."

She reached for Jenlena's hand and squeezed it tightly. But when she turned to her friend she was shocked by the sight. "Oh my god! What's wrong? You look like you've seen a ghost!"

Jenlena swallowed. "It's fine. Such great news."

"See, babe?" Jordan shook Daphne by the shoulders. "Everything's going to be okay." He kissed her on the mouth.

Daphne stood up, changed out of her pajamas, and took a cold shower.

That night was Saint-Jean-Baptiste Day, the provincial holiday passed down from the first French colonists in the New World. Jordan didn't usually like going out but Daphne insisted. She couldn't sit still. "We need to celebrate," she said. "We're alive and it's not going anywhere."

16.

Bonnie Cicero stood with her friends by one of the DJs, waiting with nervous excitement for her MDMA to kick in. She was twenty-four and lived for the summer, though believed mournfully that this year could mark her last without adult responsibilities. Come fall, she'd be twenty-five and real life would begin in earnest.

She wanted to move to Toronto and work in a newsroom, or to Ottawa and work her way up through the government, or eventually start her own nonprofit. Partly because she knew she had a way with people—it was one of her gifts. She was a natural leader and wasn't ashamed of it. No, she would not shrink from the responsibility of being exceptional. Partly because she fundamentally believed in the world, its virtues and potential. Two hundred years ago, for example, she could have been traded for sheep between her father and some drunk widower. But because thousands of brave and nameless people had put their lives on the line for change, she was here doing drugs at a loft party near Rosemont Station. She wore an oversized leather blazer and knew for a fact it looked fantastic, the same way she knew for a fact this remix of the Cranberries' "Dreams" had come on just for her, the bass creeping up her spine and tickling behind her ears.

Homelessness, for example, which she had just taken a course in. It had been nearly eradicated in Finland, and recently another study out of British Columbia showed that when you gave people $7,500 that basically solved the whole problem. These were real, tangible gains. They were within reach. And! She just also remembered too! The prisons in Norway! The collective business model of Gore-Tex! A FUCKING TIME MACHINE!

Bonnie accepted a piece of gum from a friend in a tutu and a chainmail hood. So there were real, tangible things and she wanted to be a part of them. Her deepest darkest secret was that she found herself immune to the malaise that had held hostage so many of her peers. Yes, it was a privilege but also a responsibility. She herself had already led the charge against a powerful male musician in their community who she knew for a fact had used his influence to coerce young girls into drugs and sex and then emotionally manipulated them to his every whim until their sense of self was so shattered they had to run away and join a cult.

"Hey Bonnie," said another friend, rubbing his acrylic nails up and down her cheek. "Oh my god. Bonnie, you're so beautiful. Can you feel that?"

"Yes," she said, running her hands along her friend's face, then down her own, down her neck, and along her chest. She unbuttoned her jacket to be as free as possible, moving through the music and then inside of it.

Fundamentally, she was not a vindictive person. Look at this city! The crowd was so beautiful. There was no better place to come of age, and the conditions that made it so were an ongoing project she was committed to continuing in whatever way she could.

One day, when she'd finally made her mark on the world, say at forty or so, she'd put her feet up and say to her younger sister, "See? See what our lives are worth? Turns out you were wrong and I was right because we weren't doomed. You never had to run away to join the Moon Bethlehems because we really can make this world better."

And Lisa would say, "Yes, you're right, the world is good."

And she would come home.

17.

Tonight the crowd bumped and grinded in honor of the man who over 2000 years ago foretold Jesus. There was a group with their faces painted blue and white, the colors of the provincial flag. Another couple had glow sticks; the girl broke a green one open with her teeth and began to rub the neon liquid inside across her eyelids, then the cheekbones of the boy. They kissed.

Jordan hadn't wanted to come out, but it was Saint-Jean's, and Daphne had begged him. Besides, they'd heard about the party from one of Jenlena's Québécois friends, so they didn't expect to know anyone there. This was Montreal, however, and nearly everyone had at least made out with each other.

When they saw Bonnie Cicero they felt the blood rush out of their faces in tandem. Daphne reached for his hand, but Jordan resisted her. "I, I," he stammered. "I gotta go."

He made a beeline for the bathrooms, leaving Daphne alone in the crowded room. She had never seen Bonnie before, not in the flesh, and the girl felt somehow both less and more beautiful than her photographs online. Both bigger and smaller.

The music felt louder now, the room much warmer. She pressed her back against the wall as the crowd began to move as one.

I'm sorry, Jordan texted. **I'm a pussy**

I'm sorry i'm sorry i'm sorry

I'm such a fucking pussy

C u at home

She was just about to type a reply when a voice from behind said her name like a question. "I thought that was you." Daphne turned around to see Troy from work with a temporary fleur-de-lys tattoo on his cheek. Wasn't he a little old for a party like this? Did it mean that she was old too? The thought depressed her even more than her boyfriend cowering in shame over Bonnie Cicero, who was currently dancing with her eyes closed atop a folding table where some young men had been selling PBR. Tears streamed down her face. She stuck out her tongue and licked them up.

"I'm sorry," he said before she'd even spoken a word. "It's so loud in here I can't hear you. Wanna step outside?"

Daphne nodded. He led the way and she followed.

18.

"Ancient Rome. I've always wanted to go back and see what it was like. Plus, I think it would be really good for us as a culture to once and for all know what Cleopatra actually looked like."

—FRANCIS MARQUETTE, NEW LONDON, CONNECTICUT

"I'd consider it a service to world cinema if we went back and prevented the death of Heath Ledger."

—KRISTINE HAYES, BOSTON, MASSACHUSETTS

"Lord knows I've made mistakes in my life. Focused on the wrong things. I could go back and make things right with my kids. The thought alone helps me get out of bed in the morning. I know I'm not the only one. Since all this time machine business was announced, something's shifted. You can feel it in the air, like the world's changing already."

—CARLO KLEIN, DENVER, COLORADO

"With today's medical knowledge there's no reason my father had to die. I'd go back in time and tell him to get checked by his doctor in the fall of 1992. Just a simple procedure to remove the mass, followed by a brief course of chemotherapy, and I'd have my father again. There's no telling what I'd be able to accomplish then. I certainly would never have become a drug addict."

—KELLY HWANG, LAFAYETTE, ARKANSAS

"Three words: bludgeon baby Hitler."

—KEVIN WILKS, SPOKANE, WASHINGTON

19.

Daphne knew that before the animals, Roderick Maeve had gotten rich off the American housing crisis and other complex financial maneuvers she had never seen the point in trying to comprehend. Rather, she passively consumed information about the antics of his personal life. In one interview, an ex-wife had called him temperamental and said he'd once crushed up the morning after pill into her chia seed pudding. Still, despite everything, the woman felt compassion for him because he was, as she put it, the type of person who'd order a banana split and eat everything except the banana. Daphne had read this in a magazine at a dentist's office and never forgotten. It made sense to her because she thought perhaps, at her core, she was that type of person too.

The day after the time machine was announced, all of Daphne's coworkers were talking about it. Bridget, the philosophy grad student who always wore a bolo tie, said she thought the whole thing must be a publicity stunt.

"Sure," said Yves, the French-from-France fiber artist who was addicted to kratom. "But nobody believed he could kill all the animals either."

"He's going to license the technology to businesses," said Ann-Christine, the dance student with impeccable posture and rotting teeth. "Whoever pays the most will be able to use it to maximize their profits however they want."

"We'll get the animals back, though, won't we?" Daphne refused to be embarrassed by her excitement.

"Sure, but at what cost?"

"We need the animals," she said. "That's a nonnegotiable."

"It's Roderick Maeve's world," said Bridget. "And we just live in it. He takes away the animals just because it pleases him and he brings them back just because he's in a better mood. It's just like the time my dad ran over the dog."

"I just read today that a British power company is going to pay $75,000,000 to go back to the Industrial Revolution and install their solar panels," said Troy.

"Which makes no sense!" said Yves. "So much of the technology that solar power was first predicated upon hadn't even been invented yet, let alone the materials they'd need to build it back then! Believe me, in a month we'll all be laughing our heads off."

Patricia, whose shift was just ending, said she didn't trust Roderick Maeve because he was a misogynist. Today, in addition to the jade around her neck, she had twin aloe veras hanging from her ears.

Daphne laughed out loud. "You can't just not believe in something because you don't like it," she said. "Misogynists are everywhere. You don't just get to tap out because you find it unsavory."

"I'm not," said Yves. "I am not a misogynist."

"Of course I can choose not to participate," Patricia said. "I *have*. If your lifestyle isn't ethical, then that's your problem. But you don't get to make assumptions about me based on your own apathy. Keep that to yourself."

Daphne could feel her heartbeat in her throat. "So what if you shop at women-owned businesses," she said. "That doesn't change the fact that there's misogyny everywhere you look. Every corner of this city, a misogynist probably built it or at least came up with the idea. Aren't you tired of fighting it? Everything you like, I fucking guarantee that there's a misogynist behind it somewhere regardless of how high and mighty you wanna act just because feminism is in fashion."

"High and mighty? Sorry if I don't think that the Eurocentric, white-male mindset that got us into this mess is the thing that's going to get us out of it."

"Guys, we're getting a second chance here and you're playing contrarian just to have some moral superiority. You'd really prefer talking to your plants until life as we know it ceases to exist?"

"Honestly, yes." Patricia rubbed the terrarium with the forefinger of her left hand. "I think me and Cordelia will have a lot more to do with saving the world than people like Roderick Maeve."

A woman came in then. She too had a plant with her for emotional support, an umbrella tree trailing behind her in a little red wagon with bells. "Chamomile tea," she said. "Cruelty-free if you have it."

It had happened three times for Daphne with men she didn't want. In high school, on Halloween with the older brother of a friend; in her first year of university with a man she met at a bar; and just last year with the professor. It wasn't something Daphne liked to talk about, a combined total of maybe fifteen minutes of her life, the vast majority of which she didn't even remember. She refused to be branded by it.

The rest of the day was uneventful, save for a small fire in the toaster oven, which she put out easily enough with some tap water.

But then, before close, Troy pulled her aside and asked her if everything was alright. "I mean," he said, "because of what happened with Patricia."

They were in the hallway by the back entrance, just the two of them and the smell of trash. On the bulletin board to her left was an old memo reminding employees to tie their hair back, and a poster announcing an upcoming demonstration to demand government oversight of the emerging time travel technology.

"If you're having any trouble or . . ."

She could tell Troy was trying not to be so much taller than her. That morning, she'd picked a fight with Jordan over a towel he'd left on the floor. "You've changed," he said. "No," she told him. "I was always like this before you knew me."

Troy said he just wanted to check in because he thought she was a great worker, a pleasure to be around, and maybe after the summer, if he had some money to spare, he could pay for her to take this latte art class his friend Pascal taught in the Plateau, but he just wanted to make sure she was happy with everything at the shop because he knew she'd been upset today and he really wanted everyone to feel like a family, so if there was an issue with Patricia he'd like it resolved. "You, like, understand?"

Daphne examined his face, the light sinking into his acne scars, and suddenly she wanted to know if that had been hard for him as a child, and he would say yes, and she would say, me too. I thought I'd have this big life, she might say. I thought I'd go to grad school, get a stipend. Disappointments, they'd trade their little stories. "No," she said. "It won't happen again, I'm sorry."

"Or if it's because . . . if last night." He paused. "If it was *unprofessional*." He winced at the word, even though all that had happened between them when they slipped outside the party was a cigarette and seven collective sips of Jameson from his flask before she went inside to find Jenlena, dead-eyed and aching for boys.

"The last thing I want," Troy continued, "is for you to ever feel uncomfortable . . ."

Daphne looked right into his eyes. Outside, the weather was coming down in sheets—she could hear it. They were trapped, but it felt good. She leaned forward and kissed him on the lips.

CHAPTER SIX

Jenlena Is Disappointed

1.

"But you know," her mother said when she called Jenlena after the announcement, "they said on the CBC that eventually it'll be open to the public."

Jenlena used her sleeve to wipe the snot from her nose. "So what, you'd go back in time and have an abortion like you wanted?"

"What a terrible thing to say! Jenny, that's awful."

"I'm kidding."

"Really, you're not fifteen anymore. Is it so unreasonable to expect us to have a conversation like adults?"

"Fine. Tell me what you'd wanna do."

"Oh, I don't know," her mother said in a wistful voice. "Well, sure, maybe I have always wondered what might have happened if I'd hung around longer in Vancouver. I could have put myself out there more, that's clear now. If I'd taken another acting class instead of wasting all that time with your father. But then again, for just another movie that no one watched? No, I think at the end of the day I'd probably just go with the old classic and kill baby Hitler."

Jenlena hated when her mother got wistful. Or maybe she didn't, maybe a wistful mother was fine and it was just that Jenlena happened to be in one of those moods when the only thing that felt good was to be hostile toward somebody who would be vulnerable to it. "Germany had been totally screwed over after the war," she said in her best humanities seminar voice. "Everybody was antisemitic back then. If it wasn't Hitler some other freak was bound to do it."

"But don't you think Hitler was special? There's nothing like the sting of being an artistic failure to really rile a person up."

"Sure," she said. "Hitler was really special, Mom."

Her mother laughed. That was one thing—she had a great laugh. Jenlena could remember it from when she was very small, the feeling of that sound cloaking the both of them. That was something real, wasn't it? It echoed to this day. Or could that too be erased at the whims of some distant stranger, a rich guy promising to save them all?

In Vancouver when she was a child, they often went down to the beach to eat fried fish from paper wrappers. Once, the wind blew the paper away and her mother ran to the water just to get it back. She told Jenlena they had to protect the beach because it was their friend. "It's always here for us when we're sad, right?"

There was no one more beautiful than how Jenlena remembered her mother from this time: her long hair, her soft skin and slightly crooked incisors. Her nails were long but never painted. "No, Mommy," Jenlena had said. "I am not sad."

2.

Scenic Route to Death was filmed outside of Revelstoke, B.C., in the late 1990s. A low-budget slasher film, the only movie Tina had ever starred in and a source of great embarrassment.

As a child, whenever Jenlena asked to see it, her mother would get tears in her eyes and tell her she wasn't allowed.

"Why not?"

"It's private, the things that happened before you were born."

Jenlena was fourteen when she finally saw it, stealing Christopher's credit card to order the DVD from a Swedish website for eighty-seven dollars. She watched it alone on her laptop in her room. Tina driving alone through the province's interior on her way to meet her widowed lover. The car breaks down and a sasquatch appears out of the trees to devour her in a slow, tantalizing manner. There were Tina's breasts flailing in the wind. "Stop!" Tina said. Her blood spurted onto the camera lens. "Please, help me!"

But it was all so strange. It didn't look like her mother to Jenlena, not as she remembered her from those magical days on the beach. Her mother's makeup was carelessly done. Her breasts seemed oddly shaped. She was any other girl in a bad movie, like somebody they'd picked up from the mall. The whole thing was a poor reproduction of what Jenlena knew from her memory to be true.

That night, during a frigid winter, Jenlena went to sleep with the window open, like she always did when she wanted to catch a cold. The next day, she was allowed to stay home from school. She waited until her mother had left for aerobics class to go into the basement and look through their old photographs. Not just the headshots but candid photos of the two of them in their old Vancouver apartment. She needed evidence that her mother had really been as beautiful as she remembered. But in every picture there was something off—in the angle of her nose or in the space between her eyes. It was never quite right. So clearly, though, Jenlena remembered those days before Christopher. Their old life and the smell of laundry and the downstairs neighbor's screeching violin. In one photograph, you could see the kitchen cabinets behind Jenlena and her mother. They were brown in the picture, even though Jenlena was certain that they had been blue. Then she was crying and didn't know why but since she was alone in the house it didn't matter. She could cry as long and as loud as she liked without having to explain herself to anyone.

3.

PARA-RELIGIOUS GROUP TAKES OVER LOCAL FRANCHISE

Across Canada and in many other Western countries, the presence of the so-called Moon Bethlehems has been growing steadily. Once a fringe group, the Moon Bethlehems have seen their membership rates incline sharply since this spring's mass extinction. A recent Global News poll reported that 1 in 6 Canadians know someone who identifies as a Moon Bethlehem. In Alberta, where the group has a strong foothold in response to the province's controversial oil fields, this ratio rises to 1 in 4.

"It makes sense," says Dr. Sabina Lockwood, a religious studies professor at Concordia University who specializes in religious extremism. "People are frightened, looking for answers, and not finding solace in the usual places."

But if the Moon Bethlehems' communal lifestyle, beige dress code, and antisocial ideas bring to mind the more infamous cults of Jonestown or Charles Manson, you may be getting ahead of yourself. In Dr. Lockwood's opinion, the Moon Bethlehems pose little threat of violence. "In general," she says, "the more rigid a group's ideology is, the more warning signs you'll see. But apart from a few extremist factions, Moon Bethlehems seem to lack a strong organization structure and a clear ideology. These people basically just like to live an alternative lifestyle and sit around."

The true danger, perhaps, lies within their culinary skills, or lack thereof. Case in point: Montreal's Plateau neighborhood, where a group of Moon Bethlehems have bought and begun operating a Domino's Pizza franchise. "We're happy to introduce ourselves to the community, and we want people to know that just because we have an alternative lifestyle doesn't mean they should be afraid of us," said one of the new proprietors, a young man who gave his name as Moon Beattie. "War, depression, wildfires, all Canadians worry about the same things and sooner or later most of us will accept that mainstream society is simply beyond reform."

Residents, however, have been less than enthusiastic about this change in ownership, with Yelp reviews remarking on the pizzeria's marked decline in quality. "Waited over an hour and mushrooms had mold," said one customer. "Breadsticks were raw," remarked another one-star review. The cherry, if you will, on top of the synthetic cheese? "En plus," said a third patron, "ils ne parlent pas français."

4.

Two girls on poppers were crying about how much they missed their cats. "My cat was pregnant," said the taller one. "I can't stop thinking about her babies dying inside of her." Jenlena just stood there, up against the wall, waiting for someone to fuck her. Couples moved together on the dance floor like water. Boys with septum piercings, with goatees, with lipstick and eyeliner. It was Saint-Jean's, and Jenlena hadn't been with anyone since Adam and longed to feel wanted.

"Are you okay?" people kept asking her.

"Honey, did you get too hot?"

No, she thought. *I want to dissolve.*

Finally, someone caught her eye. His name was Connor, and he would be fine. She knew him peripherally from school. That was enough. It was all decided then. She gestured to the exit and they met in the doorway. "I live pretty close," he said.

He served her a glass of whiskey and played a song by an artist he liked. He was supposed to see them play that summer, he said, but they'd canceled in protest of the government, or something like that, perhaps the corporations. "So hard to keep track of everything to be angry about," he said.

"I know. Sometimes I forget," Jenlena admitted. "I can't think straight in this heat. Sometimes I'm not angry at all."

"Me too. I put on music and I can go like, five hours without thinking about how we're all going to die."

She leaned forward across his kitchen table and asked if he really believed that was what would happen.

"What?" he scoffed. "The time machine in California? Like it's a movie and Roderick Maeve is Iron Man who comes in to save us all at the very end? Don't be naive."

His sudden coldness startled Jenlena. "I'm just saying it's something people are talking about. I'm not even sure I want the world to be saved. Honestly, I was a hell of a lot happier before anyone had ever heard of the time machine."

"Great." He rolled his eyes. "So you want the world to end just because, let me guess, you can't find a job or your boyfriend won't call you back."

"I don't have a boyfriend," she said defiantly.

"Right," he said without looking at her. The air between them turned stale. Their postures had shifted. He took the bottle of whiskey and poured himself a tall drink, downing it all in one go. At any other time of day, they might have had too much self-respect to have sex with each other now. But four o'clock in the morning was such a gnawing feeling, and it propelled their young bodies beyond dignity and fatigue.

"Is that your bed?" Jenlena asked. In bed, he would soften. There was always a chance.

They kissed for about thirty seconds before he reached for a condom from a mug on his nightstand that said *FEEL THE BERN*. His body was thick and when he took off his pants there were welts across his hips from how tight he'd fastened his belt. It hurt so bad. Connor was red-faced, huffing and puffing. Jenlena thought, *I'll be an old woman before he finishes*. Then he came on her stomach, and she was young again. She had her whole life ahead of her.

5.

Though he'd since moved out, Jordan had been right. Now that they squatted in the basement of a burned building, life was easier for the girls. They didn't have to pay rent, and they hardly worked. There wasn't power, but it was summer in a basement. On the hottest days, they lay across the kitchen floor in their underwear, pressing their skin into the cool tiles, then they'd flip over onto the other side. Daphne usually took their phones to charge at work, or else Jenlena would go to the library where she could take advantage of the AC.

The toilet clogged at least once a day, so they started going in the alley, or, if a flush was necessary, into a café on Saint-Laurent. One of the baristas kicked them out, though, so they started going to the Ultramar instead, where the cashier never looked up from his phone.

The girls traded philosophies. Daphne was chipper, which Jenlena found physically painful. Daphne was always bouncing around, singing little songs and doing yoga. "What's with you?" she asked Jenlena. "We've got our whole lives ahead of ourselves!"

Exactly. If the world went back to normal, they'd have animals again. And if they had animals again, who would pay her to dress up as one, besides a total pervert? If they had animals again, who would care about her plants, besides a total nerd? So what, she'd go to grad school? She'd take a course in administration.

Daphne said that the best thing about living in Quebec was that every day it reminded you change was possible. Barely fifty years ago, people worked together, rose up and fought for their culture against the Anglos. Now, every sign and advertisement was legally required to display its French script bigger than its English. "They nationalized the hydroelectric industry!"

"But *we're* Anglos," said Jenlena. "The change was not in our favor."

"It's just an example," she said. "It's just to illustrate what's possible when you actually try."

Jenlena groaned. She hadn't showered in days, and it felt like there was something growing in her mouth. Though just a week prior she'd been enthusiastic about her future, that person had become unrecognizable to her. Worse, a humiliation. Had she truly seen herself as an achiever? At night she dreamt about the succulents that lined her bedroom window. A great sense of peace washed over her as she held them in her arms. They were so soft, and their leaves smelled like talcum powder. Then gradually, they began to wither. She held each one under her breasts and let her milk flow into the soil, but always by morning they were dead.

The most dangerous thing about a dream wasn't that it wasn't real, but that it wasn't bound by any logical framework. A dream could change without warning. Suddenly left became right, top was bottom, inside was out, across the continent. You felt things that you wouldn't, in your waking life, dare to feel.

6.

It wasn't so exciting, to pretend to be a dog now. But she did it anyway. The same old drag, this measly world. Her next client was a woman who asked her to pee in the corner. They were at an extended-stay motel out by the highway, where the toiletries were no-name, but Jenlena took them nonetheless.

"I don't really do that," she said to the woman. "It doesn't work with the costume."

The woman told her twenty dollars, then offered fifty, and finally, they agreed on seventy-five. The woman took off her blazer and placed her pearl earrings on the dresser, underneath the TV. Jenlena squatted in the corner beneath the desk with the touchtone phone. She climbed out of her hind legs and did it, hearing the pee as it hit the floor and feeling its warmth all up her thighs.

The woman pointed at the puddle and started to yell. "Bandit! Bandit, was that you?" Jenlena could smell the coffee on her breath.

"See what you did? No. *No!*" The woman grabbed Jenlena by the scruff and threw her against the foot of the bed, then kicked her because she was so bad. She didn't deserve to be in the house. She kicked Jenlena and when her nose started to bleed all over the sheets, she made Jenlena look at it and said, "We gave you a home and this is what you do to say thank you?"

Jenlena fell against the floor, half-dressed, half-animal, halfsoiled. She tried to leave her body but she couldn't. All the usual pathways were blocked. There wasn't anywhere to go but inside of herself. Unequivocally here, present. Then the timer went off on her phone, a cloying tune, adjacent to Christmas but with a Polish flair.

The woman stood up, retucked her shirt, and walked toward her purse. "You seem like a nice girl," she said, handing over the money. "I could see us working out well."

Jenlena took the bills, then rushed to the bathroom to change into her clean clothes. She slammed the door and turned on both taps, expecting to cry, though the tears never came. Instead, she started to laugh. When she was a kid, her mother would say that wearing the wrong clothes for the weather was a sign of mental illness, as it belied a fundamental disconnect between a person and their environment. Driving around the city, she would point to women wearing miniskirts in the rain or dark, heavy boots in the summer. "That is a sad girl," she'd say. "There is another sad girl there."

And when Jenlena was in university taking classes like Finger Painting II: Priorities of Feminism, and History of the Last Six Weeks, she began to wear the wrong clothes on purpose, because she wanted people to know she was deeply depressed. What a thrill it was to wear a tube top to school in December just to prove that no one more depressed than her had ever walked the campus. Only recently did it occur to her that happiness, depending on the circumstances, could be a mental illness too.

She made her way home. A large group was protesting something by the mountain but she couldn't tell what. She didn't care. She decided to pass by the Domino's taken over by Moon Bethlehems. Maybe she was hungry; maybe that was what she was feeling. But the place didn't seem to be in operation. The windows were plastered with posters of weather and starving children. She peered between them and saw the Moon Bethlehems, six or seven of them, vaping on the counter. One saw her, pointed, and started to laugh.

"Be careful," a man walking by told Jenlena. "They're degenerates. We should make it illegal, if you ask me."

Jenlena nodded. It was easier to agree. He said the Moon Bethlehems had broken into his wife's car.

"Oh?"

"In the new world there'll be a better chance of cracking down on things like this," he said. He had ideas and had been writing to the city council.

Jenlena nodded. The man continued as she began to walk away. "No hope for the future. In my day, we called people like that losers."

When she got home, she heard Daphne on the phone with someone, giggling. She had been like that since the time machine was announced and Jordan moved out. She was washing her hair again and did exercises for her posture. "Narwhals," she said. "Don't you remember? With the horns in their faces. No, not unicorns, narwhals were real. They lived in water."

7.

FAMILY REUNITED AS TEENS DROP SUIT

Smiles abounded early yesterday afternoon in Melbourne as representatives for Nate and Brandon Richardson announced their clients' plans to drop a lawsuit seeking monetary compensation from their parents for bringing them into this world. In June, the brothers, both aged sixteen, filed a suit demanding $500,000 for what their representatives referred to as the suffering and obligations implicit in the lives they had nonconsensually been saddled with. Despite a whirlwind of bitter legal proceedings and dramatic courtroom testimonies, sources indicate that the twins had reached the decision to drop the charges after news of the American time machine. As Brandon Richardson, the eldest by fifteen minutes, explained outside the Victoria County Courthouse this week, "With this new technological intervention perhaps our lives do have some unforeseen value." Observers have remarked on changes *in the twins' appearances during recent weeks. They showed up in court in flamboyant clothing and puka shell necklaces.*

8.

Serious replies only.
I am very busy with 996 work schedule, can naturally pay high rates but to save you time and money i will be very specific about what i want: classic peanut butter fantasy

9.

EMILY: I'LL WAIT FOR YOU IN THE BAR. WEARING A RED RIBBON AROUND MY NECK SO YOU CAN TELL IT'S ME.

10.

The last time, Jenlena was just as nervous as the first. She bit her lip and chewed her fingernails. She calculated how long $200 would last her. Through the winter? She had a crate of succulents in her room but so far the responses to them online had been tepid. Jenlena of the spring, dung beetle queen, already felt like an aberration.

The client wanted to meet her in the Queen Elizabeth hotel, downtown on René-Lévesque, one of the nicest in the city and across the street from a park where some activists had beheaded a statue of the first prime minister a couple of years before. Outside, the street smelled of rubber. Inside, the air conditioning hit her like a wall, and like a ghost she walked right through it.

Jenlena crossed the grand lobby and sat down at the vintage-style bar, with its art deco chandeliers and geometric tiling, details harkening the glamour of a time before the Great Depression.

Each time a man looked at her red ribbon it gave her a start, but no one approached her. "I'm meeting someone," she told the waiter, though she knew the truth was obvious. What other reason did a girl in her cheap clothes have to be at a hotel with such decadent light fixtures?

Pouring her a glass of water, he caught a glimpse of her duffel bag beneath the table. The top zipper had been pressed open, revealing a thin strip of fur. He overpoured and the water spilled onto the table. "Oh my," he sputtered. "Oh, I'm sorry."

Once upon a time, there was a modern girl who lived in filth and her name was me. She had her notebook with her, the one with daisies printed on the front. As long as it was there, there was a chance she might write something inside of it, and as long as it was art it didn't count as real life.

She fingered the red ribbon around her neck. In literature, ribbons were famous when they went around women's necks, it was a riff off the old folktale where a woman's lover wants to know why she never takes it off. He asks her every day for many years until one day, for various reasons related to misogyny, the woman relents. She unties the ribbon and her head falls off.

It wasn't true though; it was just a story. And it didn't apply to Jenlena in any way. No man has ever wanted to know anything about me, she thought. Not my father, not any boyfriend. They might have asked questions, but they only heard the answers they wanted to hear. No one had ever been truly curious enough to burrow into her nooks and crannies: the silly preferences she had when it came to socks in bed, or small things from childhood.

The AC coated her body. It didn't have a smell, it was one big void. When the waiter returned to check on her a second time, he asked if she knew that this was the same hotel where John Lennon and Yoko Ono had had their bed-in in the 1970s.

"No," she said. "I didn't know that."

"People always think it's New York," he said. "But it was here, right on the seventeenth floor."

"Hmm," said Jenlena, watching man after man enter through the revolving doors beyond him. Some were tall and dressed in suits, some were squat and had sandals, one was just a little boy.

The waiter smiled. "I'm kind of a history buff," he said, lingering beside her with his jug. What he liked about history, he said, was that it just kept going and going. "Even now, believe it or not."

Then she saw him, a man. Just an ordinary man, but Jenlena could tell immediately that he was the one she'd been talking with online. He had a tailored suit with leather shoes and his hair was combed back, slick with gel. He walked toward her, but she felt overwhelmingly that she could not go up to the room with him. It was of grave significance that she not do it. In one swoop she untied the ribbon and her head did not fall off. It remained firmly on her shoulders as she made her way out of the bar.

"Miss?" he called to her, but she kept going. "Miss!"

Now her heartbeat was the only sound there was. She saw his reflection in the elevator doors, he held the red ribbon in his outstretched palm.

"You dropped this. You did, didn't you?" His eyes were wide and his lips sagged. Up close there was nothing very precise about him at all. "It was you, your ribbon, I saw you. Is that your costume there?"

"No, that wasn't me, I'm sorry."

"But we had an agreement. I have the money. Right here, I have it."

He padded his breast pocket, but Jenlena continued past him, quickening her pace toward the exit. She pushed through the revolving door, but at the precise moment the outside heat first touched her skin, she somehow bumped right into him again. "I told you, sir. I said, *pas de chien*!"

"Told me what?" a sonorous voice asked in amusement. "What did you tell me?"

When Jenlena looked up, it was a different man now before her. His skin was rough and his eyebrows joined together above his nose. He had a zip-up hoodie and drawstring pants. Yet he was not strange to her, she knew his face. Everyone did.

But I guess that's what your twenties are about.

"I'm sorry," he said. "But if you aren't in a rush, please let me buy you a drink. I insist."

CHAPTER SEVEN

Ricky Gets a Divorce

1.

Roderick Maeve hadn't been feeling like himself. He probably wasn't drinking enough water. It could have been more than that, but he'd have to start hydrating to really tell. At night he noticed it most, but who could drink water after 9 p.m.? He thought that there ought to be a way to make other people go to the bathroom for you. In this day and age, was that so much to ask? Pay them a decent wage, of course; he wasn't a monster. Tomorrow, he'd write an email to his assistant. "Yes, sir," she'd say. "Consider it deep-dived."

It was just that the inside of his mouth was starting to remind him of his mother. No, not in a perverted way. Of when his mother was *dying*, he meant. Her decomposing body: vaguely sweet and stringy on the sides.

2.

At first, Roderick Maeve had believed that being wealthy just came down to stuff: wearing the right brands, buying vacation homes, an extra topping of gold leaf on his desserts, half a dozen Bentleys. In his twenties, when he'd made his first million, he bought everything he was supposed to and showed up at parties eager to perform whoever it was he could now afford to be. Over the years he'd created a mystique for himself based upon the vague origins of his new money and his penchant for athleisure, only to discover that real money, the serious kind with which you coated your hands to mold the world to your liking, was subtler than what you saw on TV. That sort of wealth was in the things you couldn't see: historical friendships and speculative capitalism. Real wealth, he discovered while sitting with rich people in uncomfortable chairs, had more to do with having the right opinions about wine. True connoisseurs had a palate for identifying its layers and nuances— and Ricky was more of a beer drinker.

In his thirties, when he made his first billion, he paid for private lessons with a sommelier but could never get the hang of it. He said "oaky," but his new milieu—consisting of heiresses, old-money playboys, artists' patrons generations deep in fossil fuels—still sneered at him, even when *oaky* was objectively correct. It was the *way* he said it. So he spent six months in a private course on how to correctly pronounce words, but the syllables refused to behave in his mouth. There was just something about being raised by a Floridian teen mom with red hair and no eyebrows, a stink that you couldn't wash off yourself.

Other wealthy people, he had concluded by his forties, only invited him to parties so that they could feel better about their lives. He existed so they could look across the room and scoff as he opened a beer bottle with his left eye socket, a trick that generally only impressed the help. Other wealthy people mocked him, but they needed him too. They kept him around because despite their faults, the sins of their ancestors and family associates, and the gnawing emptiness of a Sunday morning with nothing to do, at the very least they weren't Roderick Maeve.

3.

Once upon a time, he realized he hadn't seen a rat in a long while. "Where have they gone?" he asked his assistant, a well-groomed Bard grad. "Has the problem finally been dealt with, then?"

His assistant searched on her phone. "No, sir," she read with her eyebrows furrowed. "Actually, says here there's more of them than ever. 'Cause of the weather, they're breeding like crazy, all through the winter now. I guess we're just lucky." She grimaced. "Can't stand the sight of them myself."

The animals took over, people were stuck inside their houses, and no one knew what to do. When he'd first thought up the deadly frequency, everyone said it was impossible. *All* the animals? They said it was inhumane.

But there was also a little girl in Compton who'd had her face chewed off, her one and only face! And what about that mother in Spain, raped by dolphins? These were the things, the *humans*, who kept him up at night. Besides, his entire life had been built on ideas like this. His silk sheets, his Spanish tile, his literal Basquiats—all of it was owed to some of the stupidest ideas on earth.

His assistant found him a scientist out of Stockholm who hypothesized the frequency. Ricky had more than enough to put up the money for development. In the end, the Swedish scientist put everything together quite quickly and assured him the animals would feel no pain. His one request was that when the time came, it would be Roderick Maeve, and not he, who pressed the button.

"It's *your* brainchild, after all," the Swedish scientist had said. "I'm merely the craftsman."

It was simple really. The little girl in Compton, et cetera, et cetera. Ricky flared his nostrils thinking about that little girl. He pressed the button once, then three more times in quick succession so that the moment might be diluted in his memory. He swallowed. Out the window, bodies began to fall.

People could go outside again. All the children playing on the street, and the women walking home from work without fear, that was something *he* had done. He was invited on late-night shows, where he recited scripted anecdotes and the audience laughed on cue. Such a wonderful feeling to know he was beloved under the bright lights. He tasted the makeup that melted onto his face and was convinced the moment would last forever.

But leaving the studio not an hour later, protestors stormed his limo and called him a murderer. That weekend, the woman he'd been pursuing canceled their next date in honor, she said, of her hedgehog. He'd saved the world, mind you, not that you could tell from the way people continued to look at him at parties in the coming weeks. Just the same old furtive glances, the utterly polite hellos. There was nothing goddamned worse than polite.

In May, the socialite Carolyn Van Murphy didn't even invite him to her annual Memorial Day gala, a slight that made Ricky break out in hives. A hundred years ago, her grandparents had been painted by John Singer Sargent. Today, she owned a television station and always made a big display of never remembering Ricky's name.

"Why don't people like me? I started with nothing and I've done everything right in this life."

"Is that something you'd like me to look into, sir?" his assistant asked, ever poised for a quick Google search. Her main duty was to follow his every whim. It wasn't a bad job. Vision but no vacation pay. No two days were ever alike.

After the snub, Ricky paid her $500 to take a weekend reconnaissance trip to meet Carolyn's son in L.A. A hundred years ago, the Van Murphys had financed railroads across the prairies; today their great-grandson was a noted cocaine addict with a YouTube channel.

A trip like this wasn't so unusual for Ricky's assistant, whenever he needed a particularly *intimate* brand of information. He'd thrice sent her to Washington to schmooze with congressmen and it always came with a healthy bonus. She could have said no if she wanted to; she could have faked a cold like a normal person if it really went against her morals. Never in five years had he heard mention of a boyfriend.

She came back from L.A. with a mark on her neck that suited her, Ricky thought. It gave her prim demeanor a little edge. "Give it to me straight," Ricky said, wincing. "I can take it."

"Well, it seems Carolyn's upset about her pet rabbits. I guess she had this lineage, they dated back four hundred years or something. Obviously they're all dead now, and she's inconsolable."

"Would she have rather stayed inside for the rest of her life?" Ricky could raise his voice at his assistant from time to time. He paid the girl enough for that. "The privilege!" He banged his fist on the desk.

"She's crazy," his assistant said. "Her son made that very clear. Like, she's been on pills pretty much since she was born."

"Ungrateful, all of them."

"You're exactly right, sir. You did the right thing, though. Really, sir."

He was able to breathe deeper and deeper. "Just a stupid party anyways."

"You're exactly right, sir."

"Dull people."

"Yes, sir."

"And it was . . . with the boy?" he asked tentatively.

"Oh sure." Her voice had a lilt but she didn't look up from her phone. "Total gentleman. What you'd expect."

4.

Ricky's mother saw no shame in believing everything she heard. God had a plan for us all; one must light candles on the full moon; whenever a bird flew in through the window, it was a sign of either prosperity or doom, depending on the season. Wind was a road for fairies. Why not? Someone had to be right. To her, it was quantitative. For example, Jesus Christ was the son of God who healed lepers and turned water into wine before dying on behalf of the whole world—but he was also just some guy who lived in Palestine a long time ago.

Steph-Ann Maeve knew that most people were more than one thing. Her father, for example, had once employed half the town as the general manager of the sawmill, been named godfather to no less than fifteen kids, and coached the Little League baseball team to victory in the state championship. But greatness faded. In America at least, it had a life span. The mill closed and there was so little work that her father and some of his friends had maimed themselves to collect the money from their accidental death and dismemberment insurance policies. By the time Steph-Ann was born, he had one eye and a stump for a right hand. Most people knew him as a drunk who slept all the time.

These two versions of her father taught her that the truth was not one thin line to be tightrope-walked across perilously. It was a woven network of contradictions that could, if you let it, provide safety. And thus she kept her menstrual blood in a vial around her neck for good luck. She kept her menstrual blood in a glass jar and served it drop by drop to a boy at school to get him to like her back. She fed her menstrual blood to the jade plant on her window sill to cleanse the night air of bad dreams.

Hers was a shitty town to be from. The humidity warped you. "Are you the girl whose one-handed father has been asleep for twenty years?" people sometimes asked Steph-Ann.

"He's not asleep all the time," she'd say. "He gets up to use the bathroom."

Her mother read palms and rented out a tanning bed she'd inherited from a great-aunt. "You have borrowed meridians," she was always telling Steph-Ann with no further explanation. Steph-Ann had a feeling it meant she would die young. Her family had a feeble dog that had no name. When they'd moved into the unit he'd just been there, shivering in his own piss in the bathroom. Sometimes she called him George Michael in her head. Most of the time she hated him because he was ugly and represented everything about her life.

When she was fifteen, a rich man built a hotel that glittered on the shoreline like a movie. All the older brothers and sisters from the neighborhood applied for jobs but only the most attractive were selected. Steph-Ann often fantasized about becoming a girl who wore seashells on her breasts while serving tourists candy-colored drinks by the outdoor pool, but as a redhead with no eyebrows she was doubtful about her qualifications. A day in the sun left her skin bright pink, and though her breasts had developed years ahead of her classmates', they'd brought with them a thick waist and heavy thighs. Still, one could dream of clocking in and out at the tallest building in town. Such was the reckless hope of youth.

She and her friends snuck into the hotel pool almost every day that summer, cooling off on the striped lounge chairs and talking shit about the tourists. Some of the girls their age weren't even pretty.

"When you're rich you don't have to be," her friend Danika said.

Her friend Helena snorted. "They're still girls. Just lazy is all."

"I'd be lazy too if I was rich," Steph-Ann said.

"You *are* lazy," said Danika. "You still have the Cheeto dust from yesterday under your fingernails."

They howled with laughter.

It was on a day like this that Steph-Ann had needed to pee. Why didn't she just go in the water like a normal person? That was the first clue that something monumental was afoot—how she was compelled to go inside the hotel. With its grand fountain of a dolphin embracing a sea turtle, the lobby was too beautiful to resist exploring. Fresh macaroons and pineapple were laid out on a platter by the coffee machine. Beyond that, a desk that said "Concierge." Steph-Ann tried to pronounce the word in her head.

She walked past the restrooms entirely and stepped into an elevator, just to see what it was like. *When I work here*, she thought, still dressed in her string bikini and flip-flops, *I'll get to pretend I'm on vacation.* She pressed the button for the top floor for no discernible reason other than that it was what she felt called to do. Sometimes when Steph-Ann felt pulled in various directions, she believed it was her father's phantom hand guiding her along. Other times she knew her father was no more than a drunk who stunk up the bathroom.

Exiting the elevator, she found herself in a narrow landing leading to an open blue door. Steph-Ann peered inside and saw a man walking toward her. She knew who he was. Everyone did. He was the richest man in town. She'd seen him in magazines at the grocery store and on the local news. He said in interviews that he built his hotels to connect people with nature. "There's nothing like the view of the ocean from one of my penthouses."

"Are you lost?" he asked Steph-Ann.

"No," she said, looking up at his heavy eyebrows. She could tell he was drunk, but not in the way her father got drunk because this man was happy. He showed all his teeth when he smiled, even the ones on the bottom.

"You look familiar," he said. "Does your father work for me?"

She shook her head. "My father only has one hand."

He started to laugh. Yes, it was funny, wasn't it?

It was the first time a man had ever looked at her, just her. She was alone on the top floor far away from her friends and he led her into a room with a shag carpet and a panoramic view. His heavy gold rings hit the glasses as he made them both drinks. Steph-Ann's went down like a potion. She felt her whole body tingle, like she herself reflected the ocean from all her surfaces.

Facing the bed, they saw not the water but the town. Steph-Ann looked out at the new buildings closer to the shore and the restaurants where mostly tourists went. Farther inland was downtown, the courthouse where her uncle had stood trial for insurance fraud, and the bars she snuck into with her friends to flirt with tourists for free drinks. Then, past the old baseball diamond and the bus depot was her street, where her father was sleeping and the tourists never went.

The rich man was already moving his hand down her back.

5.

Roderick Maeve was born in the middle of a thunderstorm. Steph-Ann's father arose from his slumber, resting the baby precariously on his lap, and nodded his passive approval. Her mother examined the baby's hands and said breathlessly that she had never seen such strong meridians. Though the child bore his father's heavy eyebrows, Steph-Ann never told anyone about what had happened between her and the rich man in the hotel. She knew no one would believe her. Stories like that, there would be layers to the disbelief, an intricate structure, underground tunnels.

Besides, no matter where the baby came from, he was so perfect it terrified her. His tiny hands, the gassy smiles she swore were genuine. It was too much, looking at him at her breast and thinking about all the horrible things this life entailed: shame, bad TV, eating around the mold. One day he would grow up and know what it was to be trash. One day he would have pubes and be no different from all the guys around here: Huey from the gas station or the new mayor with his butt chin and recent embezzlement scandal. All those years to come, they terrified her. Sometimes she put the baby in her handbag just to catch her breath. How could she have been so cruel as to bring him into this mess? Dark thoughts consumed her.

The only thing that calmed Steph-Ann's nerves was something from a book she'd read years before. It had said that all great spirits lived multiple lifetimes. Moses, Abraham Lincoln, and Gandhi were all examples. They occupied the bodies of otherwise mediocre people to enact change and fight for what was right. Then, when their flesh died, the spirits traversed decades to find a new host and once more direct the world as their divine wisdom dictated.

Steph-Ann had always thought her father could have been one of these men, at least the version of himself from before he lost his hand: generous and hardworking, a true patriarch of the community. But for whatever reason the great spirit had changed its mind and left his body, leaving her father deflated and without purpose.

Now the honor would befall her son. It was obvious by looking at the baby. He would lead a special life, he would be remarkable. Surely, crazier things had happened. Just nine months ago, for example, she'd had to pee and ended up having sex with a fifty-year-old man.

When the baby was eight months old, she asked him point-blank: "How many times have you been alive before?"

The baby merely blinked. But he had this *way* of blinking. Steph-Ann had never been very good at explaining things. She was more of a tactile learner. A breeze came in through the curtains and tickled her elbows.

"Who's gonna save the world for Mommy?"

"Me," said the baby. It was Roderick Maeve's first ever word.

6.

In school, he learned things easily, had a knack for concepts and vocabulary. He was driven by strong impulses and from an early age noticed that people had a tendency to say yes to him, which was strange because the opposite had been true for his mother. At the diner where she worked, customers openly smirked when she talked to them about the phases of the moon. Ricky loved her but it could not be denied that she had a strangeness that put her at odds with the world. She swam upstream, so to speak. Whereas Ricky *was* the stream. He was the whole Atlantic Ocean.

By the time he reached puberty, life was so boring he'd started to experiment with writing the wrong answers on tests: Vancouver was the capital of Canada, the school's periodic tables had all been printed incorrectly, Ponce de León had discovered the Fountain of Youth in what was now the parking lot of a Chili's. Then he'd argue his way into earning the point regardless, not even so much with rhetoric but his unwavering commitment to the fallacy. That and he could go almost six minutes without blinking. It made everyone very uncomfortable.

Where did this confidence come from? As he did with his bony knuckles and dark eyebrows, Ricky saw no choice but to attribute this quality to his father, a man his mother never spoke of. Every year on his birthday she took him to the beach for a banana split, which they ate together in the shade of the tallest, tackiest hotel in the city. "What happened to my dad?" Ricky would ask. "A million things," his mother would respond. "But your life will be even bigger."

For his senior thesis, he created an original citation manual called the Briars-Mcduff, in which each element of a source was followed by a semicolon. It was meant, he wrote, to represent globalization. No matter how independent any one of us may seem, we were all connected by dots and squiggles. Columbia offered early admission; Stanford, his top choice, a full ride.

Back then, he liked women who looked like his mother's coworkers. Before he left for California, one of them took him into the dry storage room and showed him her breasts. She said his inexperience showed in his shoulders and the rich kids would eat him alive for it. She was in her thirties, which was his mother's age, practically a dinosaur. Her breasts were big and hung heavy, lower than in pornography (some pornography, anyway). They took up an entire shelf.

"Now I'm not going behind Steph-Ann's back here," she explained. "You're talking about a good friend of mine. So I have to let you know I promised I wouldn't let you touch."

Later, once he'd made his money, he developed a taste for supermodels. They were so thin he was always hungry for more. Yes, it was a bad joke, but it had the added disadvantage of being true.

Sometimes two bad qualities really did cancel each other out, like his shameless self-confidence and debilitating thirst for acceptance. He'd never had a problem meeting women; they were always agreeing to marry him.

"What are you talking about?" his most recent ex-wife, Evie, a Québécoise model who'd been the face of Calvin Klein for almost a decade, used to say. "You're a *billionaire*."

Then she'd rub up his side like a cat and purr, "Don't you wanna fill me up?" As if they were in New Jersey. "Fill me up tonight, okay, honey?"

7.

Steph-Ann got sick at thirty-six. There were tests, more tests, then everything happened very quickly. When Ricky had flown home from California to see her, her cheeks were hollow and she'd lost her hair. All around her hospital room were the trinkets of various deities: prayer flags across the wall, crystals on the nightstand, a golden hamsa hanging from the bed rail. She clutched a rabbit's foot in her palm but let it go as Ricky's fingers reached for hers. There was nothing to worry about, she said, because so many angels were waiting for her on the other side.

"But me," he pleaded. "I'll be all alone." She reached up to touch his cheek. He told her everything. How he'd always been full of shit. He didn't study and he didn't do his coursework and everyone who knew him knew he was just a Floridian chump. Now, at Stanford, he was on academic probation after citing seven fictional sources for a research paper about the demographic shifts in the last ten years of a Pennsylvania steel town he made up himself.

"Mommy," he said. "What am I going to do with my life?"

"Shhh." She said that sometimes the worst things about us are our greatest strengths. "That's how you were born."

He didn't understand.

"It was a terrible thing but it brought me you."

"My father?"

She nodded.

"I want to know. I'm ready."

She swallowed with difficulty then began the story. Half of the syllables were caught in her throat, but Ricky knew who she was talking about. Everyone knew that name.

When she finished, he asked if she was serious. "For real, Mom? Or is this like with the fairies?"

She pressed her head into the pillow and closed her eyes.

8.

In 1982 my mother shared an encounter with you at one of your hotels. It caused him no pride to think of the old man atop his mother, but when Ricky dropped out of Stanford with no money or family, Steph-Ann's strange story was his sole asset. After she died, Ricky sent a letter to the old man's office in Orlando, with toenail clippings enclosed in a Ziploc bag. Two months later, a representative sent an NDA and a check for $50,000. A month after that, a friend called with an insider tip from his cousin in New York: all over America, poor people were buying houses they couldn't afford, and the whole thing was about to blow. Ricky sent the cousin his inheritance and within the year had his first million dollars. He bought stocks, he bought a house in the Keys, he bought his girlfriend new lips and took her to Bora Bora.

The next year, he heard about a company out of Silicon Valley that used infrasound technology to detect portals leading to alternate dimensions. The plan was that people would pay to be able to see other versions of themselves, living other lives in other worlds. It was an idea too dumb to fail. So stupid it couldn't possibly be as idiotic as it seemed.

The founders said it would help with the inequality. You know, that rising tension people were always talking about on the news. "Say a person is really struggling," went the pitch. "Maybe they look through the portal and see that they're totally thriving in another dimension. It makes it a lot easier to accept their lot in this one. Or, you know, vice versa. Successful people see themselves on food stamps and it'll help with empathy."

Six months after Ricky's investment, the company was acquired by the U.S. government, and Ricky's money was returned tenfold. He bought villas and private jets and a new chin and his own island. Then he bought nothing. Clothes, vacations, cars, meetings with the president, all of it was given to him for free, in the name of friendship, with the promise of future business opportunities.

He couldn't stop making money if he tried. He invested in Afghan dogs and a team of doctors who claimed to be breeding immortal mice. One of his companies had cataloged over three thousand feelings unique to American society and sold the data to marketing firms. "People are always so caught up in the truth," he said in an interview. "As if it isn't something we can make up for ourselves. Me, I've never cared about what *is* possible, only what *could* be."

His money was addicted to itself. Eventually, he even had enough to get invited to the same yacht party as his father. They crossed paths by the bar and a Hollywood producer introduced them. Ricky wore track pants, the old man beige slacks that were so stiff they seemed structurally integral to his posture.

"So you're the one with all these exciting ideas I've been hearing about," the old man said to Ricky. "Not that I can follow them myself. The older I get, the stranger money becomes. In my day, we made our fortunes off of what you could see. Now it feels like more and more you'd need some kind of advanced degree to understand what makes someone like you worth more than someone like me. Hard to believe, isn't it? Go to one of those poor neighborhoods and they'd never be able to tell by looking at us."

"Do you know a lot about poor neighborhoods?" Ricky asked.

The old man laughed. "I've always appreciated my employees." His young wife wore a green dress cut low down her chest. She looked at Ricky and it lasted longer than it had to. Her gaze lingered on his eyebrows.

The old man grunted.

"Bathroom honey, you have to go to the bathroom?" his wife asked before turning to Ricky one last time. "I-I-I'm sorry," she said in a low voice. "I've got to get him to the bathroom."

Ricky watched them walk away. Over the course of the next year, many of the old man's properties would succumb to the weather. He'd sell the others at a loss, according to Ricky's assistant's research. The year after that, the old man was indicted on several counts of fraud, though he died before he could be properly tried. The young wife continued to board yachts with wealthy men. Ricky even saw her again, at a party, where they locked eyes across the deck but kept their distance.

9.

"I never did this to be rich." Ricky stood over his assistant's desk after killing the animals. "I mean, culturally. I've never cared about impressing people."

"The Van Murphys?" She was eating a salad.

"I mean that's never been my goal. I'm an entrepreneur. That's a relationship with the public."

"Sir," she said, "are you practicing for a podcast?" She pulled up his schedule on her laptop. "I don't see anything here."

"Just talking," he said. It was only the two of them on this floor of the office. Ricky liked it that way, with fewer distractions, so that new ideas could flow through him unimpeded. On a slow day, he liked to sit cross-legged without shoes and have her serve him Mountain Dew. On a rough day, he made her watch YouTube videos of 800-meter races with him, narrating the careful choices each runner made in the final lap. "It's the most strategic distance," he'd say. "It's like chess."

They worked well together. She was like an algorithm, well versed in his moods and preferences. "So, what's going on out there? With the *people*." He pronounced it like an outdated term for an ethnic minority. "Do they really hate me or is it only an extreme few?"

She scrolled through her phone, eyebrows furrowed. "They were definitely talking about you a lot right after it happened. They were really excited to go back outside again."

"And now?" He leaned toward her. "What are they saying now?"

"Sir," she said, scrolling rapidly. "I'm synthesizing."

The people were sad.

"In general, they have no vision for the future," said his assistant. "There's this really interesting study out of Brown that tested foreign-language learners at the intermediate level. The subjects scored fifteen to twenty points lower on exam sections dealing with the future tenses than on questions of the same difficulty dealing with the past tense. It appears that people are literally losing the brain capacity to conceive of the future."

She lifted her phone to show him pictures from a protest in New Zealand where young children were dressed up as old people, walking with canes and wearing white wigs and bald caps. "Fight for the right to arthritis!" read their cardboard signs. "Let me be Bubbe!"

"The things they used to feel optimistic about—a new generation of political leaders, weather reforms, arts and culture, peace talks—have all just become power grifts for the elite," his assistant concluded. "The very reforms they would have been happy to have five to ten years ago, now they mean nothing more to them than a PR stunt. That's how cynical they've become."

"Mm-hmm." Ricky took it all in, massaging his temple. The people really did surprise him sometimes. He sure did get a kick out of their music and salty food.

After that was more or less a typical afternoon: he took phone calls, gave money to charity, then jerked off in his sensory deprivation tank before inexplicably bursting into tears.

Around sundown, he overheard two of the kitchen girls talking about how much they missed the animals. The first said that she felt so tempted to join the Moon Bethlehems that every time she felt overwhelmed by the urge she trimmed her bangs and now they were half an inch long.

"Oh," said the second girl. She asked if the first girl did this in their shared apartment.

"Yes. Sometimes I wake up in the middle of the night and can't think of anything but totally running away from everything."

The second girl was upset. "I've seen the little hairs. I thought they might have been from Toby. I've been keeping them."

Ricky could smell the garlic on the stove. Pretty, both of them. They reminded him of the girls from his high school, the sweet ones who did poppers in the bathroom. He liked it when the women who worked for him were attractive but only in straightforward ways. Pleasing, but without the risk of getting too caught up in anything. Every so often one of the more daring girls would give him a look. A smile or a raised eyebrow. And it was tempting, sure. But he knew from experience that sooner or later you'd just end up feeling overdressed and incontinent on a boat.

The second girl told the first that she'd been keeping the little hairs in a jar because science was changing every day and, who knows, maybe they'd get the animals back. The first girl laughed. "Right, because the future looks so bright right now."

Ricky thought of something then. That's when it came to him.

All great ideas occurred seemingly out of nowhere. They grabbed hold of him and he had no choice but to call his assistant. "I'm going to build a time machine," he told her.

"To bring back the animals, sir?"

"It's bigger than that," he said. "I could bring it all back. Hope." He felt it in his body like an electric shock. Like he was a young man again. *See?* he thought. It was working already.

"Consider it deep-dived."

There was a young quantum physicist out of Harvard who had some promising theories.

10.

Whenever Roderick Maeve worked with anyone new, he put them through a rigorous vetting process. He had to, especially now, what with all these Moon Bethlehems around. Just the year before, three had infiltrated his cleaning staff and tried to unionize. People like that, walking among him, touching his things. They reminded him of the people who took advantage of his mother when he was a kid. One year she only wore red, one spring they only ate lentils, one Christmas they planned for the alien apocalypse. Half her tip money always went toward the tithes.

But his assistant assured him that they wouldn't have anything to worry about with the quantum physicist, a twenty-one-year-old with a PhD from Harvard. "He's a real individual," she said. "A self-starter."

The physicist claimed to have found a way of manipulating wormholes to bend time. It was all very complex. Roderick Maeve would never claim to be the smartest or hardest-working guy in the room, but nobody could say he wasn't audacious. He put a team together and let it be known that winning was the only acceptable outcome.

When rumors first surfaced about the plans for a time machine, many people accused him of having personal motivations. He'd use it for his businesses or to play the stock market. People like him, they said, such capitalism! Or he was a misogynist and would use the machine to go back in time and meet women. Five or ten years ago, when they were less keen to stand up to power. "It raises serious issues about consent," said an actress he'd gone out with twice seven years earlier. "What protections do I have legally to stop him from going back in time and performing sex acts on me again?"

But despite his various shortcomings, Roderick Maeve knew better than to succumb to nostalgia. Though sure, certain daydreams had occurred to him. Lots of things occurred to him.

What would it be like with Evie again, in the beginning when they'd hardly known each other? Just the two of them at the house in Quebec—or what about the trip they took to Martinique? He wasn't even thinking anything perverted. The time they cooked the fish themselves and almost left out the salt. She made him laugh so hard he nearly cut off his finger. Had they recently made love? It was impossible to tell sometimes; in his memories there was always that warmth between them. Actually, Martinique was later, when they knew each other well, but it was not yet a problem.

Was that the trip when she had complained to him of the feeling of being surveilled? "No," he'd said. The resort was very private. They had the best security.

"Not just here," she'd told him. "All the time. I guess that's what I wanted, but I didn't know it would feel like this."

The moonlight traced her profile in the dark. "I want a baby," she said. "I want to be fat and happy and free."

He told her what he'd said already a thousand times, how fatherhood had never interested him. Rich people's kids always turned out to be such scum. "Besides, it's not something you take up for a week or two, Evie. It lasts, like, twenty years."

She gave him one of her looks then, one of her *you think I'm stupid* snarls she did in advertisements. Then she rolled over onto her side, speaking in a muffled voice, as if only to herself. "I'm so tired of me. I want to be Mom. Somebody's mom."

When she'd spoken out against him not even six months later, Ricky respected the move as a tactical decision worth about two million dollars in their divorce. "You see," Evie had said on Instagram Live, "he never had a father. And his mother is dead. So he blames the world for what most of us blame on our parents."

Then she was linked to a hockey player and by the end of the year the couple was expecting twins. Meanwhile, Roderick Maeve was always hearing phones ringing in the distance. More than just the low steady rumble of vibrate, but children crying, trees in the wind, traffic on a wet road, the hum of central air. Everything sounded like a ringtone to him lately. Was this a mental illness?

No, he did not have anything to go back to.

11.

"Ricky, are you alright?" Evie asked him. "You don't seem well."

They were at the Queen Elizabeth hotel in Montreal, Canada.

"Pills, pills, pills," he said, to the tune of the Destiny's Child song. He hadn't been feeling like himself lately. "The doctor puts me on them, he takes me off, but it still feels exactly the same."

They were there to talk through the last details of their divorce in his usual suite, the same room where John Lennon and Yoko Ono held their bed-in in the 1970s. He'd rented it for one of their first dates, though he was quick to learn she was not the type to be impressed and show it. There were yellow chairs and a brown leather couch that the manager had explained was supposed to look British. Framed on the wall were the exact signs John and Yoko had made that week: *HAIR PEACE, BED PEACE.*

DRONE STRIKE, Ricky wrote in felt marker on a piece of toilet paper as a joke during their first stay. Evie laughed and the lines came out around her eyes, down her cheeks. *I'll know you when you're an old woman*, he thought. There was always something scintillating about getting political, like putting on a cheeky Halloween costume. A sexy nurse or Prince Harry as a Nazi. The key was that you were only political once in a while. Now she was so pregnant with another man's babies that even her nose was swollen.

They sat cross-legged on the bed. Marriage was an expensive hobby and it was beginning to hurt his back. He'd sent their lawyers down to the bar to have one last moment alone with her, his favorite of all his ex-wives. Ricky pulled out his offer from a manila folder. It was generous, but she wouldn't get to keep the house in the Montreal suburbs that he'd bought for a one-month anniversary present. When they got married, he leveled all the houses in a five-block radius and built her her own forest. He bought her the Rockland shopping center where she was first discovered at fifteen for a Le Château campaign, a collection of Elizabeth Taylor's jewelry, a trip to Namibia during which he arranged for a pride of lions to attack the jeep. She peed her pants but the sex that night was transcendent.

"Shrewd," Evie said, scanning the contract. "Even for you."

He wondered how long the room would smell of her perfume after she left. "We're getting a divorce." He shrugged. "It's how you play the game."

"But you don't even like it here."

It was true that the Québécois made him nervous. They were guttural, Florida but with a touch of communism. "Maybe I've acquired a taste."

"Since when?" Seeing her socked feet felt more intimate than seeing her breasts, how he could just make out the tip of her toenail stretching the dark fabric.

"Last year or so. I've been doing a lot of thinking." If he wanted to see her breasts he could google them. It took 0.72 seconds and there were many examples. "I'm building a time machine," he said.

"So I've heard."

"What do you think?"

She laughed. "I'm sorry. Who am I speaking to? It's not like you to second-guess your own idea."

"I mean it," he said. "I could save the world, but what if that's not in the world's best interest?"

"No offense, but do you really think you're smart enough to tackle such a big question?"

"Even if it worked, I'd still get blamed for something."

"It's the animals," she said. "You're letting people get to you, but those animals had it coming. Someone had to make a move."

"I dream about them," he said.

"Well, don't. I dream about all my high school teachers dancing cabaret in bear costumes. It doesn't mean anything."

He shrugged.

"Ricky, I think it's great. Really. We might have a chance against all this weather. My boys, they'll owe their lives to you if you pull this off. So why not do something for yourself? Take a vacation."

"I've already been everywhere."

"I read that you're dating again, I think that's good. She looks a lot like me."

"Everyone looks like you," Ricky said, shaking his head. "But it's over. I'm, I don't know. I'm tired of girls like that. I'm bored."

"Well, then I don't know. Go to a psychic medium, start working through all the Benjamin Franklin crap your mom saddled you with. He owned slaves, you know. By the way." She looked down at her phone. "Bobby's here with the car. I've gotta go. Just give me the papers and I'll tell my lawyers it's fine."

"Do you feel different now that you got what you wanted?" Ricky looked down at her belly.

Evie smiled. "We'll see."

12.

Evie Forget. It was easy. You used your fingers to type the letters into your phone and then you pressed "go" and she appeared. You clicked on images of her body from all angles.

Evie Forget boobies

Why not? Why goddamned not?

It wasn't perverted because he wasn't aroused.

He either felt taller than any other man who'd ever existed, Rasputin and Michael Jordan combined, with the world in his palm, or he felt the way he did now, alone in his suite, staring out at the city he didn't know, looking down at the woman he didn't know anymore. Anything in between was impossible.

13.

Dreams. Lately, he'd been having such fascinating dreams. Almost every night: intricate plots and characters. People he hadn't seen since middle school. Sometimes it felt like even when he was awake he was inside of one. The muted tones and his immovable convictions.

All his life he'd either been incredibly poor or incredibly rich. What did normal people think about? What motivated them? He hadn't been with anyone since the animals had died. Not on purpose, though the longer his dry spell lasted he began to wonder. What was that place women were always talking about? The subconscious?

He went down to the hotel lobby for a drink. The girl who ran into him had sweat dripping down her face and babbled nonsensically the moment she laid eyes on him. He thought she reeked of the suburbs, miscellaneous monotony.

"I'm sorry," he said. "But if you aren't in a rush, please let me buy you a drink. I insist."

CHAPTER EIGHT

Girl Talk ft. Jenlena and Daphne

1.

When Jenlena told Daphne about meeting Roderick Maeve in the lobby of the hotel, her friend did not believe her. It was just like when they'd been in the same classes at school and Daphne was always correcting other people's pronunciation. She who had won all the prizes told Jenlena, "You know, I had a friend who slept with a guy just because he'd told her he was Shia LaBeouf's stunt double, but in the end all that was remotely true was that she got chlamydia."

"So what are you saying?" Jenlena asked. "You think it's some hoax?"

"I'm just telling you to act *prudently*," Daphne said.

"But it *was* Roderick Maeve. I swear to god."

"I just don't get it." Daphne scratched her head. "Don't men like that usually date supermodels?"

"Sure," said Jenlena. "But you have to understand, I acted like a totally different person. I almost made him choke on his drink, I was being so witty. I was like a girl from the movies who has double Ds and rides a motorcycle and also goes to Yale and her mom has early onset—"

"Right," said Daphne, cutting her off. "Are you going to see him again?"

"Sure. He gave me his finsta."

Daphne cringed. "*Finsta*? Isn't he a little *geriatric* for that?"

"He's forty-two," Jenlena said. "But you wouldn't know from far away. What? It's exciting. I haven't liked anyone since Adam."

"What are you talking about, *anyone*? He's *Roderick Maeve*. Don't you watch the news?"

"What?" asked Jenlena. "Because of what that woman said he did to her in the hotel?" Was Daphne jealous? The proposition excited her.

"No," said Daphne, scrunching her face like it itched. "Not like that. Let's be serious. This is the guy who killed all the animals. What makes you think he couldn't kill you too?"

"Oh, I don't think he'd want that. I can be charming, you know. I told you, I was very charming."

"When he gets tired of that, when he gets bored. These people have, like, *procured* the U.S. government. I'm saying it's too much. You're outmatched here."

"Out*matched*?" Jenlena said. "What are you talking about? You know I faked my period for all of gym class."

Daphne rolled her eyes. "Stop trying to be so cute, okay? You know it's just me. What I'm saying is that despite whatever they want us to believe, men and women will never be equal, so the closest you can get is if we each have our own weapons.

"Like with Jordan," she continued. "It never would have worked between us if he wasn't canceled, because he'd have beauty and talent and popularity. Really, I'd been to his shows and he never even looked at me. But then he was canceled and we were more evenly matched because I have intelligence and a *modicum* of beauty. Troy, the guy I'm seeing now, is hot too. He's tall and has a lot of money, but I'm not out of my depth because he's fucking stupid. He's so culturally barren he thinks that show *Ozark* is premier television."

"I think Jordan really loved you though."

Daphne flicked her wrist like he'd been nothing more than a summer flu, a pregnancy scare. "I just thought, well, we're going to have a new world. Better start fresh, clean, uncanceled."

Her point was that Roderick Maeve had money, ambition, influence, success, fame, and connections. "And what do you have, Jenlena? No offense, but name me one thing."

"A young body," she ventured. "Men have ruined themselves for just that."

Daphne conceded her point. It was late now. Both girls yawned in unison.

2.

Men didn't always care what you wore or even how you looked. Certain men, certain times of day, only needed someone to look them right in the eyes and tell them—not with words but how you held your shoulders—that they weren't as big as they thought they were. Or, alternatively, that for twenty minutes or so, with you, they didn't have to pretend to be as big as they thought they needed to be. Despite her shortcomings and habitual neurosis, there were several key moments in her life when Jenlena understood this on a cellular level. It was like the time she met Adam at a loft party and made the joke about Hunter Biden that essentially got her pregnant. Like all great responsibilities, it also carried danger.

Roderick Maeve looked old for his age and somehow smaller than Jenlena felt he should have been, though he was a full head taller than she was and it showed even sitting down.

He asked her normal questions: what her name was, where she was from, and what she did for work. When she told him how she'd been selling plants he laughed out loud. "Really? Is that normal?"

"More and more," Jenlena said. "People need something to love." Was it real or was she having a dream?

He looked at her deeply then, and she remembered looking at his eyes on her phone in the clinic when she'd had an abortion. He had thick chestnut-brown hair and a tattoo of a semicolon on his wrist so small it took her until she finished her drink to realize it wasn't just a mole, of which he had many. The zipper on his sweater was pulled halfway down his chest so she knew this for a fact.

"I write poetry, too," she said. If it was a dream, she could say whatever she wanted, be bold and admit to her own art.

"Poetry," he repeated, as if he was sure it was something he'd heard of before. "I quite like the arts. Don't understand them much though, I'm afraid." He had the posture of a man who understood the room would conform to him, not the other way around. This must have been true no matter where he went. "But you do know that I'm changing the world."

Jenlena said she was familiar. The waiter dropped off a plate of food she couldn't recognize: small, round pieces of it. She put it in her mouth and chewed.

"I think when the world changes," Roderick Maeve continued, "art should be more important than it is now."

He took a bite, then spoke with his mouth full. "What my machine will do is give everyone a second chance. No one's saying we've been perfect." He leaned forward. "But who's ever said it's so bad we don't deserve a second chance?"

Everyone I went to university with, Jenlena thought, though she understood that he meant the question rhetorically.

"And that includes me too. In the new world, I think I'll develop much more of an interest in the *arts*." He said the word as if he wasn't sure how it was pronounced. "For example, what if I told you I've only ever read five novels in my whole life?"

"I'd furrow my brow and give you a disapproving look," she said.

This pleased him; he laughed so hard his eyes got tiny in his face. Then he asked if she wanted another round, but when she said yes he looked at his watch and said he had to get back to New York.

"I would like to see you again, though," he said. "If you'd like. If that's something that you'd be comfortable with, something within the realm of possibility for you."

Jenlena nodded. Again, she thought about her phone and how she had zoomed in on his face in that waiting room not even two months before. In that time, not counting the night with Connor, it had just been her alone in her body. When he looked at her like that, with his lips parted only slightly, she could feel that emptiness. It called to her, *feed me!*

"But we'll need an excuse," he said, biting his lip. "For your privacy as much as mine. Because when people see us together they'll ask questions."

Jenlena looked over her shoulder to see if anyone was doing it now: the waitstaff, a table of men in shiny suits, a young woman with her hair in a high ponytail, carrying a large duffel bag with a black tail sticking out the side.

"Can't you feel it?" he asked. "I can always feel when someone is watching me."

"I can feel you," she said, looking at him. "You're looking at me now."

He coughed into his martini. Then he laughed, nodding with approval, "*Poet*. So what if you wrote something? An article, a profile. It'll give us a pretense for spending time together. And you'll have total freedom. You can decide the length, the tone. I'll even place it for you once you're done. It'll grant you a lot of exposure."

"I don't know," she said. "I guess I should warn you, it's never been my specialty to dabble in complete sentences."

He shook his head. This was serious: "You have to write about me, you'll love it. I'll call up my contacts and get you on all the big websites. You'll center-part your hair and wear glasses for photographs in the *New Yorker.*"

So it was settled, they'd see each other again soon. He motioned to the waiter, then pushed his chair out from the table. Jenlena saw how tall he was—it washed over her. He touched her back now, lightly but with purpose and the feeling made her dizzy. She remembered who he was: Roderick Maeve. The man who killed all the animals. The one who said he'd turn back time.

"Hey," she said, trying to shake herself out of thinking about it. "D-did you know? This is the same hotel where John and Yoko stayed for their bed-in?" But try as she might, her voice was thin and trembling.

"Of course," said Roderick Maeve. "That's my suite."

Following him to the lobby, she left the duffel bag with the Dalmatian costume on the floor. "Miss!" said the waiter, running after her. "Miss, you left something."

Jenlena looked right into him. "No," she said. "That isn't mine."

3.

None of it mattered now, all of it was null: A cat rubbing its spine along your calf, a dog following you home, you of all people! How a mama bear would stop at nothing if you got near her cubs. The one weird girl from high school who had a hedgehog. *Yeah, I heard she does porn in Japan now.* Richard Gere put a gerbil in a bottle and lit a fire at the bottom of the bottle so the gerbil would run into his asshole. Buying a leather jacket with the first paycheck of your big new job, telling the guinea pig your secrets, asking the bunny to marry you, rigging the vote on what to call the class hamster. Did you know that Edie Sedgwick had a cat who was the son of Bob Dylan's cat but it died in a fire? Yes, you read it in a book and told everyone you knew. "Uh-huh, uh-huh," they said. You read that a horse on the battlefield would never step on a dead person. Can you picture it, with the fog and stuff, a horse making its way around the bodies? "Uh-huh, uh-huh," they said. Why were you the only one who cared about horses stepping over corpses? It was so lonely inside your specific thoughts and feelings.

4.

M●●N_cicero_666 @Moon.Cicero 1h

Everything thats happening was decided a long time ago

M●●N_cicero_666 @Moon.Cicero 1h

We took this land that wasn't ours and shit all over it

M●●N_cicero_666 @Moon.Cicero 1h

I'm not even talking about settlers v. native americans, but our own grandchildren

M●●N_cicero_666 @Moon.Cicero 50m

Three days on the road. It is almost enough to make you believe change is possible

M●●N_cicero_666 @Moon.Cicero 50m

Yet from an early age we're just taught to buy things and become obsessed with america

M●●N_cicero_666 @Moon.Cicero 45m

Driving cross country right now, hard to believe how beautiful it is

M●●N_cicero_666 @Moon.Cicero 30m

Ppl give me shit for hating on albertans, saying that i'm too harsh but i mean have you ever seen one in real life?

M●●N_cicero_666 @Moon.Cicero 29m

Famous albertan exhibit A:

M●●N_cicero_666 @Moon.Cicero 29m

 Ted Cruz, born in Calgary, AB December 22, 1970

M●●N_cicero_666 @Moon.Cicero 29m

wouldn't fuck him if it would bring back the animals

M●●N_cicero_666 @Moon.Cicero 25m

Just kidding. I would do anything.

M●●N_cicero_666 @Moon.Cicero 1m

boosting this one more time just in case the universe gives a fuck

5.

So there it was: Daphne, patron saint of big words, was jealous of Jenlena, 2.9 GPA. Jealousy was like sarin nerve gas, to be handled with the utmost care in glass cylinders in a movie starring Nicolas Cage and Samuel L. Jackson. It was the king of feelings because it rendered everything else inadmissible. What a delicious sensation. She could have run for president. And she would, wouldn't she? Figuratively. She'd write a big piece for the *New Yorker*, she'd gain fifty thousand followers, she'd be a whole new person. In all probability, Daphne would be jealous of this new girl too.

The only problem was that since their meeting, Roderick Maeve hadn't messaged once. He hadn't even followed her.

The heat lingered well into September and everyone seemed to be taking it personally. A couple outside was arguing. The woman asked the man if he even loved her, he said he did most of the time. She said he was such a pig she was surprised he hadn't died too.

"Well, didn't you know, baby? We're going back in time. You'll never be through with me!"

Jenlena went upstairs to see what was left of her scorched apartment. The fire had kissed so many things: their photos on the fridge, the IKEA couch, boxes of all their fun cereal. It had whispered sweet nothings and had its blatant way. In her room, the dresser was crisp, her closet was covered in soot. There was her old New Religious Movements textbook in the corner, singed on the chapter about the Manson Family, an outlier according to Professor Sabina. "The vast majority of people with strange beliefs practice peacefully," she'd stressed, "and with little fanfare. Some of you here in this room might even be doing it as we speak, if you'd only admit it to yourselves."

Jenlena sat on the bed covered in ash and googled all the women Roderick Maeve had ever dated: models and performance artists and movie stars and women who said he was cruel. "Ricky," said one in an interview from over a decade before, "is the type of person who'd order a banana split and eat everything except the banana." Jenlena leaned back and thought about how ice cream didn't exist anymore, not the kind that was made from real milk. But she could taste it then, vividly right on her tongue. *I would eat the banana for him*, she thought. *I'd make little faces while I did it.*

Women, she thought, were interesting creatures. Some of them would have you believe that because they didn't have the exact same power as men did it meant they didn't have power at all. But that wasn't true. Unemployment, when used correctly, allowed one to think about things quite deeply. She felt she was being objective. She wasn't a woman right then, not at least in the specific sense she was thinking about, which only ever happened in front of other people.

Her stepfather, Christopher, for example, who earned multiple hundreds of thousands of dollars a year, was a flagrantly weak man, easily undone. He wore specially made shirts from a company targeted toward office workers, cut slim in the arms and wide in the belly. But his strong jaw did do him some favors. She was mature enough to understand this now.

He'd been afraid of her for years, treading so carefully whenever he took her out for one of their biannual lunches to talk about the things he wanted to buy for her mother. "Or a coat, or leather boots. Has she ever said anything to you about Peru? We've had a good year, honey. What do you think we could buy to really show Mommy she's our number one?" He talked like a soccer coach in a movie where the star player turned out to be a hamster.

When she was sixteen, he had an affair with a woman from his work, and a group of Moon Bethlehems sent her mother photographs of them together in a motel. The glossy eight-by-elevens came in a manila envelope. He'd broken down in tears, begging her mother not to leave him. It was the first time Jenlena had seen a grown man cry like that, great gasps, and his whole body shuddered. Her mother stood over him, stone-faced, not even blinking. Jenlena watched from the stairs.

Her mother told her not to look at the photographs, but she left them around the house so brazenly Jenlena could tell she wanted her to. Now, years later, she could still remember how the glossy finish felt between her fingers. Christopher kissing the other woman and the shadows of their jaws splashed across the wall. The woman was not as beautiful or thin as her mother and this had truly perplexed her as a teenager. There was a sexual undercurrent to the adult world and she could not grasp its customs. To this day, the photographs came to her during sex from time to time, which she didn't understand and had no choice but to succumb to.

That summer, Christopher sent the two of them on a trip to Europe and they weren't even expected to call. They went shopping, saw a concentration camp. From what she knew, her mother didn't even cry.

6.

M●●N_cicero_666 @Moon.Cicero 1h17

Lets talk a little 'bout briteKor, one of the leading oil and natural gas companies in the world, responsible for the majority of produce in alberta tar sands

M●●N_cicero_666 @Moon.Cicero 1h17

Junior executive christopher campbell who makes $250,000/yr literally threatened peaceful protestors with an electric drill last winter

M●●N_cicero_666 @Moon.Cicero 1h17

New reports name him as PERSONALLY responsible for the 1mil liters of toxic waste from a containment pond into the Athabasca river in 2018

M●●N_cicero_666 @Moon.Cicero 1h16

A year later suncor leaked human sewage into the same river

M●●N_cicero_666 @Moon.Cicero 1h16

100% in violation of treaty rights

M●●N_cicero_666 @Moon.Cicero 1h15

100% in violation of Canada's clean air act

M●●N_cicero_666 @Moon.Cicero 1h15

But do these people face jail time?

M●●N_cicero_666 @Moon.Cicero 1h15

Dont make me lol

M●●N_cicero_666 @Moon.Cicero 1h14

drinking water from local communities has been found to contain benzene, a carcinogen linked to bone marrow failure, anemia and leukemia

M●●N_cicero_666 @Moon.Cicero 1h14

there is NO safe exposure level

M●●N_cicero_666 @Moon.Cicero 1h14

Literally one of the poisons nazis used in their death camps

M●●N_cicero_666 @Moon.Cicero 1h14

Just in case anyone thought i was exaggerating

7.

In the end, it took four days for him to get in touch, which felt both forward and aloof at the same time. **Testing,** he sent in an Insta-gram message. **One, two, three . . .**

That made her blush, thinking about him typing out all the numbers in full.

BORN_IN_FL: **HOW ARE YOU?**

ADRIENNEB1TCH: **OK. YOU?**

BORN_IN_FL: **VERY GOOD. THE SKIES ARE BEAUTIFUL IN CALIFORNIA.**

ADRIENNEB1TCH: **RAINING HERE**

ADRIENNEB1TCH: **:(**

ADRIENNEB1TCH: **BUT I LIKE IT WET**

BORN_IN_FL: **HAVE YOU BEEN WORKING ON YOUR PIECE?**

Yes, she'd been working. She'd scrolled all the way to the pay-wall reading *New Yorker* profiles: a Saudi prince, an Ohio mayor caught cheating on his wife with a woman in a pangolin costume, the Judaism of Ashton Kutcher.

BORN;IN;FL: **NO PRESSURE. I JUST CAN'T SLEEP RIGHT NOW SO I WAS WONDERING**

BORN;IN;FL: **I'M JUST CURIOUS TO SEE WHAT YOU COME UP WITH**

ADRIENNEB1TCH: **TO WRITE ABOUT YOU?**

BORN;IN;FL: **TO KNOW WHAT YOU THINK**

She typed and then deleted, I think you're in possession of a personal fortune which rivals the GDP of multiple countries, a degree of wealth many of my contemporaries deem highly unethical.

ADRIENNEB1TCH: **I THINK YOU HAVE NICE EYES.**

BORN;IN;FL: **IS THAT A JOKE?**

ADRIENNEB1TCH: **U TELL ME. YR THE ONE WHO'S EARNED A BIL-LION $**

8.

Haiku for Feb 1
So much rain today
A fox ate all the groundhogs
You came on my face

BORN_IN_FL: **GENIUS!**

When he sent her a screenshot of a poem she'd posted months ago, it meant that Roderick Maeve was doing research on her and wasn't ashamed to let her know, whereas while she had been doing research on him incessantly, she was careful never to reveal any trace of it in her messages to him. It was not a power dynamic they taught you the name of in school, but there was power there; she could feel it, alive and pulsing between them.

ADRIENNEB1TCH: **WHICH ONES BTW**

BORN_IN_FL: **?**

ADRIENNEB1TCH: **YOUR 5 NOVELS**

BORN_IN_FL: **AH**

BORN_IN_FL: **DUNE, THE FOUNTAINHEAD 2X, ONLY COWGIRLS GET THE BLUES**

BORN_IN_FL: **AND SULA, THAT WAS FOR AN EX**

9.

After the heat, autumn lasted three days. All the trees in red and orange like that, Jenlena was reminded of the fire. Nobody ever cried for the dying leaves; it was always implicit that they'd be back again the next year.

BORN_IN_FL: **CAN I MAKE A CONFESSION?**

ADRIENNEB1TCH: **IF YOU WANT.**

ADRIENNEB1TCH: **WHO AM I TO SAY NO?**

BORN_IN_FL: **WELL. I LIKE YOU**

BORN_IN_FL: **CANT STOP THINKING ABOUT YOU**

She googled how he earned a million dollars in the housing crash, how one of his companies was alleged to have proven the existence of a parallel universe, how no one knew who his father was, what his body looked like waterskiing, how he had killed all the animals, how allegedly he had pressed the button himself.

But there was something she liked about him, precisely because he was the type of man she remembered being afraid of as a child: the principal at school, or her friend's dad who had thick wrists and was always dirty from his work in the garage.

ADRIENNEB1TCH: **DITTO**

10.

Now he was scrolling through the Instagram of a normal girl, he was liking her posts from his private account, and despite the growing promise of his new machine, Ricky was obliged to admit to himself that double-tapping on her selfie with the caption *wut a bastard monday mornings on yr period are* was the most excited he'd felt since the time machine got started.

CHAPTER NINE

A First Date to Remember

1.

All around the world, people rejoiced in celebration of the time machine. Business boomed, stocks soared, product prevailed. It was what the world deserved, wasn't it? A second chance after all their mistakes. So all along there had been nothing to worry about, the strife and demonstrations.

Ricky set up the boy wonder physicist in a basement room of the laboratory with a five-by-ten-foot chalkboard he'd brought with him from Boston, his one demand coming west. The physicist was tall but not graceful. Ricky had come to see him at his work twice, and both times his short pants gave the impression of a recent growth spurt.

"We could get you a better room, you know," Ricky told him. There were three thin windows lining where the ceiling met the wall and some dust reminiscent of a spiderweb. A decent view, at least.

"What's to see out there?" he asked, facing the chalkboard. The math—shapes and arrows and numbers—spilled out like gibberish.

"And you can call me Ricky, by the way. It's what my friends call me."

The physicist was not like other people. There was a lot of talk about some sort of great sadness, but he had just never bought into that kind of thing. Sure, he had been sad once or twice (when he carried his own sister's coffin through the cemetery, for example), but you have to move on with your life.

Though he was no historian, the one thing he understood about the past was that as long as it had existed, people had been told they couldn't do this, they couldn't do that. Then about a half a dozen times in a generation there were people who said no. They did what they wanted anyway. Ever since he could remember, the physicist had always intended to be one of those men.

At fourteen, he was accepted to Princeton on a full scholarship. He wanted to be the smartest person in his class, then he wanted to be the smartest person in his year, then he wanted to graduate in three years, then get his master's degree during his PhD degree where he would be the smartest person in the whole school, maybe in the history of it. And he knew at the base of his gut, the same place where all the numbers came from, that none of this would be very difficult.

His first year at Princeton, he looked so young that a janitor mistook him for a child when he was eating alone in the dining hall. An *ordinary* child, something weak and disoriented. "Can I help you?" she asked, touching him gently on the shoulder.

He told her no, he was doing math. She looked down at the proof he had spread across sheets of loose leaf on the table. "Honey, those are drawings," she said.

In the end she insisted on taking him to the security office on the other side of campus and one of his professors had to come down himself to explain that no, he was not a child but one of the most promising young physicists they'd had with them in years. By the end of the week, the dean even sent him a letter apologizing. Two separate reporters from the school newspaper asked if they could interview him about the incident but the physicist declined because the thing about him was that he was not like other people, so addicted to the past that it dominated every thought and feeling.

He wanted to manipulate light, then he wanted to stabilize a wormhole, then he wanted to bend time. He lay awake at night picturing it, reaching his hands out in front of him into the dark and twisting it to wring out the imperfections.

Before his sister died, their father took them on a trip to Poland and killed a deer. He showed it to the children afterwards, splayed out on the table in the shed with its head hanging off the edge, tongue slack and eyes open. The physicist's sister burst into tears.

"What?" their father said. "You love animals." He'd thought she would revel in the opportunity to see one so up close.

"No, Daddy," she kept saying. "Make it go back, make him like he was before."

His sister was like this, unbound by logic, a child in every sense of the word, taken with flora and fauna to a spiritual degree. She'd pick flowers and press them in his math textbooks just to drive him crazy. Once, he heard her whispering to a rock.

Then one day, that autumn back in Virginia, she never came home from school. The physicist had left early because of an argument over fractions with his teacher. There was nothing he hated more than when people acted like math was something it wasn't. When they made it sound like it was all about rules and rigidity, though sure, maybe you had to get through a bit of that until you got to the good stuff. Then it was more like wind. You were free.

They lived a seven-minute walk away from the school, but even after two hours it remained possible that his sister had been distracted by some flowers or a wild animal. And it was true that three days later, they found her body in the woods.

So, when the woman claiming to work for Roderick Maeve first approached him, it was no surprise for the physicist to be asked if he was only building a time machine to bring his sister back.

"No." His answer came easily. "You have to consider the variables."

Because, say they were a happy family. His mother never ran off with the guy from work and his father never started drinking. The physicist would do what, play soccer? They'd have dinner every night? Go to Applebee's and eat the grotesque cheesecake together as a family. How would he have any time to study?

Besides, his sister, as he saw it, was just a little girl. You had to think it through. So she would have grown up. She'd probably go to a state school or maybe just learn how to cut hair somewhere. Knowing how irrational she'd been, she might have even ended up as one of those Moon Bethlehems. And he'd teach somewhere mediocre, only slightly above average at math. God forbid one of those philistines who only paid attention to the rules. Then the weather mounting around them and one day all the birds fall from the sky.

"You have to think about it rationally," the physicist told Roderick Maeve's assistant when she appeared that day in his graduate lounge to ask about his time machine. "Is the life of one little girl worth the math that would save the planet? Because rationally it can't matter how much she loved nature or that she happened to be my sister."

2.

Of all the companies that lobbied him for use of the machine, it was the British Gardenamore that caught Ricky's attention, because their CEO reminded him of his mother. She had red hair and talked about introducing solar panels into the Industrial Revolution. "By our projections," she said, "it would pretty much solve the weather crisis. A huge PR win for you ever since, you know, you killed everyone's pets."

His assistant spoke up. "He actually—"

Ricky motioned for her to heel. "It's alright, I've always been one for candor. This weather thing," he clarified. "People are really so concerned?"

"It polls particularly high among the college-educated."

He considered it.

"You'd be a hero." Another executive, a man, stepped in. "Because you know what a lot of ecologists are saying, that the weather was particularly important for the animals. It would have, you know, polled well across all species. So we have an opportunity to, um, kill two birds with one stone. So to speak. Solving the weather, bringing back the animals—the people would love you. They'd follow you anywhere after that."

The tension was thick, corn-fed.

"To be awfully frank," the CEO said, "we had our hesitations coming here. A time machine, could it be? But this here"—she looked at the diagrams Ricky's team had projected on the screen, then at Ricky, before her face broke out in a wide smile—"is magnificent!"

Their proposal was simple: send two of their technicians back in time and introduce solar technology into the Industrial Revolution. It was foolproof. "We have all the best historians," the CEO said. "Believe me, we'll have it worked out down to the most minute detail. So it's a clean swap. Nothing else changes, then *boom!* The weather won't know what hit it!"

It was beginning to appeal to him. Fuck yes, he wanted to be a part of something like that. They shook hands with great voracity and afterwards he called on his assistant for a champagne toast.

"You know," said the male executive, "my daughter was deathly afraid of spiders all her life. Woke up in the middle of the night screaming from nightmares that they were crawling all over her."

"And now?" Ricky asked. His three drinks hit him in one fell swoop, like a bird into a window. He leaned back and let the feeling swaddle him.

"Well, we've got this weather now, 'aven't we? She wakes up from nightmares that a flood's come into her room and washed away all her toys. Which makes our job all the more crucial, doesn't it?"

"Yes," said Ricky. "Most definitely. I've always believed the past belongs to us all."

"Beautiful, sir," said the CEO. A lock of her hair had fallen out from her bun.

After the meeting, Ricky searched for vintage windbreakers on eBay, then sat cross-legged without shoes for a long time, thinking about nothing, and for dinner the chef once again made an uninspired salad. As always, the girl who brought it to him was appropriate.

Afterwards, he played an unreleased Spike Lee movie in his screening room but just scrolled through his phone to read about people who hated him online. He called for a pad and paper and wrote longhand the things people said about him in two columns marked "pluses" (saving the world, so funny, a pleasure to serve, great style, "such interesting taste, sir," the world is grateful, unprecedented visionary), and "minuses" (animal murderer, fake teeth, total hoax, scam artist, "forced me to give him a blow job in 2009," unprecedented capitalist). Somewhere in the middle must have been who he really was. In the morning he'd give the paper to his assistant to file with the others.

At 4 a.m., he woke up with a sensation that something had just brushed up against his foot, but no, the animals were gone. His name was Roderick Maeve and he had done it himself. It was to save the people. Sometimes he didn't know where he was and sometimes he couldn't recognize his own hands. He tried to remember the last time he'd been on a run but for the life of him could not.

Ricky rolled over onto his side to see if anyone was next to him. No. So there was nothing stopping him, nothing to save him from that Sunday morning feeling when he couldn't come up with anything else to want and the world was empty. It was 4:45 a.m. on a Tuesday. Maybe he'd stay up to watch the sunrise, give that a try. If it didn't work he could text that girl, the normal one. He liked her really, those normal silly poems. Next week he had four hours between meetings and decided to see her. He had that house in Quebec left over from his marriage to Evie and could invite her there for normal things.

3.

Winter came in the middle of the night. It splooged atop cars and all the roofs. Jenlena's jaw ached from clenching her teeth so much while she slept. They bought a twenty-dollar camping stove just to boil some water to warm up their feet. "Thank god the world is ending," Daphne said. "Can you imagine how scary it would be if we weren't getting a new one?"

The next day, Roderick Maeve picked Jenlena up himself. He didn't explain where the car came from, only told her it was his culture to give rides to girls, an American tradition. He stopped right outside her singed building and sped down Parc Avenue, the exact same route as when she went to get her abortion.

"You look nice," he told her at a stoplight. It sounded like an evaluation. His hair was thinning on the top, she noticed for the first time.

On the side of the highway, two cars had spun out on the black ice. "Can you believe this weather?" Jenlena asked. "The last time we saw each other was so hot, and now look at this."

He declined, keeping his eyes on the road. "It's my job to believe it."

They drove off the island, then into a suburb where all the streets had the names of wine: Beaujolais, Champagne, Merlot. He told her his house wasn't anything special, just a holdover from his last marriage. "She was from here," he said. "Spoke the French and everything."

Jenlena nodded. Evie Forget, one of the supermodels of her childhood: tall, blond, pouty. In high school, Jenlena used to picture her Calvin Klein campaign whenever she was trying to curb her appetite.

He stopped in front of a wrought-iron gate, keying in a password for them to enter and drive along the narrow road. There were trees to either side of them, and he told her that when he'd first started dating his wife, he'd leveled the surrounding neighborhood just to build her a private forest. "Turned out in the end, she didn't even give a fuck about trees, though." He shook his head. "The crazy things you do for love."

Jenlena did a little laugh. "Right."

He turned his head then, looked at her with both his eyes. "You've been in love?"

"Sure," she said. "As a figure of speech." Sometimes she felt like the rough draft of a Lorrie Moore character. Worse, a pastiche. Or, as her computer had once autocorrected in a paper, *pistachio*.

Inside the house, a grand foyer opened up onto both floors and a gaudy chandelier. Roderick Maeve led Jenlena toward the living room, a suede couch positioned under a life-sized oil portrait of his ex-wife. "Oh that," he said. "Just ignore it. Or would you rather I hung a sheet or something?"

Jenlena's lips were chapped from the cold. "No," she said. "I hardly even noticed."

The sprawling back window opened up onto more trees. "Total privacy," he said, draping his puffer jacket along the mantel. "Nobody can see or hear a thing."

He wore a vintage Nike sweatshirt and she had baggy jeans with one of the legs bleached. His skin had that plasticky sheen you'd expect from a rich person, the opacity. She found his teeth unnaturally white, and his forehead didn't move while he spoke. He sat beside her on the couch and they both stared forward for a moment, just blinking.

At first, they pretended it was all about the article he'd asked her to write for the *New Yorker*. It started out like this. Jenlena pulled out a coiled notebook with daisies on the cover from her bag. She tucked her hair behind her ear and asked him about his morning routine.

"So, I've heard you like to run," she said.

"No, but that's exactly why I do it so much," Roderick Maeve replied. "Builds character."

Jenlena wrote it down.

"One thing I should make clear," he continued, "is that if you want a sob story about how I'm doing it all to find my father or return to some long-lost love, then I'm sorry but you'll have to find another angle. The thing is that with me not everything has to be drowning in pathos. Sometimes it's not any more complicated than the fact that I saw the demand and I put together the team. I have the means. What is it good for if I can't pull off something bold and revolutionary like this? If I can't do that then it's just money."

4.

He'd said this kind of thing before, in interviews, all the time. Repeating himself like that made him feel as if his whole life had already happened and he was just following the stage directions. One of those feelings: happy, dopey, sleepy, alienated beyond belief. Grumpy, horny. He didn't know what it was about this girl Jenlena. That was what fascinated him. She was so unusual to him; he'd never known anyone like her. Not rich, not poor, just normal. She had the energy of a knapsack (a new one for the first day of school, crisp in the pockets). What was that smell? It wasn't bad, not necessarily. A taste he could definitely conceive of acquiring, like that time he ate all those live maggots covered in saffron.

He wondered if she was bulimic. Evie had told him that all girls were, to a degree. The same way they were all lesbians. It was so bizarre to him, the sight of girls locking themselves in the bathroom en masse, with the faucets running and spurting their guts. All boys ever wanted was to get inside of them. All girls ever wanted was to get their insides out. There was a comedy routine in there somewhere. If he wanted he could pay some Lampoon kid to find it.

After he got through his usual spiel, he mixed two cocktails at the bar using ingredients he could only assume had belonged to Evie:

a three-quarters-full bottle of tequila and a bottle of syrup with a light green tinge. The fridge made its own ice cubes from scratch.

"Tell me a secret," Jenlena said after her first sip.

"Excuse me?"

"That's why I'm here, isn't it?" She took another drink. "You want to tell me, to show me secret things. You're tired of having them all to yourself."

It startled him but he liked it. He grinned and leaned toward her so their knees touched and he could feel it in his teeth. "But it's a secret," he said. "Off the record." Was he the dumbest man on earth? Always telling women things.

She closed the notebook and slid it onto the glass coffee table in front of them.

"We're supposed to say that nothing's going to change besides the energy source," he said.

"Supposed to," Jenlena repeated.

"Well," he said. "We have this whole professional team, they're helping with the side effects. Doing all kinds of research and practice scenarios to make sure. But I'm not sure I actually believe in it."

"So it's like a sci-fi movie?" she asked. "We'll all wake up one day and everything's unrecognizable?"

"Sure," he said. "Maybe. My point is that what if that's a good thing? When you've seen the things I have, you start to realize that most people, well, they really don't know what's good for them. With the people we've got today, I'm not sure the weather is even our biggest problem. My hope is that there could be a philosophical shift. When we realize that there's this power in the sun and it teaches us to use what we have. It's the sun. Think about that mentality, think about what that could do for people to be more grateful for the things they have, instead of always pining for more.

Because you wouldn't believe the requests I get. Ever since we announced the machine, people I haven't even spoken to in years who expect me to help them go back in time to save their marriages? It's been five, ten years, and you're still hung up on some marriage? No wonder we're in the shape we're in."

"But it *is* tempting," Jenlena said. "You can't deny that it's tempting to think about where you'd go. With the time machine, I mean. Into the past."

"Honestly?"

"No," she said. "Tell me a lie."

He laughed, but suddenly felt conscious of his teeth when he did it. They were too white, weren't they? Yes, for the rest of his face. "Honestly I don't think about it. Not seriously. It was just an idea I had. And I didn't think we'd actually make it, not until we found the scientist who could do it. Even then." He shrugged, taking a big swallow of the taste of his mouth. "What's always excited me more is the future. Don't you agree?"

She shook her head. Her eyes seemed to swell and he watched her posture change. "It's just that for some of us the future doesn't always hold much appeal," she said.

When his face softened, she seemed to brace for the usual mythology: *think positively, drink lots of water.*

He leaned forward and said, "In that case, maybe the better option is to embrace the present." Then he kissed her.

Ricky was like this, totally tacky and uncouth when it came to women. He had a thick tongue and put it in her mouth. He pulled her thigh over his lap and could feel her nipples through her sweater against his chest. His knees buckled like a cheesy song he knew all the words to. He wanted her whole entire body spread thin over his and he tried to take off her pants but she moved away.

"I think I'm hungry," she said.

It was literally impossible for him to parse what she meant. He cleared his throat, stood up, and said he'd look for what he could in the kitchen. "No promises, okay?"

5.

Jenlena went to the bathroom and was disgusted by how yellow her teeth were. She was pale and practically looked like she had cancer. What if Daphne was right? She had no business mingling with a person like this. Despite whatever strange alchemy had occurred during their first meeting, Roderick Maeve already knew this, and that was why he was acting so strange. Soon he would return her to where she belonged. She'd be usual forever and then she'd die.

What was he thinking right now, on the couch in the other room? *What a joke this girl is, if you can even call her that.* She barely had the parts. He had probably just invited her over for some illuminati practical joke and by the end of the night lizard people would eat her alive. *Well, okay*, she thought, putting on a smidge of lip gloss. *So all along, my life's been worth nothing. All along, I've had it figured out.*

When she came back, he'd put on music, an old rock song that had been used once in a movie for a famous dance scene. He grabbed her hand and they started moving. It was awkward and they kept stepping on each other's feet but it was nice to laugh and he put his hand on her back and she liked that too. She liked feeling his belt buckle against her stomach. Yellow light came from the outside, though it was fading.

The song switched to something slower. Now they were barely moving but it felt very important. She went through the parts of her body and thought about how she had prepared them for tonight.

Her wrists and neck, between her legs and other obvious places. Everything was true but the most true things happened late at night.

"You owe me one," Roderick Maeve said.

"What?"

"A secret."

"I like you." She pressed her feet into the floor.

"No." He was boyish when he smiled. "A *secret*."

"I'd really like to get to the bottom of you. I'd like to put you into words."

A timer went off in the kitchen. "We'll eat a little," he said. "Let's get something in our stomachs."

6.

He'd prepared a simple pasta, just noodles with some oil and a couple of spices left over in the cabinets. "My wife was never a big eater," he said. "My ex-wife."

The dining table stretched the length of the room. From the window, Jenlena saw the mountains in the distance doused with snow. He asked her for her sob story and she told him about her stepfather in the oil industry and how her mother had wanted to be an actress. "One of those classic giving-up-on-your-dreams stories," she said.

Ricky made a joke about how he wouldn't know anything about that. It was bad and he knew it, in which case it might have been good, it could have been charming. "So you really wanna sell flowers and write poems all your life?" he asked.

"No," she said. "Not really. Really, I don't think I'm very good at wanting things. It comes from my mother's side."

He asked her to elaborate.

"When I was a kid I was always trying to be so dumb," she said. "I thought the dumber I was, the less anyone could hurt me because I'd be so dumb I wouldn't even notice. So ever since then, I guess you could say I've been pretty laissez-faire."

She had a strong delivery but the notion of her apathy was almost laughable because desire ran down her face, she was absolutely dripping in it. Desire for so many things at once he struggled to parse them individually. He knew then what he would do—maybe it was the reason he had brought her here to begin with. Had he been dying to bring someone here?

"Come outside with me," he said.

He led her out the sliding glass doors, where they faced the man-made forest, a thick wall of trees. It was dark and Jenlena made out only shapes: the shape of branches, the shape of underbrush, the shape of wanting to do anything he asked her to, the shape of being afraid to do it.

"C'mon." He clasped her hand.

She took a breath and stepped after him into the snow, so crisp it barked as their feet broke through. More snow began to fall, large soft flakes that coated her eyelashes. Roderick Maeve said nothing, Jenlena watched his breath pool in the cold air then disappear. She labored to keep his pace, leaning on tree trunks for balance. Above them, the moon hung low, taunting them with meaning.

It was a few minutes before a large barn appeared in the distance, beyond it a break in the trees that gave way to a sprawling field, where the snow was muddied and the grass beneath it torn up into piles. A familiar smell had appeared, though Jenlena couldn't place it. She rested her hands on her knees to catch her breath, but Roderick Maeve did not stop.

He led her to the door. It was made of steel, and the barn had long, thin windows stretched horizontally just beneath the roof. He was wet too. She could see the light bounce off the melted snow on his cheeks, like a girl with too much highlighter. He gave her a big smile. "Are you ready to go inside?"

Yes. No. Jenlena had the feeling that she had somehow misunderstood the question. "Uh-huh," she said.

He opened the door.

Again, the smell. More so now, but still she couldn't place it. Then he turned on the lights and a brown horse stood before them. It hit the ground with its front hooves and neighed.

Jenlena fell backwards, into the wall. "No," she said, adamantly, like a child who wanted to stay up all night watching TV. "*No.*"

The animal exhaled through trembling nostrils.

"No." Softer now, unsteady on her feet. "Is it," she asked, "a robot? You're making robots now, for sad and lonely people?"

Roderick Maeve laughed at her. He couldn't stop laughing. It was like she was the animal, she was a cat playing with string, a dog trying to walk on its hind legs. "You didn't think," he said. "You didn't really."

"It's real?"

The horse breathed not three feet from her.

"Darling," he said. "Who do you think I am? No, I couldn't do that. Not to all of them. Of course, I kept a few."

The smell was incredible. It washed over Jenlena. Many things bubbled up from memories: namely, the sight of nine or ten of them together, running. At a summer camp, she and the other children rode them through the trees, downhill even. Horses lived inside the stables that also smelled like them and her mother would take her to the fence with carrots. They held out their hands and felt their soft lips against their palms and it tickled.

"You wanted a secret, didn't you?" Roderick Maeve touched her back but she barely felt it. The horse turned its thick neck, shapes of light across its fur, ovals and triangles, each one was her favorite. It looked at her, she could feel it and she was real because a horse was looking at her and the horse was real.

"I knew you'd like her," said Roderick Maeve. "You can touch her if you want."

She wanted to, she did. Jenlena moved her hand through her coat both the right and wrong way, like velvet. What not everyone knew was that the streak down their faces was called a blaze and they were born covered in slime but ready to run. To this day, she sometimes watched videos late at night of foals oozing from their mothers and other dead things and she cried her eyes out.

"I feel like I'm dreaming," she said. She looked at Roderick Maeve then. The shadows from the beams crossed his face so all she could see were his teeth.

"I have a man who comes to look after her," he started to explain. "Very discreet, of course, he's been through all the paperwork."

"Why don't you keep her in California?"

"In California, I keep my dogs."

"*Dogs?*"

"Don't tell me you wouldn't have done the same. About a week before the frequency went out we decided to develop an implant that could spare some of them from the damage. Most of them we keep in a lab, but yeah, sure, a couple friends called in some favors. So sue me, I have a heart when it comes to my friends."

"What are they?"

"Entrepreneurs, some humanitarians, supermodels mostly."

"No. The animals."

"Majority dogs. Cats too. One angora rabbit, just gorgeous, I think a parakeet somewhere. Billy wanted to keep that sloth for his daughter."

"How many?"

He began counting on his fingers then quickly gave up. "Couple dozen?"

She felt weak in the knees, certain she'd throw up. "Roder—" She grasped his fleshy hand for balance.

"Call me Ricky," he said, laughing once more. "It's what my friends do. We're friends now. See? We know each other's secrets."

She swallowed and the taste burned the back of her throat.

"You like secrets, don't you?"

"Yes," she said, but the word congealed.

"What was that?"

"Of course."

"And you understand how they work?"

She nodded. "Yes, sir."

"Call me Ricky." He wrapped her up in his big big arms. "We're going to be good friends."

Jenlena couldn't keep her eyes off of the horse. She saw herself and this strange man reflected in her black, glossy eyes.

"Come on now," he said, and Jenlena realized that she'd started to cry. "Why don't we let her out?"

Unpeeling himself from her side, he pressed a button by the lights that made the wall open into the night. The horse exhaled, stamped its front foot, then took to a gallop. The moonlight draped across her body like it was made just for that moment and Jenlena knew it was not a dream because she only ever dreamt of breast-feeding plants.

"I think I'm ready to go home now," she said to the California billionaire. "My roommate will be waiting up."

She watched his eyes narrow as he made his decision.

"Okay," he said finally. "I'll give you a ride."

CHAPTER TEN

Daphne Sees an Old Friend

1.

Daphne had put on weight from eating so much bread since the animals died and the chemicals in "cheese" made her skin break out. But as long as she avoided direct confrontations with the mirror, it was possible to rationalize these changes in her appearance. She could map out the five-paragraph essay in her head. Beauty was only one thing. It was big, sure, like money—for women it was even bigger—but whatever didn't kill you made you stronger.

So she would be an ugly woman. Sometimes you had to consider the benefits that sort of adversity could grant you. If as a moderately attractive five-foot-eight bottle-blond she could earn a 3.98 in school, as an ugly woman she would surely be unstoppable. Daphne could learn Mandarin, she could go to law school. She'd get a stipend and spend it on new clothes or fancy juices that made you glow from the inside until she was pretty again, with the added depth of having been to the other side. "Listen here," she'd say around the campfire. "Have I got a wild story for you."

Most days, save for when she was at work or asleep, she surrounded herself with narrative. Daphne listened to a podcast about how Mao Zedong swam the Yangtze River seventeen times to prove his virility. She listened to a podcast about a woman and a gay man who were best friends. She listened to a podcast in which Moon Bethlehems spoke about what the animals had been like during the siege, how in hindsight they'd never had a chance because their goals were unclear and they had no organizational structure.

"It was like, well, I mean you had some of them who'd been told what to do their whole lives," said one Moon Bethlehem who had been within the animals' ranks. "Then they taste freedom and it's like, well, what if I don't wanna be a dog anymore, what if I wanna be a bird? Which in retrospect I think led to some misfires."

Soon they would be approaching a year since the animals had died, and mainstream opinion was split on what to think. Was the mass extinction a global tragedy or a necessary evil? It didn't really matter. Soon, the time machine would make all that null. Mice would live in the walls again, wasps would ruin brunch, pigs would be slaughtered. They'd be covered in salt and taste delicious.

2.

"You know we haven't talked yet about what we're going to do," she said to Jenlena one day that winter when it was so cold they got knots in their shoulders from shivering all the time. Their lips were chapped and they wore four pairs of socks at once. "In the new world, you know. I mean, I'm probably going to move in with Troy. I expect he'll ask me pretty soon and I'm definitely applying to grad school. I was just curious to see what your ideas were."

"Oh," said Jenlena, seemingly caught off guard. "I guess I haven't thought about it."

"But you're looking at apartments, right?" Daphne said, hand on hip like a CEO or pubescent beauty queen. "I mean, if the world isn't ending, is it really appropriate to be squatting in a burned-down basement?"

Thinking about the time machine gave Daphne the feeling that anything was possible and everything was available to her. It was the way things had been in university when problems solved themselves the moment they arrived and she had won all the prizes. She was smarter than anyone else she knew, except for Jordan when he talked about music. Except for Jenlena when she flirted with guys. She was so excited she'd started staying up nights just to research the future online. She was thinking of applying to grad school, she was seriously considering buying an LSAT study guide online, or backpacking in Thailand. She bought two hundred dollars' worth of new clothes from Forever 21, then a $400 Reformation dress, and signed up for three credit cards online. *Be who you want to be in the new world now, that way you'll be off to a running start*, she read in an infographic on Instagram and it made a helluva lot of sense. She wrote a list of traits she intended on cultivating: punctual, optimistic, tactful, polyglot. She ordered *Swann's Way* off the internet and worked on her glutes.

"You better get cracking," she said to Jenlena. "All the good professional degree programs are gonna be overwhelmed with applicants."

"I mean," Jenlena responded, "I'm probably just going to see where this thing with Roderick Maeve goes."

"Just make sure you have a solid plan in case it doesn't work out."

"Why wouldn't it work out?" In the past month, he'd pushed back her trip to California three times, but there remained in her voice the hollow lilt of hope.

"I'm just saying," said Daphne, opening a jar of peanut butter and then diving into it with her fingers like a sex act.

"You know, I'm writing this piece for him and it'll grant me a lot of exposure. Sometimes that can be more than money, I think. Once I'm in the *New Yorker* I could get an agent and write an entire book. I was thinking maybe like Ayn Rand. Something really influential? Like Ayn Rand but for people like us, people who just want to sit around all day."

"Jenny, I saw a picture, like yesterday, where he's out to dinner with a supermodel."

"That's just for the shareholders," said Jenlena. "He has to project a certain image."

Her mouth fell open midbite, like a bird feeding its children. "You don't actually believe that."

"Look," said Jenlena, showing Daphne a blind item, suggesting Roderick Maeve's relationship with the model was set up by her billionaire father as part of a tax evasion scheme. "See? It's all publicity," she said. "Nothing's real."

"Can you imagine?" Daphne asked, changing the subject after a plastic bag outside the window caught her attention. "All our problems, just gone?" She snapped her fingers.

"Do you think we'll still be friends?"

"Oh, definitely," said Daphne, but her thoughts had drifted, slipped free from their cage. There was no better feeling than actually wanting tomorrow.

Maybe, she thought, at dinner parties in the new world (she could see it clearly now that she'd been up for forty-eight hours researching TEFL programs), sitting over the roast duck breast with her friends in geometric earrings, they'd talk about how close the world had come to losing itself. "Remember how when the weather was so bad we started blaming each other?"

"It was the only thing we could do."

"It gave a semblance of control, blaming each other for the things we said in passing, or what had happened years ago."

"Clotting, did we call it? Clotting, right?"

"Canceling," she would say.

"Ah, yes."

And she would lower her voice so that the others had to lean in close and say, "I knew a canceled man."

"Oooooo, do tell!"

"Well, it was very much exciting."

3.

In California, there was a big press conference. There were photographers and television cameras everywhere. Roderick Maeve wore a suit with Air Jordans. The Gardenamore CEO stood beside him on the big stage. Her hair was down today, stick straight. The two technicians who would actually be going back in time sat in plastic chairs to the left. Roderick Maeve didn't know how or why they'd been chosen, simply read off the remarks the company had written for him, espousing their bravery and qualifications.

"For the last fifteen years across Britain and Europe," he said, "Gardenamore has become a leader in solar energy, one of the planet's last hopes of combating the weather crisis. And though they've made considerable strides, the brutal truth is that any progress we're making is linear, while the weather moves exponentially."

As directed, he paused for effect.

"Until *now*! With this machine we'll send two of our most-qualified technicians back in time to the birth of industrial society to reroute the world's energy dependency for the centuries to come!"

As directed, he paused for applause.

"Know their names," said Roderick Maeve. "These are the brave individuals sacrificing their presents for our pasts."

The female technician had short hair and a round body with a ruddy complexion. She wore tortoiseshell glasses. The male technician was younger. He was handsome, but in a familiar way. Anyone had seen his face a thousand times. He had a young son in the crowd who wore a T-shirt that said *My Daddy Is a Superhero*. His wife was pretty and crying.

Everyone knew that they would not be coming back. Once they had successfully completed their mission, the technicians would retreat into a quiet, monastic life in the countryside with just each other for company. Indeed, they were to pose as husband and wife, though they were to have no children, so as to disturb as little else as possible.

The CEO spoke for a little while, a speech about how the one thing she liked about the weather was that it brought them all together and for that she would always be grateful. Then there were about a thousand questions, or rather five, and each individual reporter had to formulate them in their own specific way. And even then most of it amounted to *Are you serious?*

"Yes," Roderick Maeve said. "Of course. I for one am not prepared to just lay back and let the weather have its way with me."

Afterwards, there was a big luncheon with all kinds of important people. They shook Roderick Maeve's hand. Some had smooth skin, some had rough. They congratulated the CEO, who said, "Yes, it's very exciting, our solar panels will be everywhere, it's a dream."

The technicians must have been nervous around so many important people, so to make them more comfortable, Ricky told them a funny story about his house being infested by butterflies. "Butterflies!" he said, his face slick with the desperation of an aging showgirl doing jazz hands. They laughed politely. Then, for a brief moment, he realized that exactly no one was looking at him. Soon a young senator appeared.

4.

MAEVE FETED IN WASHINGTON

Much to the chagrin of his critics and naysayers, Roderick Maeve unveiled further developments for the launch of his time machine in Silicon Valley this weekend. Maeve, who initially made his fortune shorting the housing market in 2008, came to prominence early this year, when one of his companies developed the sonic frequency crucial to our success against the winter siege. Since then, development of his time travel project has advanced rapidly.

While this breakthrough technology offers unprecedented hope within the global weather crisis, critics have doubted and even mocked the feasibility of Maeve's predictions, and in particular the remarkable speed at which the technology has been developed. Such negative press, however, has done nothing to discourage the British company Gardenamore from offering a rumored nine-figure payment for one-time use of the time machine to rewrite our energy dependencies. The plan would retroactively revolutionize the world's energy consumption by sending two of Gardenamore's technicians back to the early days of Britain's Industrial Revolution to introduce solar technology, thereby erasing three hundred years of environmental damage to planet Earth.

"It's quite remarkable," spoke US congresswoman Emily Rameri from Washington, D.C., following the news. "For those of us who'd given up on anything more than the incremental changes our government has offered so far, Roderick Maeve is giving us the bold moves we've been praying for. And not a moment too soon."

5.

There were serious questions: What would happen to the briteKor
Garden and Event Center? Would MeeMaw rise from the dead?
And how would it affect the stocks? Experts were interviewed on
television, explaining away. *Here's a graph, this is a chart!* They
assured the laymen, "See, it's data."

But as far as Daphne was concerned, the time machine was like
a Mark Rothko. Bitter people only wished they'd thought of it first.
Bitter people—she could picture it, a whole mass shaking their fists
up to the heavens and asking *Why not me?*

And who didn't know how bitterness, like jealousy, could
undermine even the most rational objections. *Oh, she didn't really
mean it, she's just jealous. He didn't really mean to get you so
drunk you passed out and then fuck your unconscious body, he's
just bitter, he doesn't have much of a readership these days.* Bitter
foods, though, they kept you taut.

It was like recently, when she told her new boyfriend, Troy, how
she had a friend who was dating "like, a really rich guy. Like, so
rich I'm almost scared to even tell you about it, let alone his name,
but you'd totally know who he is, and he wants to take her across
state borders."

They were in the Plateau, at what he called his "place" and
she called his "condo," sprawled out on the white leather sectional
but not touching. The heat was up so high you could literally
hear it.

"Aw." He leaned in close and stroked her wrist with his pointer
finger. "Sweetie, you're jealous."

Daphne felt her heart deflate, tie itself into a noose, and suicide off her spine. Why was everyone so addicted to grade school?

There was no reason for her to be jealous of Jenlena. Tomorrow, she'd have to write a list, itemized, of all the reasons Jenlena should have been jealous of *her*.

Though it was true that she kept thinking of her friend's body. Those puffy pink nipples. A man with a billion dollars could cut her into a billion pieces. "I just think it's kind of pathetic," she tried to clarify. "She's putting all her eggs in one basket, but when he leaves her, what'll she have? Nothing. Best-case scenario will be to run to some tabloid and 'tell her story.'"

"Stones," Troy said.

"What?"

"Stones in one basket, that's what people are saying now."

"What are you talking about? Why would I put stones in my basket?"

"You put stones in your pocket," he said. "All of them, in one pocket, like Virginia Woolf."

"To kill myself?"

"Well, exactly. That's why it's something you're *not* supposed to do."

"But I'm not jealous, okay? That's sexist, anyways, for you to even suggest that."

They'd been seeing each other since the end of the summer. Now it was winter, which meant they'd firmly survived one season. It gave them depth to have seen each other in all manner of layers. Once he bought her a popsicle, once he bought her a beanie.

Troy was the type of guy who'd been to every continent and owned his own camping equipment; he kept it in the shared storage area in the basement. He donated money to political campaigns and had the same bell hooks book on his bookshelf that Daphne had bought for Jordan. He had a copy of a Roxane Gay book, too, and the spines were even cracked.

Her orgasms were very respectable. They didn't make a big show of themselves. It was good this way, healthy like a balanced diet. Sometimes when they had sex, she wondered what it would be like not to have a body. She supposed that with nothing to hold her thoughts in place they would spill out across the world. All her thoughts, feelings, and memories in the air mixed with all the thoughts, feelings, and memories of everyone else whose bones and brains had decayed, and maybe in some ways that was the weather. Everyone all together across the world, their happiness and disappointments jumbled together so that for their children the air became so thick it was difficult to breathe. One night he didn't pull out fast enough and some of the cum landed on her stomach. He told her he was sorry. While he went to the bathroom for a fresh towel, she touched it with her finger then brought it to her lips just to see what it tasted like. He wasn't bad. There was nothing bad about him at all.

He was even interested in reading her poetry.

"My what?" she said. He might as well have asked to fuck her in the ass (which he had not).

"Your writing. I remember you telling me that a while ago, that you wrote." This was over breakfast: underdone toast with cauliflower butter.

"Oh," she said. "Not really. Not anymore. It was just something silly. Kind of, like, a hobby?"

He wrote, he told her. He was writing a novel about a thirty-something white guy who owned a coffee shop in the Mile End.

"Oh," she said, stretching the word into two syllables.

"I'm kidding." Troy gave a silent laugh. He leaned his head back. She laughed too, out loud. She forced herself to do a little snort.

That night, though, he did manage to peel through enough of her that she agreed to read him a poem, naked on the bed, dewy in the lamplight:

Lifewish for a Turgid Boy
I had followed the rules into darkness
And learned that every time a euphemism
Comes true, a fallen man earns back his wings
Believe it or not, I remember what
It was like to be born, Ontario
Ontario, in June, the afternoon
Like a hatchling tearing down its world
We knew bravery before we knew light
Then forgot it along the way from youth
Poison ivy and some old-ass bathtubs
Just some worms your mom chews on your behalf
When I look at my phone, there's a baby
'N an old crone, trapped inside that selfie
Ladies, break me open. Ladies, fly away.

He kissed her on the nose and said he wouldn't pretend to know what it meant.

6.

But not a single time did she see one of those girls she'd been friends with at school.

7.

JORDAN: **I HAVENT BEEN ABLE TO SLEEP I JUST CANT REALLY BEE-LIVE U WONT SEE ME LIIKE ARE YOU ACTUALLY SERIOUS? I FEEL LIKE THIS IS SOME NIGHTMARE OHW CAN YOU JUST SAY THAT TO ME LIKE IM JUST SOME GUY WHEN YOU KNOW WHO I AM.**

Since their breakup, Jordan had been living with Gabe and together they made experimental music everyone hated. They posted it on YouTube, but all the comments were about Moon Cicero.

"Whoa," said Gabe one day, drowning in his phone. "I had no idea she was this famous."

"She's not," said Jordan. "She just gets retweeted sometimes by famous people."

"And you punched her? Dude, you better watch out, she seems pretty wild."

"I don't think I'm on her radar anymore. She's too preoccupied with the end of the world."

"Oh," Gabe said. "That."

When Daphne first told him about Troy, he threatened to kill himself and told her he was serious. "Boys are better at killing themselves than girls," he said. "Everyone knows that. They take it more seriously, with ropes and guns. Because when men want something done, they do it. Girls are so wishy-washy. They do it in sentimental ways, they're always trying to do it in the bathtub."

Daphne took a long sigh. They were sitting in bed, it was one of the last hot days. "Jordan, the world's about to change. Do you realize what a massive opportunity this is? I'm sorry but I've got to take advantage of it, and that means really striving to meet my full potential. The way I used to do, before we met."

"But you were miserable," he said. "You threw an air fryer out the window."

"No." She meant even before that. "You didn't know me then, but I was basically a well-adjusted person. I had a bright future. I've decided it really is what I deserve."

He reached for her, but she pulled away. Then he started to cry and said he loved her so much he'd set fire to their apartment just to prove that life was something you could mold with your own two hands. "Even when I used to write music, the songs never just came to me when I wanted them to. If I begged, maybe, but only the most derivative versions. And I was so tired of feeling small. It wasn't hard, I had enough saved for the gasoline."

"Jordan, you *what*?"

"Didn't you know?" he said. "You wanted me to. You were so worried about money and afterwards, the next day, when you kept sucking on my fingers you must have tasted the gasoline."

"What if someone caught you?"

"You know the police are incompetent. My friend's place once burned down and they got over a thousand dollars from insurance. Now they're getting married."

"Baby," she said. "You don't have any friends. And wishy-washy's not so bad. Just so you know. If it means girls are the ones who get to stay alive while the men are dying, maybe wishy-washy's not such a bad quality to have."

"I'm talking about taking control," he said.

"I know," she said. "That's what I'm doing now." She stood up and hid in the bathroom until she heard him leave.

When her father first left to chase tornadoes across the prairies, Daphne's mother said it was because she made so much more money than him. Men had been feeling so emasculated lately, it was an epidemic. "I think he was trying to teach us a lesson," she told Daphne. "And he did, it just wasn't the one he intended. But I'm happy for him." She'd have her friends over and drink from big plastic wineglasses. "Everyone deserves to make a big decision at least once in their lives."

He sent Daphne a jar for her fourteenth birthday, her father, from somewhere in Saskatchewan, and said it was filled with wind. He said he'd gone all the way up to the storm just to get it for her. She kept it on her bedside table until one night in high school, drunk after a party, she knocked it onto the floor and it smashed into so many pieces she cut her finger five months later on a rogue shard, packing up for university. It wasn't a story, not really; she'd only dwell on it until the new world arrived.

8.

Now it was so cold that once, when Daphne was dyeing her hair, she'd called Jenlena over so that she could warm up her fingers in the active bleach. "You wanna get in on this?" She only ever used the highest-grade chemicals.

"Oh that's nice. Oh, that's the warmest I've felt in days." Jenlena moved her fingers around her warm, goopy mass of hair. "I could spend all day like this."

Daphne looked at her friend and wondered how much time they had left together before the world changed. It was normal to outgrow your best friend, especially if part of the reason the two of you had grown close in the first place was a shared malaise in response to an impending existential doom that was now on the verge of dissipating completely. Before she started getting really into the world ending, Daphne never would have been friends with someone so vague and unambitious.

("I'm not unambitious," Jenlena would have said. "I submitted to the *New Yorker* twice last week, a poem and a story. Flash fiction. I just changed the line breaks." Wasn't there a name for the syndrome when people had such lofty and impossible dreams that it amounted to the same thing as having none at all? Like Munchausen's, but with even more miscellaneous vowels.)

But Daphne knew she'd miss Jenlena. She'd miss her funny stories, her off-kilter neurosis. When you thought about it like that, it was almost sad that that the world was going to change.

There were still thirty-seven minutes left for the chemicals to seep into her hair follicles so that she could look the way she wanted. Jenlena felt like lying down so Daphne sat on the edge of the tub and went on her phone. She could have scrolled forever, it came to her so naturally. Everything was exactly the same size and lasted less than a second. Then she saw Moon Cicero in a video linked to by a friend's brother she once made out with at a party. Her thumb froze. Even though Daphne went on the girl's Twitter every few days, it was different seeing her face. A face made someone real. Looking at the beautiful woman your boyfriend used to love was like taking a bump of cocaine. Even if he wasn't her boyfriend anymore, she felt hot and cold at the same time.

Daphne clicked on the link, an interview on some YouTube channel. The host's name was vaguely familiar, though she couldn't place it. He had a podcast, he was somebody's son. They sat in a dark room in front of netted microphones. Moon Cicero's oatmeal sweater had a stain down the front, but her deep auburn hair was shiny and reflected the studio lights. The host had a clean blue shirt with a bolo tie.

"At this point it's just cruel to keep humanity going," Moon Cicero said. "I mean, even the movies have dementia. What is it now? They're remaking *Babe: Pig in the City*. But this time machine is probably the most pathetic thing we've seen so far. People only believe in it because they're scared. But I haven't been scared in years, so I can see clearly. Scared is just one letter away from sacred, though they could not be more antithetical to each other."

The host just sat there, nodding along, letting her talk. He was the type of guy who never blinked when discussing economic populism, Asperger's chic. Daphne had been out with guys like that before, done some of their ketamine and felt nothing. That's when she realized the whole interview was a joke. Everything Moon Cicero said was so ridiculous he didn't even need to point it out. He kept looking into the camera, like by default whoever was watching wouldn't take her seriously either. The mockery united them.

"Even if they do manage to give us this so-called new world," Moon Cicero went on, "it isn't right. You can't just erase. You don't get to. There are very specific people to blame for this. When you erase the weather you'll erase the blame, but I think blame deserves to have its say."

Daphne sat in the empty bathtub and propped her phone against an old shampoo bottle so she could chew her fingernails. The bleach started to sting, it was working. *Soon I'll love the way I look.*

Moon Cicero's face was flushed. She was talking a lot with her hands. She said that as a Moon Bethlehem it had been her duty to study all the terrible things humanity had done along its road to no return, but nothing was as disgusting to her as the time machine. "You have people in the government who say they're drawing up proposals to erase the residential schools," she said. "Can you imagine?"

"But that was a cultural genocide," said the host. "Seventy-six percent of Canadians support undoing those actions."

"So they don't have to feel guilty anymore! They just want to feel good about themselves! Most people all over the world just want to feel good and I'm telling you that's our first big mistake. I'm here to say that if you're watching this on your iPhone or your flat-screen TV, you should feel very bad and get used to it because it'll all only get worse and fast!"

She took a breath. "But if you're lucky, the really cool thing that's happened to me and my friends is that eventually you look at enough pictures of the Holocaust that your feelings get so big they seep out of your body and into the atmosphere, mixing with all the other junk out there until you can't even recognize them or believe that something like that would ever have been inside you and then you are free."

The host smirked. Daphne hated it when men smirked. They were all so damn apathetic. The video already had thousands of views. Soon there could be memes and eventually parents might even know about it. For the most part, the people in the comments section agreed that Moon Cicero was crazy. They were rolling on the floor laughing, they were doing it out loud. But if you scrolled far enough, which wasn't even so far, in the grand scheme of the internet, people began to agree.

She's right tho? Not sure why people here think this is funny.
Preach!

it's true because i feel it every day we are dying inside. every-day more dead than the day before and yet it is called life? this world was not made to last ha.

The timer went off on her phone, a Pavement song, something Jordan had shown her. She was still finding his socks all over the place, tucked into the bed, between couch cushions. But now it was time to kneel on the tile floor with her head over the tub as Jenlena filled a yogurt container with warm water from the camping stove and poured it over her head. Then she slathered thick, chemically scented conditioner through her hair and kept it lubed up like that till morning.

9.

It was a Christmas for the end of the old world. The girls bought four bottles of wine and six bags of chips and a rotisserie chicken made out of tofu. You could even eat the bones—they were made out of cauliflower jerky. It wasn't even so cold that day, actually. It was eight degrees Celsius.

"Do you ever think the cauliflower will get fed up like the animals did?" Jenlena mused as they set out their plates on the coffee table. "It's definitely been doing the lion's share since the animals died."

Daphne said she was more worried about the snow. "I heard on a podcast recently that that thing they used to say about each snowflake being unique isn't even true anymore. Some of the designs have started repeating themselves."

They got drunk and read aloud from a book Jenlena's mom had sent: *101 Things to Do with Chickpeas.* The first few chapters had some neat recipes but by the end they were really pushing it: *tell them your hopes and dreams, put one underneath your mattress to see if you're a long-lost princess, glue them together in the shape of a heart and give them to your Valentine.*

During the second bottle of wine, Jenlena talked about how proud of herself she was for not texting Roderick Maeve. She'd hardly been on her phone, which was now dead, and she didn't even know where to go to charge it until at least the day after tomorrow. Except perhaps at the gas station, maybe, even though she hadn't thought about it, just in case her mother called, because it was a pretty shitty thing to not even talk to your mother on Christmas. "Maybe I'll go to the gas station after this," she said, motioning to her glass.

"How much do you think it's worth?" Daphne asked, uncorking the third bottle. "In this economy, what you're going through right now?"

Jenlena took a big sip. Nothing was as good as the last drink, so they had to keep going to find that feeling again. "What do you mean?" she said.

"Just knowing him, all the text messages. That's gotta be what, a few thousand dollars? Ten, fifteen grand? If he's gotten really personal?"

"We've gotten personal, sure," Jenlena said.

"And he's causing you pain, you're suffering. I've been witness to that. I can attest. He's out there at beach parties and you're alone, crying in a sub-basement without power. That's gotta be worth something. You go to the right people, fifteen grand at least, throw in a couple embarrassing sexual things. You can get money."

Jenlena sat back onto her palms, considering it. "Sexual things." She exaggerated the shapes of the words with her lips.

"You have them, don't you? Details?"

Jenlena shrugged.

"Don't tell me you've been putting yourself through all this agony and you don't even have sexual details!"

"Only through his pants . . ."

"*NO!*"

"What do you want me to say?" Jenlena started to laugh and Daphne started laughing too.

They laughed so hard it was a near-death experience. They floated up and out of their bodies and saw each other, spilled off of the futon onto the floor, surrounded by green wine bottles and red bags of chips.

Every now and then it was necessary to love your best friend. Sometimes just a little most of the time and other times very intensely for just a few hours. "But, like, for real." Jenlena squinted, trying to focus her eyes on the tall, tall girl who sat in front of her. She slurred: "Okay. Ya wanna know a secret?"

"What?" Daphne asked. "Oh, please, tell me something good."

"It's friggin' insane. Oh my god, I can't believe I have the hiccups, I'm not even drunk."

"Oh my god, what?" Daphne sat there begging and it was the last thing either of them remembered.

"Did you know they kept some of the animals for themselves?"

The next morning, they woke up head to toe on the futon and raced to the bathroom, making it only as far as the doorway and the bathtub, respectively, before vomiting.

For the rest of the day they talked about their feelings:

"It's like my organs don't want to be a part of my body anymore," said Jenlena, lying on the floor in her underwear with a wet sock across her forehead.

"I seriously can't imagine that dying is worse than this," Daphne replied from the futon, soaking her feet in a pot of cold water.

"I mean I've seen people with cancer and they looked better than you."

"If I die you can have my books of insects," Daphne said.

"If I die, you can have my—what would you want? If I die, will you put out a chapbook of my poems? They're all in my coil notebook, the one with daisies on the front. Just make sure everyone knows I'm dead. Wait, Daphne, why are you crying?"

"Oh, I don't know." Daphne covered her face as her voice broke. "I guess it's just the first time in a while that I've thought about those bugs."

"You miss him, don't you?"

"No," she insisted. "Soon I won't miss him at all."

10.

M●◐N_cicero_666 @Moon.Cicero 5m

Planning such a fun surprise for you guys.

M●◐N_cicero_666 @Moon.Cicero 4m

We give up our names. We give up our lives. The new world begins only then.

M●◐N_cicero_666 @Moon.Cicero 4m

I want to formally apologize for my participation in last month's chatelaine issue. I should have known better, but i didn't

M●◐N_cicero_666 @Moon.Cicero 3m

I've been crying six days straight thinking about seeing my picture next to an advertisement for air canada

M●◐N_cicero_666 @Moon.Cicero 3m

I hope u know this but the tourism industry is even worse for the planet than construction

M●◐N_cicero_666 @Moon.Cicero 3m

But i have to live with that

M●◐N_cicero_666 @Moon.Cicero 2m

the fact that i was swayed by vanity + sick ambitions of those I sought advice from.

M●●N_cicero_666 @Moon.Cicero 2m

It just proves that i am as inexorable from the human experience as i
ever was . . .

M●●N_cicero_666 @Moon.Cicero 2m

a difficult reminder but i am grateful for it

M●●N_cicero_666 @Moon.Cicero 2m

I have never felt so violated in my life than when i saw my picture
like that

M●●N_cicero_666 @Moon.Cicero 2m

+ i was once abused by boyfriend

M●●N_cicero_666 @Moon.Cicero 1m

Screaming in the face and shoved me into the wall

M●●N_cicero_666 @Moon.Cicero 1m

Then had the whole story shared in explicit detail on the internet by
my own sister

M●●N_cicero_666 @Moon.Cicero 15s

But whatev we all gunna die :)

11.

"You realize," Troy said the next time they saw each other, "I know
what you think."

"Oh?" Daphne was fishing a glove from the sleeve of her
coat.

"About me."

She stood there blinking. They'd just had breakfast and she was running late for her shift.

"I was the same when I was younger with my older friends. You've got such big plans for yourself, you have such big ideas. But what you don't realize is how the years chip away at all that stuff. I have a master's degree, not that you ever asked."

"Okay," she said, putting one boot on and then the other.

"Do you understand what I'm trying to say?"

"One day."

"Please." He laughed, revealing a sesame seed stuck between his teeth. "You don't have to be so scared. Believe it or not, life's pretty good on this side of thirty. All I'm asking is that you trust me a little more."

"I'm not scared," she said. "I haven't been scared since they announced the time machine."

For New Year's, he took her to a party at a friend's place in the Old Port. Across the street, Moon Bethlehems stood wrapped up in fleece blankets, attempting to distribute leaflets to the passersby, who mostly ignored them. One woman accepted the literature only to toss it a few meters down the block. As it left her hand, the paper caught the wind and soared briefly before landing beside the curb. Inside, there was a rumor that the girl by the window was Grimes. No, it was later confirmed, she'd once sucked on Grimes's nipple at a party. The men had intricate facial hair and the women wove little wild flowers into their eyebrows.

Daphne wore a dress she hated, something pleather from SSENSE, a third generation from what Kim Kardashian had worn to the Met Gala several years before. Seeing her reflection in the floor-to-ceiling windows made her want a drink. Then she'd have another and basically feel like a well-adjusted person.

Everyone was talking about the time machine and how grateful they were that someone was finally stepping in to save the world, this world, the place hundreds of thousands of people had been working so hard to build and improve and preserve over the last hundred years. The world was good, didn't they know?

"Some people wanna tear down the whole system," said one man with moss on his shoe. "But in poor countries people are still able to recognize how far we've come. The things we take for granted. You know, light rail transit, vacation time."

"It's the white people who've become so blasé. They're not in charge anymore so all that's left is to tear it all down," a woman in a green velvet dress said to Daphne, then proceeded to pull her into a corner and tell her all the crazy things she had heard about white people: that they did not wash their legs, they were addicted to pornography, and genetically predisposed to pedophilia. She was white too, at least as far as Daphne was familiar with the term. She had blond hair—genuine, Daphne could tell by her eyelashes.

"To me, the new world's already begun." Troy kept saying this. He wrapped his arm around Daphne's waist and said he had the new world right here. Her shoes pinched her feet.

After her fourth drink, Daphne leaned against the back of the couch for balance but missed, touching a woman on the neck. "Oh, I'm sorry!"

"It's okay—Daphne?"

When Daphne looked down she saw Mellie, one of her old friends from university who had stopped talking to her. She had a ring of four-leaf clovers for earrings.

"Oh my god, *Daphne*!" Mellie ran around the couch to wrap her up in her arms. "Oh my god, you're back from the dead! You know, when I heard about you and Troy, I was so happy. I've been meaning to get in touch, but I've just been so busy."

"It's really nice to see you," Daphne said, feeling her stomach stick and unstick to her dress.

Mellie told Daphne that she was doing law school at McGill. Everything was going exactly as she'd planned and life was wonderful.

Daphne offered her congratulations. She felt wobbly.

Mellie leaned in close. "You'll never guess who I saw the other day."

"Who?"

"That guy you dated. The crazy one. I was shopping for groceries and I swear he just appeared out of nowhere in the bulk aisle. I quite nearly spilled cashews all over the place, Daph. It totally freaked me out." Mellie mock-shivered but it was clear she really meant it. "What was his name, Jackson?"

"Jordan," Daphne said, and it felt obvious she enjoyed the shape his name made in her mouth, like stretching her shoulder against a door frame. Were her cheeks burning? It was hot in here, wasn't it?

"You know, I've really missed you," Mellie said, touching Daphne on the arm. Then her eyebrows had a great idea. "You should come to one of my salons. We all get together the first of the month and analyze Will Ferrell movies from a feminist perspective."

Daphne took a sip from her drink but it went down the wrong tube. "How did he look?" she asked. "Was he with anyone?"

"To me, the new world's already begun!" Troy burst between the two girls and clasped Daphne's hand. He was drunk. She'd never seen his face so shiny before.

"I want a cigarette," Daphne decided out loud. There was just over half an hour left of the last bad year of their lives.

But you weren't allowed to smoke out the window. It was a safety issue, said the host, who caught her giving it an honest try.

Outside, it was snowing and each flake looked exactly the same as they landed on her face, hemorrhaging her makeup. The Moon Bethlehems were still across the street in front of the Metro station, shivering. Of course they were, they had nowhere else to go. All kinds: old and young and strong and frail. Daphne wondered what they'd do in the new world when their convictions were proven superfluous.

Then a smaller man emerged from the back of the crowd and she knew that it was her old professor, the one from university who had so admired her poetry. He wore a black blanket that hung heavy over his otherwise beige garb but atop his head was the same Kangol hat, exactly the same.

What possessed her? Or had she always been like this, bold and unwavering in her pursuit of self-respect? Was that why she'd hardly ever told anyone about what had happened, not even Jenlena, when she'd asked her how their meeting had been. ("Fine," she'd said. "And he's totally going to publish you?" "We'll see," she'd said.) Not when other girls started talking about him online, not even when he was dismissed from the university. She only ever told Jordan because it was the first time she'd had sex since and she was just trying to explain why she might have been acting stiff. ("What? Are you serious? No, Daphne. I'll kill him.")

"Are you interested in learning more about our growing movement?" the professor asked as she approached.

"I know who you are."

"Moon Sears," he said, extending his hand forward. He was so skinny and the tips of his fingers had turned yellow.

"No," she said. "You can't pretend you don't remember me."

"As Moon Bethlehems, ours is a palliative nihilism. We invite people of all walks of life to join us in bearing witness to the destruction of our planet."

"You had some luck when you were young," she said. "Wrote a couple good poems that nobody noticed were total rip-offs. But they never told you that sometimes luck can be the worst thing to happen to a person, especially when you know in your heart you were given something you didn't earn. You hate yourself so much you can only be vulnerable with unconscious people. That's deep inside of you."

He blinked three times before a smile broke out across his face. It made Daphne nauseous, the same look he'd had in class praising her villanelle and she'd felt so happy. She was going to be a real poet, famous and everything.

"So, you and I agree more than we disagree," he said. "Because we're the ones"—he gestured to the group around him—"who think the people should suffer for their crimes. Whereas people like you want all that washed away, forgotten about."

"You don't know anything about me," she said.

There were a hundred tiny lines on his face and they all curved inward. "I know the look on your face when I did it to you. How you squirmed and kept waking up but I didn't stop. See? That was our culture. Even I'm admitting it. It's easy now that I've renounced my humanity."

Daphne took a step back. The cold had sunk into her teeth and she couldn't keep still. Yet he was perfectly still and he didn't even have gloves on. The other Moon Bethlehems too, their fingers and ears were exposed to the weather like it didn't even touch them. "I think you're disgusting," she said.

He shrugged. "Aren't you old enough now to recognize that the individual has never mattered in the long run?" Then he handed her a brochure, rippled from the weather. "So don't you want to see the world burn? Wouldn't it feel good, Angela?"

"Daphne," she said. "My name is Daphne." Then she started to laugh. "Pathetic," she said, taking a step back and regarding the group at large. "The lot of you. Come two months' time, what are you going to do? Good luck getting into any programs! Like you've ever won a prize!"

By the time Troy called her, she was already in a car home. She was crossing the mountain and the driver was telling her about his accounting course.

"Where are you?" Troy asked.

"I jumped out the window. Didn't you hear the splat?"

"I'm in the snow, calling your name."

"I'm not feeling well."

"Mellie said she saw you talking to those Moon Bethlehems. She said you were out there for a long time."

"You really wanna know what happened?"

"Daphne, I'm begging you!"

If she didn't care about him then why couldn't she tell him? There was nothing to lose, except that she couldn't think of a way to say the words without sounding just like any other girl.

"Daphne?" Troy asked. "Are you still there?" She could hear the party behind him, hopeful and Lady Gaga.

"It's my friend," she said. "My friend Jenlena once got totally hurt by this guy she didn't even like but he, well, he forced her to do things and she can't even remember exactly what." She wanted to be the only person who had ever lived in her body.

He took a big inhale. "Oh, I'm so sorry. That must have been so hard on her. On you too. I know you're close."

"Not really. We just live together because we're broke."

"Daphne, are you okay?"

"I'm not your girlfriend, just so you know."

"Um, okay. I didn't realize this was the discussion we're having right now."

"It isn't a big deal." The driver turned around to check if she was alright.

"What part?"

She could tell Troy's wires were starting to blow and it made her feel good. She could feel her fingers again. "I mean, what would you do? Say you were her boyfriend, my roommate Jenlena, and she tells you her story, she goes through the whole presentation, then what would you do?"

"I'd listen." His voice lurched. "I'd tell her how I was there for her, whenever she was ready to talk. Even if she wasn't. I'd tell her that was okay too, I'd tell her how strong she was, what a remarkable woman. Most importantly, I'd let her know that there's no right or wrong way to deal with these things."

"Really?" she asked.

"Yes, one hundred percent."

"What if she doesn't feel anything?"

"Then that's great, that's one hundred percent okay."

"But it's not," she said. "My friend Jenlena's an idiot, she's one of the dumbest people I know." She didn't know who she was talking about anymore, but chances were, they were a goddamned fucking idiot.

"Then it's okay, it's all gonna be okay."

"How would you know?"

"Well, because I—"

"Have you forced girls, Troy? Have you?"

"Hey now!"

"You've thought about it, haven't you? You've seen it in movies and always wondered what it would feel like."

He denied it and she called him a liar.

"Whatever you're trying to be, I'll never believe you," she said and hung up the phone. All her life men had been trying to hurt her, but each time it ended up being a gift because she had to work harder.

When she hung up the phone, the driver asked her why she was crying. "We've got to enjoy this old world while it lasts," he said gleefully. "That's how I see it. Goodbye potholes! Goodbye hemorrhoids!"

i'm sorry, Troy texted by the time she arrived at the front door. **i'm never going to know the right thing to say but i am in love with you.** Daphne made her way underground in the dark and opened the door to their apartment, where Jenlena was packing a bag with one hand while holding her phone's flashlight with the other.

"What's happened?" Daphne said. "Did someone find us? Are we getting kicked out?"

"No," said Jenlena. The light from below made her wide grin ghoulish. "He texted! He finally texted. I'm going to California!"

12.

Daphne sat with the book of insects Jordan made for her on her bed. She had the book open to a page of two daddy longlegs and balanced a votive candle between the soles of her feet, butterfly pose. *We tell ourselves butterfly stories in order to live,* she thought.

Everyone was addicted to saying you went into a cocoon to grow wings and emerge as a beautiful miracle. But what no one ever mentioned was how the caterpillar's body actually broke down inside the cocoon, turning to mush before its reconstruction. Sometimes the hardest part about your twenties was knowing what stage you were in: if you had been mush, were currently mushing down, or had mush yet ahead of you.

Most of the bugs had come from behind the fridge or in corners of the cupboards. Jordan made the book for her because he said people were going to tell them all kinds of things about what had happened to the animals but they needed to keep a record for themselves to remember the truth. As long as they knew the truth they could be a civilization just of each other. She traced a tiny body with her finger.

The truth was that she remembered how he tucked his hair behind his ears and frowned a little when he was thinking about something deeply. Spiders had eight legs. They were frightening to some people; others were grateful because they ate the mosquitoes who stung you during the summer and it itched. Mosquitoes stung some people more than others, always Jordan more than her. He had special blood, he told her. Or else it had to do with eating bananas. Spiders lived in webs or they made webs to have their babies. The webs were made out of something that came from their own bodies. Or were the webs for hunting? It all felt so far away now.

Yes, because they were sticky. She remembered using her fingers to pull one down in her old room and feeling like it was touching her all over. When she told Jordan about her professor he had been so angry he threatened to kill him. "It's okay," she said. "It's not a big deal, I've never even talked about it before." Then they were both crying and he held her tightly until she fell asleep with her ankles wrapped around his legs. Later, he followed Professor Sears home and vandalized his apartment. "And what would you have done if they caught you?" she'd asked. "They'd have sent you to jail. Then people would like you again. They'd care about your civil rights."

He had told her that being trapped inside with her was one of the best times of his life, just the two of them together. One day, they saw a group of animals gather in the alley, some they hadn't seen since childhood and others just from storybooks. An antelope turned his head from the circle of animals out the window and looked at him. They looked into each other's eyes. "Not even you have ever looked at me like that before," he said to Daphne. It was like the antelope with his long neck and wide horns could see right into Jordan. The antelope's eyes softened and Jordan knew he was neither good nor bad. "I'm not even Jordan, just a part of this one, giant body. One tiny part like a hair or piece of skin."

If you killed a spider it was supposed to rain. Others could kill you. In Australia or other parts of the world you wouldn't even realize you'd been bit and then you died. A black widow, she remembered, a girl-boss spider. *See?* she thought. *I am remembering. Are you happy? Where are you now?*

She picked up her phone and called him. "Hey," she said, all casual as if it were any other Tuesday. It was 2:30 a.m. on the first day of the new year. When he answered, she could hear a song in the background, one of the old ones they used to dance to. She wondered if he had a girl there with him, one who was pretty, and if he was mean to her. *He's only ever been nice to me*, she thought, and it broke her. Even when he had mocked her prizes and done all the cocaine himself, it wasn't enough, she needed more.

"Why are you crying, what's happened?"

"Nothing," she said. In the grand scheme of things nothing had ever happened to her. Fifteen minutes she didn't even remember.

She told him she was sorry.

"For what?" he said.

"It was too confusing," she said. "At first we were so happy. So I didn't understand why I'd sometimes still feel sad. And I'd get angry at you for no reason, I'd feel like popping out your eyeballs with my thumbs."

Jordan admitted that he'd also loved and hated her at the same time. He said that between the weather and microwaves and GMOs, it was impossible for anyone to think straight. "But all I've ever wanted was to be with you. What if I told you I figured out a way we could really make it work?"

"What?" she said, blowing her nose on the bedsheet.

"Isn't it obvious? The time machine! I could go back to that night when I first met Lisa. I'd treat her like a queen. Better yet, I wouldn't even talk to her. I learned something, Daphne, when I set that fire. Every so often a man's gotta grab his circumstances with his bare hands and wring them into submission. What do you think, Daphne? Would you still meet me at that party above the lamp store?"

"Yes," she said. "I'll wait for you by the stove."

CHAPTER ELEVEN

A Momentous Occasion

1.

A lot of TV shows talked about the Industrial Revolution and what it meant, how it birthed their entire society because men in Britain disagreed with men in France about the fundamental qualities of wealth. In France, they said only so much wealth existed in the world and the only way to make more for yourself was to take it from other people. But in Britain, they started to question this. They started to say that, what if, like, maybe, wealth was not so finite? That, have you ever thought about how, wouldn't it be crazy if we could create value out of nothing? So these men did just that, made up a new economy where people could buy things like Wedgwood china and the miser's snuff box that other people made in mass quantities at places called factories. There was also new money from the slave trade, lots of it. Wealth that came "out of nowhere."

That was how much Jenlena garnered, at least. That's what she would have said if she was really going to see Roderick Maeve again, and if he ever asked about it and she wanted to sound impressive.

She watched a special on the two technicians from the solar panel company. They were going to go back in time and infiltrate the salons of London in the 1720s. "What if we could harness the power of the sun?" they'd say to all the top intellectuals. "What if we, like, paid a little more attention to that sun up yonder? Do you think that maybe, perchance, if we found the right materials we might be able to harness the photons?"

There was a montage: the technicians taking notes from a PowerPoint presentation, the technicians in a costume fitting, the technicians with a linguistics coach to work on their accents.

"In today's London," the female technician said in an interview at her home in London, "I couldn't pass for his wife in a hundred years. But back then, life was so difficult. It'd make sense I'd look so much older. They worked out a whole story for us, ten children who've all passed on, I'm afraid." She was mournful when she said this, then recited their names.

The male technician was from Manchester and enjoyed playing sports outside his rigorous work for the company. There was a short segment with footage of him running with his son in a field.

The female technician had no hobbies; it was explained that she was at the top of her field. "So many sleepless nights," she told the camera. "I was just a shopkeeper's daughter. And never the smartest one in school, mind you. But I always worked hard."

"She worked harder than anyone else," said her husband.

"He thought I was crazy."

"I always told her to relax. She worked herself to the bone."

She touched his arm. "But I told him you had to." She looked at the camera. "I understood it was my purpose. We aren't spiritual people so it can be hard to explain. But when I'm working I have this feeling of peace. It doesn't exist for me anywhere else."

Her husband looked into his lap, then used the hem of his shirt to clean his glasses.

"And darling," she said, "I told you. I always told him I was doing it for a reason. I was driven by a purpose. We just didn't know what it was, until now."

He held her hand tightly. The camera panned to an old photograph of the couple on their honeymoon in the countryside. The husband explained: "We met at Oxford and married right away. For the honeymoon, I took her to the country. You see the photograph here. It's a plastic bag in her hand. We were collecting the fresh air to bring back with us to the city."

Sometimes, Jenlena lay in bed and believed everything she watched on her phone. Other times it all just seemed like stories. People told you things all the time: sit down, wash your hands, memorize Louis Riel's birthday, here is a picture of your father. And for the most part you said, "Okay, sure."

That was what she struggled to comprehend about the time machine. Not the science (though that too, like history, was not something she'd identified with for many years). It was the gall, really, the sheer bullheadedness it required to comprehend time as something malleable, something you could have an active role in, and exert yourself accordingly.

For Jenlena, it was easier to think about herself until she went numb. She typed "pre" into the search bar on her phone and the rest of the inquiry appeared automatically because the device knew her better than Daphne or anyone she had ever had sex with: "mature dead babies." Little seedlings. Some of them were beautiful and she hated herself. Some of them were horrifying and she hated herself for hating herself because what year was it and she had the right to do whatever she wanted. She threw her phone across the room even though it was the most expensive thing she owned and her closest friend. The problem was that without her phone all she had was a body. She pulled herself out of bed and crossed the floor.

"I'm sorry," she said to the device. "I didn't mean to get so angry with you like that. It wasn't your fault."

Her phone told her about a sizzling-hot new romance online, between California billionaire Roderick Maeve and a supermodel-actress-entrepreneur who had, allegedly, gushed to her friends about a weekend getaway to Acapulco. "He's hung like a horse."

Jenlena felt no choice but to embark on a research project on the woman, the scope of which spanned centuries. The supermodel's diamond-dealer ex, her Cambodian mother, her Jewish father. Jenlena kept clicking on the blue words, which brought her to genocide then through to ancient dynasties, references to haute couture, genocide again, Esther Williams, swimming.

By morning, the sun rose garishly and a rumor surfaced that Ricky and the model had broken up to focus on professional pursuits. The time machine was less than two months away. Her phone said *Seeking deep voice woman of african descent to read descriptions of asian tsunami during bondage play. Very discreet.*

2.

Once the time machine solved all their problems, where would all that fear go? It was a serious question. What would rise in its place? Sometimes Jenlena felt like she had been afraid for so long she wasn't sure what was underneath.

The U.S. government and Central Intelligence Agency, men, getting a job, never getting a job, Mom dying, dying before Mom (having to watch her face while I do it, having her make it all about her), food shortages, income inequality, getting fat, the internet, French people.

She took out her coil notebook with daisies on the cover and wrote down everything she could think of. Then she left her phone at home and went to the gas station bathroom to drop each scrap of paper into the toilet and then flush them away for good. *What am I without my fear? Without my fear,* she thought, *I will float up and up into the sky, I'll hit the ozone layer, just me and all those lost balloons waiting to pop.* When she came back home, he hadn't texted her. He hadn't called or sent a message from his finsta.

3.

Then, when he called on New Year's Eve, she came. She, the only girl in the world who knew about a pony, packed lace underwear, painted her nails, and shaved everywhere except her armpits. So all along it had existed, this version of life on earth where you went places, you saw things, people noticed you, indeed they were waiting for you to arrive. It had been true, what they said about life in all those movies, the dense glamour: sights, sounds!

The private airport was usually just for hockey players, but that day Jenlena herself boarded a jet that was just like in the movies. Many surfaces were shiny while others were made from leather. Jenlena had the feeling that multiple animals had gone into the making of it. The pilot shook her hand and said he took pleasure in accommodating her. He really meant it, Jenlena could tell. He could tell she was really that kind of person. Roderick Maeve had christened her so. She was glowing, alive in the way God intended, regarded by others. The service industry had been invented for people like her.

The flight attendant was a woman in her forties who offered her whatever she wanted. "Shirley Temple with a splash of tequila," Jenlena said. She was excited, and took photos of herself in

collaboration with the light, but could only think of heinous cap-
tions: *Where in the world is Jenlena San Diego?*, (Angel emoji)
among (cloud emoji, cloud emoji, cloud emoji), *Catch me if you're
a cunt.*

Then she ran her hand along the leather seats and thought about
how in the near future, it would all run on the sun. Nobody would
fight over food anymore. Or water, or places to grow their food.
She thought about the episode of *The Simpsons* where Mr. Burns
builds a metal shield to block out the sun from all of Springfield.
She didn't remember how it ended, though. And Mr. Burns wasn't
anything like Roderick Maeve. He was old and decrepit, for one.
No, she would never have fucked Mr. Burns, not even on a dare.

As they entered California, the pilot announced it over the
speakers as if it were its own country. When they landed, everything seemed foreign to her, even the parts that were the same: cars,
a Starbucks, miserable people on their cellphones. A limousine
picked her up, but they hit traffic on the freeway because of the
fires up north. Jenlena could see the smoke, so thick the hills
were muted in the distance.

Roderick Maeve lived on a large estate. The house was three
stories high and had no right angles. There he was, waiting for her
by the main entrance, dressed in tear-aways.

"I missed you!" Jenlena said, wrapping her arms around his
neck like a rash.

"Darling," he laughed. "If you wanted to see me so badly, why
didn't you just turn on the television?"

He led her inside and they sat down in a room with hideously
ornate wallpaper and a view of the smoke. The air-conditioning
was so strong she felt all her tiny hairs swell from her skin, as if
trying to protect her. *You idiots*, she thought. *You know nothing.*

A dark-haired woman in a maid's uniform came in with a platter of food and Roderick Maeve told Jenlena that it was candied pieces of smoked salmon preserved from before the siege. It was rich and sweet. Her body felt it too. Ricky used his fingers to pick a piece of bone out from his teeth, then used the bone to pick out a piece of fish.

"Hey," she asked. "Have you ever seen that episode of—"

But his phone rang and he left the room to answer it.

4.

"Yes, uh-huh."

"I see."

"Alright, fine."

5.

He came back into the kitchen and asked if she felt like going for a drive. In the car, they said nothing. He drove too fast but people allowed him to. It was as if they could tell who he was. Nobody even honked. He emanated his identity and was therefore accommodated without pause.

The air was still, not stale but vitally rigid, like a child playing freeze tag. They didn't talk about the fires, they didn't talk about anything. Once again, she didn't exist, had no Wikipedia page. *Tell him about your draft*, she told herself. Putting words on paper was a way to solidify her existence. At the very least, a metaphor or two could make him laugh. Or had Daphne been right? From the beginning, it had been one big Illuminati game. Tonight, the lizard people would peel off her skin. They'd drain her blood and make a fun cocktail. Blended with salt on the rim. Had the ritual begun? Was it beginning now?

It was very sophisticated to think like that, she thought, tapping her foot. *I see things so clearly, like someone with a PhD.* A body wasn't much, scientifically. It could be dissolved in a tub of acid. And afterwards everyone would say that she had been beautiful. Daphne could say that she'd had a best friend who was murdered, and she would be made more beautiful too by a proximity to tragedy. She would glow in the dark.

Roderick Maeve changed lanes. Their bodies lurched as he merged onto the highway. In some ways it was the most physical they had ever been together. Jenlena fingered the armrest on the door, where there should have been a button for the window but there wasn't. Then she pressed into each of her toes one by one, like a doctor had told her would stop her from fainting when she had dizzy spells in high school. She counted to ten seven times and hated the sound of her own swallowing. Roderick Maeve turned on the radio, a macabre weather report.

"You know," he said, clearing his throat. "About a month before the animals, I went to Europe and while I was gone there was this nasty infestation in the house. Rats, I thought when the staff first told me. I hadn't seen a rat in years. But do you know what it was?"

Jenlena looked at him, his pristine forehead, his wet lips. "No," she said.

"Take a guess. If you can remember. What animals do you think it could be?"

"Ummm."

"Any animal!" Each time he spoke he pressed his foot down on the gas.

"Turtles?"

"Butterflies."

She could tell he loved tasting the word.

"I came back from Italy and they tell me there's been thousands of them flying around the house, hatching eggs. Nobody knows how it happened, one of the girls must have left a window open upstairs, but we had a contractor by to look through everything. Butterflies! Can you picture it?"

"It's beautiful."

"The only problem is when they die in such large quantities. The bodies decompose and it turns into this sort of goo. This black goo, and in such large quantities. Even after the fumigators, I keep finding this gunk in strange places. Inside a drawer. Another time, I put on a pair of shoes and they were just filled with it.

"That was, how long was that now? A year ago. And I always tell that story. After it happened, in all the interviews I did for television, it was very charming to be this big man invaded by butterflies. Everyone likes that story. But I've never been able to describe that gunk. Why was it so dark? Because butterflies had such bright colors. It was a year ago but I'm still seeing it everywhere. When I wake up, I get this feeling like it's on my teeth and in my eyes. I can feel it at the bottom of my pockets but I've had the house cleaned six times and they always just tell me it's gone."

"Uh-huh," she said.

"*Uh-huh* what?" He merged off of the highway onto a quiet street.

"I just mean, okay, I'm listening. I'm picturing it, all those butterflies melted down."

"Maybe I just wanted to hear how it sounded. I say all kinds of things out loud—you know how sometimes you don't realize how crazy you sound until you hear yourself out loud?"

"Do you feel crazy now?" She wasn't putting on a voice, not a little girl, not her sexy cousin. Still, somehow, her mouth made the sounds.

Now they were parked outside a rectangular building that was entirely reflective. "I know I'm being a bad host," Roderick Maeve said. "Believe me, I'm aware. But I'll make it up to you. There's just been one last-minute emergency. With the machine, you know. Very important business." He leaned over and kissed her on the lips, but when she pulled away, Jenlena somehow had the impression that his eyes had been open the whole time.

6.

Ricky hardly ever went to the laboratory in the basement of the office. He didn't need to. He supplied the vision, put a team together, and let them do their best. The physicist had some of the brightest minds at his disposal for assistance, scientists from all around the world who'd stop at nothing to touch the past. There they were huddled around the young physicist who lay passed out on the floor in front of a prototype of the machine.

"What is it?" Ricky asked, leaning against the prototype to steady himself. It was a big black box, disarming in its simplicity.

The young physicist said he was scared. The sleeve of his T-shirt had torn completely from his body and he used the fabric to wipe his nose.

"Of what? Have they gotten to you?" Ricky knelt beside him.

"This has never happened to me before." The physicist looked frantically around the crowd.

Ricky cleared the room. "Son," he said.

"I can't find the math." The physicist's voice broke. "I've never been stuck for this long. The numbers, they're just not *complying*.

They won't listen to me and at the end of my math there's only darkness, this one big nothing and it's calling to me, it's telling me to jump inside."

"Son," Ricky repeated, like he was addicted to the way it sounded though he had never had a child and did not intend to, no matter how beautiful the world would soon become.

The physicist whimpered.

Ricky cursed those freak Moon Bethlehems.

You had to live just one step away from utter failure, oblivion. That had been his motto for years. Otherwise you got soft, figuratively. You wrote some tepid memoir and went heli-gliding. Almost failing, getting so close you could feel failure's clammy palms, smell the fried food on its breath, that was what exhilarated him. But you had to be careful. Sure, he'd always been a flirt. He'd dabbled, but never more than just the tip.

"So you've had a setback, big whoop. I've had three before breakfast. But now's not the time to be like other people. You haven't got another choice."

Ricky slapped the boy, just lightly the first time. The physicist blinked. "Tell me you'll do it," Ricky said.

"Yes."

Ricky slapped him again, harder than was necessary. "No, *tell* me."

"I'll do it."

Ricky slapped him a third time. "Tell me, now. Tell me like you mean it."

"I'll find it!"

"You'll what?"

"I'll do the math!"

"Again!"

"Those numbers are mine!"

"Yes!"

"I'll change the world!"

"That's my boy! You had me worried. Here I was rushing over because I thought you'd become one of those Moon Bethlehems."

The physicist laughed. "Those imbeciles? No way." He cleared his throat and said, "But we're building the time machine for people like them too, aren't we, boss?"

7.

When they got back to his estate, he took Jenlena underground. Roderick Maeve was like a new man since they'd left the offices. He was the way he was supposed to be: confident, shoulders back, showing her animals. They took an elevator, stainless steel, and it even played a little Christmas song. "I told you," he said. "I told you I invited you to visit for a reason."

The doors opened and she saw grass. It stretched out into the distance, at least a football field's worth, as far as she could see. Adjacent to the entrance was a garden shed with green linoleum siding and there was shrubbery and three tall trees marking the center of the pitch. Wooden benches too, like a real park. Then, right along the horizon, a group of shadows. They started to move as Jenlena and Roderick Maeve stepped onto the grass. "I told you about my dogs, didn't I?"

He said it like it was a joke but what was funny about the way the animals, one by one, rose from their slumbers, stretched their paws out in front of them, and bounded toward her? There was even a breeze somehow, though they were belowground. Jenlena looked around. It must have been coming from the wall.

Seven, eight, nine, three more in the corner! They had long, glossy fur and their ears flapped in the wind as they moved faster and faster. Roderick Maeve stood there, watching as she touched them. They licked up and down her arms and she giggled.

"It's the right thing, isn't it?" he asked. "It was the right thing to do?"

"Of course," she said. She couldn't stop touching them, sitting on the grass like a child and pressing her fingers deep into their fur, the way she knew from experience would make the smell linger even after they were gone.

Roderick Maeve sat down beside her. "This is nice," he said. "Sometimes I forget how nice it is. I don't come down here as much as I should."

"But with the time machine," she asked as one of the tawny hounds made its way to her, "will it bring the animals back?" The dog had a swollen belly with nipples wide as toes.

"I don't know," he said, too quickly.

She turned to look at him. "I mean, isn't that the point? It'll work, right?"

"Yes," he said, too forcefully. "It'll all work out."

For a moment she looked at him and he could have sworn she knew exactly what he was thinking. Further than that even, that she'd deciphered what he had yet to admit even to himself. All his life he had wanted to know what it would feel like to have someone really see through the bullshit. What if he was feeling that now, here, with this girl? He adjusted his hips. It felt pretty good, actually.

Jenlena put her hand on his knee, it was so small she barely made the cap. "So relax!" she said with a big smile. "Have some fun!"

He texted the staff to bring them a bottle of wine. They sat with their backs up against the shed and once she was relaxed, she told him some of the things she thought about animals, how a really good one, touching it especially, was like a poem. An animal might have seemed simple but they were actually very complex. It had taken thousands of years to have colors like that, to learn how to walk on land.

"For me, it's not like I even had a pet," she said. "It wasn't like I necessarily had any plans for adopting one, I was mostly thinking I'd go to Australia or apply to grad school, so I mostly miss seeing animals casually, just the little interactions like when a cat follows you half a block and it really feels like they're trying to tell you something. It makes you feel like you're special."

He poured her another glass.

"Maybe this'll sound stupid but I used to do this thing when I'd get upset, like, you know how people are always saying, *think of the children in Africa*, but it's so overdone. So, like when I'm upset I like to think about how my problem would sound to a pigeon, like, really trying to break it down. Okay so there are these places called universities where we get our parents to pay thousands of dollars so we can listen to mostly grad students recite information we could probably get for free on the internet, which by the way is like an invisible something you connect your phone and computer to and a computer is a machine and a phone's a smaller machine and you see what I mean? Try to explain something to a pigeon and sooner or later you start to accept how little most things matter." Her cheeks were flushed. "You know what I mean?"

Ricky made a face, then a noise to go with it. "Power, prosperity," he said. "I could definitely explain that to a pigeon."

During his fourth glass and her third he asked if she thought it was strange he was so much older than her.

She took a long sip, then told him no. "I think it's probably very normal."

He took her into the little shed where they kept kibble and she raised her arms in the air for him to take off her shirt. He got on his knees to kiss her. She kept her mouth closed, then opened it, and she was breathing very loudly.

8.

You put your dick in a warm wet vacuum and felt like King Kong. You felt like you were on the verge of saving the world, a god, an emperor, Han Solo. The girl said your name but it wasn't your name really, just sounds. Because you were more than syllables, always had been. You reached down and took a big squeeze.

9.

He wasn't the only billionaire in the world. You heard rumors. One, allegedly, implanted a vibrator along the shaft of his penis. That was really something. She wondered where the buttons were kept and what happened if it ever got stuck on the Morse code setting. Or maybe he'd have two penises, perhaps three, maybe it was the length of a forearm, thick as a wrist and she'd have to take a deep breath when he entered her, like at the doctor's.

The only thing that hadn't crossed her mind was that it could be normal. Normal size, normal coloring, neatly circumcised. Like usual, the feeling started in her root chakra then floated up her spine. In California, surrounded by dog food, she made the oohs and aahs. So this was what it felt like to have a whole Wikipedia page inside of her. She arched her back and moaned. She closed her eyes and really meant it.

They finished on the floor of the dark shed and he ran his finger up and down her back as she counted paddle brushes hanging on the wall. "Do you know why I wanted to wait?" he asked, tracing shapes along her back.

It was easiest to talk about sex when they weren't looking at each other.

"I thought I was the one who was waiting," she said. "Playing hard to get to keep you begging for me. Now you won't call me anymore. You won't remember my name."

"Impossible," he said, then swallowed and changed his tone. "I'm serious."

"Until I finished the article?" she asked.

"Huh? Oh, that."

"Well, what?"

"I wanted for you to be safe. For us both to be safe. Be sure it was what we wanted."

"What *do* you want from me?" Sometimes she ran out of her personality and had to ask earnest questions.

"I honestly don't know. You're too unusual, too strange."

"Oh?"

"I've been all around the world. Every girl has nice eyes and laughter. You are harder to describe. That's what I like best, that I couldn't have thought you up myself."

A chestnut dog rounded the corner and sniffed along the entrance to the shed. Jenlena gathered some rogue kibble spilled along the wall and, turning away from Roderick Maeve, presented it in her palm.

"Does it make you uncomfortable?" he asked.

"What?"

"Me talking like this. I know for some people receiving compliments can be an acquired skill."

"No," she said, looking at him only so much as how his naked figure was reflected in the dog's eyes.

"You've had a lot of practice at it?"

She shook her head. "My ex-boyfriends," she began, pronouncing the word like it was in quotations. "They never took me seriously." The dog licked between her fingers, left a sheen.

"Young people aren't always so good at taking things seriously," he said. "It's your superpower."

She turned then, beheld the way his body had a heft to it, not fat, just flesh accumulated through time. There was white in his body hair; it occurred to her that the hair on his head must have been colored. This saddened her, that a person could achieve all the way to time travel but still color their hair. A man no less.

Later, in the even less forgiving light of his bedroom, she saw the white hairs down his chest, leading to his genitals (she even called them genitals in her head, the sight to her was so antiseptic). But she didn't like pitying him. It was unnatural, like a cat in high-heeled shoes or the time she saw her mother's breasts in the one movie she ever did when trying to make it as an actress. She didn't want to feel bad for a man like him, so rich and so powerful. If she could feel bad for a man like that, then god only knew what she felt about herself.

So she started to kiss him, first on his neck, then down his chest. Except she didn't believe in God. She'd heard on a podcast that guys liked it when girls tickled their balls during a blowjob. Except she honestly wasn't sure. Pity hurt everyone involved.

10.

For dinner, a young woman served them roast chicken like it was nothing. Jenlena took a bite and the flesh parted for her teeth like it wanted her to do it. Yes, she thought, this was what life was supposed to be like. Her real life started today and would continue forever.

Ricky took a drumstick with his bare hand. The skin caught the light, shiny, like an ice rink in moonlight. "You know I value your discretion," he said.

She smiled. "Yes, I know."

"I mean it," he said. "Let me prove it to you." Six, seven staff members stood in their vicinity. They were unremarkable, just the ideas of people really. They had ordinary faces. Even the one who had a big scar down his cheek, even the beautiful one with wide-set eyes and pouty lips. They weren't real in the way she was because she still had Ricky's scent on her skin. She was a part of him now, tonight, like a limb or a memory from childhood. "Tell me what you want," he said.

"I-I," she stuttered. "I don't know."

"Oh, come on. Tell me what you think about at night when you let your mind wander. Write it down on a piece of paper if you'd like. And I mean it, anything. You want a pretty necklace or a book deal?"

"I just like seeing them," she said finally. "It's worth it to just keep seeing them, the *animals*."

He sat still with no expression, as if waiting to see if she was joking. Then his face broke out in a wide smile and he clapped his hands. "Aha, fabulous! Well, when all this is through I'll take you to Dubai and show you my friend Rami's sloths."

"*Sloths?*"

"Two," he said. "And they're having a baby."

Before she went to sleep, Jenlena spoke directly to her reflection in the bathroom mirror. "Didn't I tell you our life would change? All along, didn't I tell you we were so much more than our circumstances and pedestrian body?"

"But didn't you feel pathetic," her reflection responded, "just waiting around for him?"

"What does it matter if I'd feel pathetic anyways?"

His toothpaste tasted like sage, his soap smelled like pine, she could see the ocean from the bay window. There were various pill bottles lining the medicine cabinet. She lifted three-year-old Zoloft and saw what he had been talking about, the dark and sticky butterfly remains. They'd formed a light film along the back wall of the cabinet. She leaned forward and took a whiff.

11.

Roderick Maeve woke up for the fourth time to check his email, though now, 4:35 a.m., there was good news. The physicist had submitted his final calculations to the engineers and construction on the machine would be completed on schedule. This afternoon was just a blip in a long life of everything going as planned. Yet again success was in his blood. Whether you liked it or not you couldn't fight what you really were.

The girl was beside him, rubbing her toenail up and down his calf. He liked her, he really liked liking her. He liked her nose and the way her top lip curved and how he could see the light reflect off a glimmer of her wet tooth.

"Would you ever want for me to live out here?" she had asked before they fell asleep. "Not with you, I mean, I know we're not ready for that, but just like closer so we wouldn't have to do the long distance and I'm honestly pretty tired of Montreal which is essentially a college town."

"Hmm," he'd responded. "Lots to think about."

Below, there were already sounds in the kitchen, his people preparing for him to be Roderick Maeve. There would be interviews and appearances and meetings. He'd shake people's hands very firmly to show he was a strong man. "Yes, sir!" they'd say in response to whatever he wanted.

Who am I in a different life? Sometimes when he was happy for no reason, he pictured this other version of himself with a woman somewhere; she'd be looking deeply into him and he into her, brushing hair off each other's faces and rubbing feet. Sometimes when he was unhappy for no reason, he pictured this other version of himself all alone, unloved by and even repellent to the women he desired. Sometimes it was even so bad he was sure he was dying. On this other plane there must have been a cancer inside of his body slowly eating him alive, that was the only explanation of how he could feel so bad, even with the big house, even with the view of the ocean, even with the paintings on the wall.

12.

In the morning, Roderick Maeve had already left for the office. Jenlena's bag had been packed on her behalf and because the driver was busy, Roderick Maeve's assistant drove her to the airport. She was attractive, if not a little rigid, maybe like one of those girls Daphne had been friends with at school. "We've prefilled the customs form for you," she said without looking at Jenlena. "Are you returning to Canada with any goods worth over $10,000?"

"What?" How was she supposed to have $10,000?

"For example, gifts."

"No," said Jenlena. "I'm not returning with anything."

The woman nodded with a little smile. *You hate me*, Jenlena thought. *It's our culture to hate each other. You've spent your whole professional life bending over backwards for him and I bet he hardly even notices. Me, I don't even have a professional life and he's taking me to see the sloths.*

"You liked California?" the assistant asked as they merged onto the freeway.

"Sure," said Jenlena. "It's just like in the movies."

"So, you like things, like, in general?" She was changing lanes.

"Sure," said Jenlena. "Writing in my notebook, sitting around."

The assistant considered this. "I used to think I liked society," she said finally, while making a left-hand turn. "It was what I studied in college. Bard, you know. Society really fascinated me, I really couldn't get enough. Six courses a semester sometimes, I just wanted more and more. And I guess I haven't really kicked the habit, you know, asking you questions like this. Some things are hard to quit even when I know they aren't good for me."

Jenlena asked her what she meant.

"It's like a toxic ex-boyfriend." She banged her hands against the steering wheel. "What has society ever done for me?"

"You seem pretty dedicated to your job."

The assistant shrugged. "I'm just curious, that's all. That's why I like to ask questions. All this talk about saving the world and I wonder, does anyone even *like* it? Do *I*?"

Soon they arrived at the airport. Smoke thickened all around the runway. When Jenlena boarded the plane, it was the same crew as before. They waited over an hour because of the visibility and when the flight began it was so turbulent a glass broke. Jenlena clutched her arm rests. She looked at the flight attendant, who was calm, seated without a belt, and smiling.

13.

"Forget all this fantasy stuff, if I had the chance I'd use it to go back to work. But I'd take it seriously this time. No

more messing around. Show the bosses that I understand the bottom line and really be the beacon of productivity that the company needs."

—FRED ADSIT, HOUSTON, TEXAS

"October 21, 2007. A man in my building won the lottery, $25 million jackpot. So I'd go back to that morning, when I saw him buying gas at the 7-Eleven. I knew he bought the ticket then, he always did, with this shit-eating grin on his face like everything was going to be okay. I'd always hated people like that. The positive-thinking people. So I get in this time machine and I win the twenty-five mil. We pay off our debts, buy a place in Hawaii, send the girls to college. Fuck, they won't even need college with money like that. We'd live like kings. And it would work better for my neighbor too, because he just spent it all on cocaine and prostitutes."

—DANIEL HOPPER, NEW YORK, NEW YORK

"He wasn't feeling well that morning. My wife said we should just let him stay home, but I pushed it. I didn't want to set the precedent, I guess. Of course that's something I've had to grapple with every day. I dropped him off myself. Just about an hour later we got the first call from the police that something had happened at the school. If I could go back? If I could listen to my son about his stomachache? You're damn right I would."

—JEFF McEACHRAN, NEWTOWN, CONNECTICUT

"For me, I understand why this is controversial. I think a lot of us are really attached to believing that everything

happens for a reason because that's how we've kinda been gaslit into accepting all the shitty things that happen to us. Or that we make happen to other people. I just mean that the idea of a time machine is a pretty crazy thing to wrap your brain around. At least for me. I've been thinking about it a lot and it's funny because I still very much am a believer in the old-school ideology. I've been through some shit myself, but I like my life now. Is it perfect? No, but I have this girl in my life and have started feeling excited for the future for the first time in a while. Still, is my happiness the only thing that matters? Because like I said, I've made some mistakes. Big ones. Sure, things have worked out for me, but do I have the moral responsibility to go back and right the wrongs that have harmed other people? Even if it means jeopardizing the present I have now?"

—JORDAN BELLECHASSE, MONTREAL, CANADA

14.

Moon Prendi knew the girl she drove to the airport was trying to cast her in some role. Mr. Maeve's girls always did, sizing her up into friend or foe, stripping her for any necessary parts. It used to drive her crazy, the bimbos he associated with, his regular harem. But since the animals, a friend from college had been sharing some really fascinating stuff online and it made her realize it wasn't only women that she hated. It was the emails, too, the late-night meetings, the noise pollution, crash diets, notifications, shitty guys from high school and how they were non-binary now. It was the droughts, the fires, premier television, the relentless "I told you so's" from her communist parents every time they talked about society. Target emissions, Shein, history in general. TED Talks and the constant upkeep of having a body. It was even her own name until one day she realized "crazy" was the only rational choice she had.

15.

M●●N_cicero_666 @Moon.Cicero 30m

I am not trying to make anyone angry

M●●N_cicero_666 @Moon.Cicero 30m

am not angry myself

M●●N_cicero_666 @Moon.Cicero 28m

Have not been since i gave up my name

M●●N_cicero_666 @Moon.Cicero 27m

Do you want to know a secret? After my bf pushed me into the wall

M●●N_cicero_666 @Moon.Cicero 27m

he thought he was a big man, bigger than the weather

M●●N_cicero_666 @Moon.Cicero 26m

But all it taught me was to identify with the earth

M●●N_cicero_666 @Moon.Cicero 26m

All along, i dont think i was ever meant to be a person

M●●N_cicero_666 @Moon.Cicero 26m

I understand him now tho, wanting to be bigger than the weather

M●●N_cicero_666 @Moon.Cicero 20m

What if I identified with the weather from now on?

M●◐N_cicero_666 **@Moon.Cicero** 5m

Arrived today in Calgary and was taken in by my 3 comrades with warmth and kindness

M●◐N_cicero_666 **@Moon.Cicero** 2m

Ready for a nice long sleep then comes the rest of my life

CHAPTER TWELVE

Ricky Talks about His Feelings

1.

The night before the transports, Roderick Maeve called Jenlena in the middle of the night. "You have themes, motifs?" he asked.

"What are you talking about?"

"Notes, at least. About us?"

"Sure," she said, yawning. "I've been working really hard, I swear."

"Do you keep a diary, I mean? Have you told your friends?"

Jenlena sat up in her bed. "I've told my friend Daphne a couple things but I'm very discreet, otherwise."

"Good," he said. "So you'll have witnesses."

"What are you talking about?"

"You could go to the *Daily Mail*, the *Washington Post*. Don't listen to anyone who says they don't pay for stories, and hold your ground until you find a good price."

"I don't know what you're talking about."

"Listen, most of my equity's tied up right now but I want to help you. If things don't work out. After tomorrow. If it doesn't work, for whatever reason, and if something were to happen to me because of that. I want you to know that I care about you and your well-being. Go to the newspaper with a story about us. Tell them everything they want to know, embellish the details if you have to."

"I don't understand. What's going to happen?"

"It's just a scenario," he said, then inhaled very deeply. "A possibility."

"Do you need to get some sleep?"

"I want to see you."

"Are you nervous about tomorrow?"

"I need to see you. I'm flying up. I'll be there in four hours."

2.

They had seen each other three times over the last two weeks. They had sex often now, mostly in his suite at the Queen Elizabeth hotel, the same place where not so long ago she'd gone in desperation to pretend to be a dog for a strange man. The same waiter from that day still prowled the dining room, though he'd since grown a chin strap. "There is an alternative to war," she overheard him telling a customer. "It's staying in bed and growing your hair out."

Once they drank champagne together in the Jacuzzi tub and she asked Ricky, "What if in the new world I'm the billionaire and you're the young girl, wouldn't that be funny?"

She was giddy from the drink. Being drunk like that, especially in the middle of the day, had always made her feel that anything she wanted could have been true. "Oh, but I couldn't imagine forgetting you," she said, stretching her toes so they grazed his shoulder. Each time she took another sip the bubbles burned her throat.

But his phone was ringing in the other room and Roderick Maeve stood to answer it.

He didn't even dry himself off, dripping instead all the way to the bed where Jenlena could hear him giving short answers, "Yes, no, yes, *why*?" And she knew that in about five minutes' time, he'd walk back into the bathroom and mouth to her that it was time to go. He would make a gesture with his hand even though the water was still warm.

In moments like this, there was an edge to his demeanor that reminded her of her stepfather, Christopher, when his tone dropped all niceties and he chastised her over the dishes or leaving food out in what they called the bonus room. It was how men told you they were angry, and more so because it was you who made them that way, you who was worthless but nevertheless manipulated them into having an unpleasant emotion, which they'd then deflect until you carried the whole thing yourself. It was yours, do what you want with it, write a little poem.

Out the window was the statue of the first prime minister, the one that got beheaded just a couple summers ago in a protest against racism. Now it had a new head and different activists had given it had antlers. Jenlena had learned a lot about herself during that period, mainly that her whole existence was humiliating for an entirely different set of reasons than she had previously understood.

It was her first year of university and she couldn't think of anything worse than being a white person, affiliated with the oil and petroleum industry no less. So she wrote down all the racist things she had ever done and thought about and enjoyed watching on TV: *pointed at the black man in Jasper, made jokes about gasoline, watched my mother lock the door when we drove downtown, was sexually attracted to Jason, didn't know who Fred Hampton was, told everyone I wished I was Japanese.* And she couldn't sleep that night because she felt her life ahead of her as a cleansed, nonracist person, and it was her generation that would change the world.

But then there was the drama when her roommate tried to overdose on aspirin and the project had to be put on hold. Jenlena forgot about the list (*crossed the road when I saw the Native man, misspelled Camila's name, said nothing when they called Miko an "Asian temptress," was honestly happy when my mother locked the doors*) until she moved out that spring, when birds were singing and the flowers bloomed and she ripped the list into tiny pieces and flushed it down the toilet.

Now, a new world beckoned once more. It was so close, just a handful of days. Nothing really, in the grand scheme of things. In the context of all of history the new world had practically already begun. And flocks would grace the sky and schools would dot the rivers and clouds would come out at night, caravans across the desert. Glarings in the alley, destruction o'er the hills, quivers in the sand, murders up the lamppost, basks in the swamp, a labor underground.

3.

Other times Roderick Maeve was hardly like a man at all. He was so soft and silly with her he might as well have been a girl. Once he even let Jenlena put a braid in his hair. He closed his eyes and told her how sometimes he felt like he had never been a child because his whole life had happened so fast and now sometimes he didn't recognize himself.

"I have no idea what I look like," Jenlena said. "You could show me five pictures of plain girls with brown hair and I don't think I'd be able to pick myself out of a lineup."

He told her she was pretty.

"But *am* I?" They hadn't even fooled around yet. That day it was like that, just talking. "I had a boyfriend who told me that he thought I was really pretty but only until he got to know me. He meant it as a compliment."

"Because you aren't vain," he said.

"Oh, I can be vain enough."

"No. I've seen how you look at yourself in the mirror."

"What does that mean?"

"Believe me, I've dated models. It's what I like about you."

"Hmm." Her eyes caught something in the distance, focused as if on the cusp of some nuanced revelation. She went on her phone.

4.

Generally, he was morose after sex but giddy after blowjobs. The next time they saw each other, Roderick Maeve handed Jenlena a towel and told her that when the board approved time travel for civilians he would take her wherever she wanted. "What would you like? A weekend in Paris in the twenties? I could take you on a stroll through Montmartre, have Picasso do your portrait. Versailles in the 1770s, get you done up to rival Marie Antoinette. Oh, I'm sure they had the most decadent parties. Arrive in time for the height of debauchery and slip out just before things start to turn."

"Maybe I could fuck Rasputin," she said, tossing the towel down on the floor as she slipped into the bed to watch some television. "You know, they say it wasn't even communism that undid the Romanovs but his dick? It's in a museum somewhere now, I think."

Roderick Maeve blushed. "I could arrange it."

"Or maybe Fidel Castro." She enjoyed imagining it. "I heard on a podcast he was a most tender man."

"And I could try to fuck . . ." He rolled out of bed and made his way to the bathroom. "Marilyn Monroe? Too cliché. Everyone's going to try Marilyn Monroe, it'll really wear her out. Sophia Loren perhaps. Jayne Mansfield, Ann-Margret."

He brought his toothbrush into the shower. "Brigitte Bardot, Cleopatra." For the life of him he could only think of obvious women.

"Evie Forget?" she called to him.

But the water was loud enough that he could pretend not to hear. Even when she called to him again, he pretended. Then the muffled sound of television and he knew the conversation was finished. She would go home soon, anyway. He would go back to California to facilitate the time machine and change the world.

5.

One and only one picture surfaced online of them together. Daphne texted it to Jenlena with a big exclamation mark. Jenlena loved imagining what people thought of her with Roderick Maeve. The admiration, sure, for she was no doubt to be admired, but their disdain too. There was no way she couldn't have existed.

But this photograph, taken in his office parking lot that day in California, wasn't what she'd been expecting. She looked washed out, her face flattened by the camera flash that also gave her red eyes, like one of those albino rodents who looked trapped in their own bodies. *That's not what I look like*, she thought. *At least not when I'm with him.*

Roderick Maeve and his assistant, read the caption.

"Are you ashamed of me?" she asked the next time they saw each other. "You never take me anywhere. Not to any restaurants."

"Because I like having you to myself," he said, too quickly.

"Maybe if you bought me some new clothes," she ventured carefully, "I could look nice for you." She pictured the fabric soft against her skin. "Wouldn't you like that? We could go to a restaurant or something."

"No," he said. "I've had a lifetime of that. Several."

Her disappointment was palpable between them. "Oh, honey," he said. "You know it's not like I can just be going around giving women money. How it would look, with the internet these days."

She nodded. Of course she knew the internet, had been there herself, was familiar with its contours. Her boyfriend Roderick Maeve had drank the blood of children, killed JonBenét Ramsey, made a woman suck his dick in a hotel room in 2016, donated money to Republicans, donated money to Democrats, owned a house a hundred miles beneath the surface of the earth, had had sex with Beyoncé.

They had sex then but she wasn't there, not really. He was so familiar to her, his stubby knob moving in and out of her until it felt like nothing. She made a noise or two, all the while trying to remember what had less calories: cucumber or watermelon, and what her high school teachers' first names were, then went through the alphabet to come up with a celebrity she would have sex with for each letter and what she would think about during that.

"Baby," he said. "You feel so good. Do I feel good to you too?"

"Yes, yes," she said. "So good, Daddy, so good."

Roderick Maeve came on her back, told her she was pretty, cute, sexy, wet, hot, tectonic. And it was true that something inside of her was unstoppable. When he fell asleep, she turned on the television to test how deep he was gone then slid out of bed and tiptoed over to his side as lightly as she could. She took his trousers into the bathroom and went through his pockets. There was his wallet, smooth black leather. She opened it up, spread it wide, but inside of the leather there was nothing. Just nothing, just darkness. She went on her phone.

Seeking professional-grade parrot impersonator

Petite woman who can pass for a maine coon. No sex, i just want to give my cat a bath like the one time in grad school chester had ringworm. You will pretend to hate it, pee everywhere and tremble, but i will keep the medicated shampoo on for ten minutes, telling you it is for your own good. Then rinse you off and as i dry you with a towel you will cling to my chest like a baby.

Old school here, man of traditional tastes, simply barely legal (or looks it) start with oral and we'll see from there

Later, trying on a $100 dress with puffed sleeves at the mall, Jenlena wasn't surprised that she'd chosen to perform the blowjob over an impersonation. Sex was something you could literally do with a machine, a piece of silicone. But animals meant a lot more than that. Her body may have understood it more than her brain but it didn't make it any less true.

The dress was beautiful, she thought, with little yellow flowers that made her feel less alone. She spun around in circles for Daphne back at the apartment and told her Ricky was the one who paid.

"Really?" Daphne looked up from her phone. "Roderick Maeve shops at Aritzia?"

That night Jenlena wrote a poem, her first in a while:

cuffing season
woof, said the girl.
meow, said the old man.
the little boy was drinking from a dish on the floor.
a father stung his own daughter,
dropped dead.
i live in a wire cage
on your dresser in the corner of the room,
spinning my wheel,
watching you watch
sexy dolphins on your phone,
biding my time until
you flush me down the toilet.

She posted it online, but in the morning, when she saw that few people had liked it (no one had commented), she felt small and embarrassed. She felt stupid and wanted to die. Then she was angry. I'll show them, she thought. The amorphous haze of people online. They'll regret dismissing my work.

6.

He was, altogether, a pretty optimistic guy. As an entrepreneur you had to be. Entrepreneur meant moving forward. That was what Roderick Maeve hated most about Moon Bethlehems: their deep-throated embrace of stasis. It was worse than communism because at least with those people power had been a common denominator.

He was not a cruel man. When one was found on his staff and confessed, they received all the help they needed. He even gave money last year to a charity that helped reformed Moon Bethlehems learn how to code. For he too had faced that darkness, believe it or not, the wide nothing that hid under the bed and waited until all the lights were out to tell him his mother was ugly. It knew his name as well as anyone else's. Nevertheless, he got up in the morning and put on clean clothes. It was called being alive.

But these Moon Bethlehems were rot. They infected everything they touched. Despite the thousands he'd spent on psychological consultants, there was no cure for that dead look in their eyes. Of course he took it personally, and that was something he was proud of. A true American success story and he considered it his privilege to inspire by example.

But since the scare with the physicist, his staff had only given him more reason to worry. At the end of January, a pilot came forward and said a flight attendant had propositioned him with sexual favors if he let her crash the plane. "It was all about the time machine," he said. "She's so scared to live in a world without the weather to blame everything on. She'd rather everybody suffer than let you save us, sir."

Then the next week, a junior VP in marketing sent a company memo stating his resignation: *There is no further to go. Even backwards is a direction. Moon children unite!*

"But he's not a *real* Moon Bethlehem," his assistant tried assuring him. "It's only some woman he met. She's a Moon Bethlehem so he's saying he is just to impress her but he doesn't actually believe in any of the principles." She'd been in a strange mood that day, sluggish and behind on her emails. Her hair looked dirty and her blouse was familiar. Was it the same one she'd worn the day before? The color washed her out.

"What principles?" Ricky asked. "Don't tell me these people do anything more than sit around on their asses all day and complain!" That morning, all the smoke alarms had gone off at once in the valley and he heard it even from his house, high on the hill.

"They're not complaining," she said. "You're the one who's trying to save the world. They accept it for what it is. If we can understand it's cruel to keep a person alive past a certain point, then why not apply the same logic to the world at large? It's kindness, actually."

He noticed that she wasn't reading anything from her phone. She was speaking from her heart. He had a vivid memory of years ago when she got bangs but they didn't stick. A man was not supposed to notice these things about his employee, yet certain tendernesses were unavoidable and, in his experience, best succumbed to within reason. *When she's finished talking*, he told himself, *I'll tell her she looks nice today. I'll scrounge up a gift certificate.* But she did not finish talking for some time.

"You know, people think they're environmentalists but they're not necessarily. Nobody's trying to save the environment. They just want people to be honest about what's happening and sometimes that involves retribution. The first ever Moon Bethlehem, he was from Ohio, some small town just down river from a chemical plant, and all his life he said that was the reason so many people in his family had cancer. Then, on his deathbed, he admitted that he too had loved the chemical plant and was actually so afraid to enter whatever realm awaited him where chemicals presumably didn't exist. They made food taste good and clothing cheaper and he loved it when his wife put the chemicals in her hair and on her face. He didn't expect anyone to change, he just wanted us to be honest.

Now some people say it doesn't mean anything to be Moon Bethlehem but I think it means a lot to some people."

"This was in the junior VP's resignation letter?" Ricky asked.

"Right," she said. "Sure."

The next day, she didn't come into work. She called him around
noon and said she wasn't feeling well. "These migraines."

"Hungover?" He wondered if he'd forgotten her birthday and
that was why she'd been acting so strange the day before.

She mumbled something.

"Take an Advil and get down here."

"It's the gamma rays, the brain can only withstand so much."

"For fuck's sake, what are you talking about?"

"The time machine," she said.

"Is this some kind of joke?"

"You can't go back more than two or three times before it really
starts to throb in the frontal lobe."

He was desperate to laugh.

"And I've been doing it so much just this week."

"Get in here," he said. "Report to your desk."

"It was just to see," she said in a singsongy voice. "To make
sure everything worked. I had my fun but it was just practice. I went
back seventeen times, can you believe it? Just to put progestin in
your coffee and see if it made you go bald, just as practice. After
ten, my vision really started getting wobbly, I don't see surfaces
anymore, barely, I can only see what's really inside."

"Practice for what?" His voice quivered.

"Aren't you so tired of believing in yourself, Ricky?"

"Practice for what?"

"Ricky." She started laughing. "I always wondered how it would
feel to call you that."

"It's my name," he said.

"No it's not, not to me."

The line went dead. Ricky ran to the bathroom, certain that he'd puke, but he found himself in front of the mirror, contorting to see the top of his head. He pulled out his phone to take pictures but his hands were shaking so badly it all came out as a blur. He stumbled backwards against a window. Outside, all the sins of the past hung above the parking lot, so thick that you couldn't even see the sky anymore. It was just gray, the dull reflection of everything everyone had wanted and the boring places they'd gone in their cars.

7.

In the beginning, when the machine was first announced, he'd been accused of having personal motivations. Even now, the girl made jokes about going back in time to have sex with Marilyn Monroe and he wondered if that was already true. It could have explained so much. Some sadnesses only made sense in the context of the cutting-edge technological achievements he was only beginning to scratch the surface of.

He always knew he was losing women when they got really into yoga. Such an intense interest in their bodies but they never wanted to share it with him.

"I'll buy you a flying pigeon!" he said to Evie once, up to here with her ujjayi breath.

"That's *not* what I mean."

He horrified her, he could tell, and it wasn't as sexy as it used to be. He was Michael Jackson's nose, Osama bin Laden.

"Relax Ev, I'm kidding." He really was. The next day, he found a surgeon in Mexico who could realign the ligaments in her knee.

"The problem with you," she told him, "is that you think that life is supposed to be easy."

"What do you mean?" He was bewildered. "It is."

No, he didn't have anything to go back to.

8.

The night before the transports, they met in the usual suite at the Queen Elizabeth hotel. Roderick Maeve looked horrible; he had bags under his eyes and the gray was coming through in his thinning hair. There were Band-Aids all over his fingers. "What's happened?" Jenlena asked.

"Am I balding?" he asked her.

"I like that you're older." She rubbed his chest.

He told her he wanted to run away. He didn't want to be who he was anymore and this was possible because he had so much money he could buy a completely new life.

"But you were going to take me to see the sloths."

"Oh, who cares." He let out a cry. "She had a miscarriage anyways!"

It wouldn't be easy, but that was what made it valuable. If it were easy everyone would do it. He could buy one for her too. Then they'd be new people, live somewhere far away and have total privacy. He started to talk about places near water, remote parts of Eastern Europe.

"An island?" she asked.

No one would want anything from him ever again. There, on that specific hill or valley, they could have normal lives, where nobody looked at them and nobody expected anything from him. Nobody took his picture or wrote pithy things about him on the internet, like how he drank the blood of children or single-handedly caused their feelings.

"It's what I learned from you," he said, looking her square in the eyes. "To want simple things. Run away with me."

He sat on the bed with his head in his hands. She reached down to hold them. "Okay," she said. "Let's go."

Roderick Maeve looked up at her. He had tears in his eyes and she touched them with her finger as they slid down his cheek. Eventually, she took her clothes off and he put his tongue inside her and said he loved the way she made him feel. Yes, he was a grown man, but he had feelings too. Jenlena knew for a fact he had a whole range of them. Just the same as anyone. When he dreamt he saw himself as just the same as anyone. He woke into his circumstances, which soon became exhausting. They bore down on him worse than the weather, all the people waiting, watching.

9.

She wasn't supposed to be like other girls, always reminding him of things, even when you stripped away all their clothes and asked them to wipe off their makeup and closed your own eyes if necessary. How could he never get rid of his feelings? Even when he said them out loud they stayed there, taunting him like skin tags. He was always reminded of something or other, which in turn reminded and reminded: ketchup and trees, chicken feet, running, even bowling, some TV show where the actress lost her teeth and sooner or later there he is back in his childhood body, listening to sounds through the wall when his mother was with the super, sounds that could have been anything but he knew exactly what they were. What was the point of anything if he can still remember it like yesterday. What is all the money for? Just to feel old and incontinent on a boat? Then he saw himself reflected in Jenlena's pupils and wanted viscerally to die or fuck her. *Shit*, he thought. *I'm already doing that.*

10.

In the morning, he was gone. He was on the television.

CHAPTER THIRTEEN

The End of the World

1.

M●●N_cicero_666 @Moon.Cicero 5m

I'm nervous. I'm not feeling like myself, but I'm ready.

2.

No, Christopher Campbell didn't believe in this time machine and no, he never had. When Tina first told him about what she'd seen on TV he thought it was a joke, at the very most some elaborate piece of "art."

His stepdaughter, Jenlena, was interested in these kinds of things, she was one of those kids who blamed everything on their feelings. A couple years back, she even sent Tina this "essay" where she said the weather was the reason her real father had left them, this man being the one who kept an otter in the bathtub and ran away before she was even a year old. "Generational nihilism," she called it. Even Tina found that a stretch. "I didn't realize she even still thought about him," she told Christopher. "That's the part that worries me."

So people were saying that this time machine was going to eradicate his whole industry (the number-one in Canada) and make people happy all over the world. So what? He wakes up on the sixteenth of February negotiating solar panels? Tina was always saying to him, "But we could have Trevor back!"

And his wife was not a dumb woman. He wouldn't have married her had she been dumb, not at least deep down. So he'd say, "Yes, dear, but were it not for our society's dependency on nonrenewable energy we'd never have been able to afford Trevor in the first place, him being a purebred Scottish terrier from a breeder in Ardrossan. Certainly not his dental surgery a year before that. And that there, my love, is the problem with conspiracy theories: you pull on one thread and it all unravels."

But at the same time, Christopher couldn't say that he wasn't a sucker for that look in her eyes when she watched all those television specials about Britain and the sun. She leaned over and squeezed his knee. "Trevor!" she said. "Remember how he did the little dance for walk time?"

They'd even had sex on a night like this. From some angles she looked just the same as she did that time they first met, her cheeks and the big forehead that she hated. From other angles he liked her even more now. He couldn't help himself, especially on nights when she was open with her body and said his name like it was something she made up herself.

Company policy was not to talk about it at work. But sometimes he walked into a conference room and it was obvious the time machine was all anyone had on their minds. They said it was going to solve all the weather, bring back winters like they had when he was a kid. A friggin' time machine. He knew more and more people who were really talking about how the whole world was going to change. So maybe he was the one who wasn't real.

———

Protestors outside, just like always. Those damn Moon Bethle-hems, yes, but others too. Kids like his stepdaughter who didn't seem to realize there's been weather since the dawn of time. Most of them hadn't even finished high school but somehow felt they had the wherewithal to tell a multinational corporation what to do. Well, sometimes he just had to throw his head back and laugh.

People needed his products, even the ones who hated him the most of all. The gangs outside the office, or, god forbid, the Moon Bethlehem freaks who'd done to him even worse. How do you think they got here from their parents' houses in Meadowbrook, in Ocean Terrace? Do they ever think about how all their clothes got here from China? Believe it or not, he took pride in this. He facilitated the extraction of the country's God-given resources for people like them too. What else did the dinosaurs die for if not to give their melted bodies to the future?

So no, Christopher would not be ashamed.

At work, they made them see this therapist. It was mandated for all the men who'd been "harassed," and that was fine. It was fine, he thought. He was willing to be an adult and sit in a room with her. It didn't challenge him like with some of those guys who felt their masculinity was threatened, or the paranoids who put up a big stink about how the sessions were tape-recorded. For him it was fine. He answered all the questions about his childhood. Yes, yes, no, et cetera.

"Did it make you angry to have Tina look at the pictures of you and Trudie from the Houston office?" she asked.

"No."

"How did it make you feel?"

"Relieved," he said without thinking.

"Are you in love with Trudie from the Houston office?"

"No," he said.

She told him it was common for men to want to get caught.

He leaned forward and asked if other men sometimes felt like they didn't exist. "I don't recognize myself in the mirror sometimes," he said. "Sometimes I wake up in the middle of the night because I can't remember what I look like and when I look in the mirror I don't look like my mom or my dad."

Since then he'd been going on long drives. Anywhere, just anywhere, with his own car. Past the high school where Jenlena got in trouble for skipping gym class, past the mall where she got caught shoplifting earrings in the shape of marijuana leaves. He'd been thinking a lot about Jenlena lately, for no particular reason.

Sometimes he knew he was relieved she wasn't his real daughter; other times he was convinced if only he'd tried a little harder to get to know her she might have been the key to his whole life. He wouldn't be in the car so much, driving into nowhere through stop signs just to see if he existed. Out past this way there had been a water-ski course, though it was all dried up now, just marsh and some beer cans. That was his fault too. Didn't you know? All this time he'd been the most powerful man in the world.

3.

M●●N_cicero_666 @Moon.Cicero 2m

Then again does the wind get nervous? Does the rain second-guess itself?

4.

The night before the transports, Christopher brought in Trevor's plush bed from the garage and set it up with a bowl of water in the living room just in case. In the morning, Tina made his coffee, just like normal. "You'll be careful," she said as he made his way out the door. "Just in case? I love you."

It was 8:30 a.m., an hour ahead of California, where the transports were scheduled for 3 p.m., and two hours behind Jenlena in Montreal. Christopher found it strange how quiet the streets were—even outside the office the protestors felt muted. The driver let him off in the usual spot underground. "Thank you," he said.

"Sir."

He walked inside the building and rode the glass elevator up to the seventh floor, just like always, like any other day. There was a young woman with dark hair and a package in her arms but he hardly noticed, not at first. It was only when the sun came through from behind the clouds outside that he noticed her hair was actually red, this deep, dark, blood-colored red. Her package was covered in brown paper. She got off at his floor and made her way behind him to the front desk. Christopher heard something and for one split second believed it was a bird. The package was ticking. Moon Cicero looked right at him, then a great bright light and Christopher saw everything all together, brighter than darkness. They turned into pieces, just specks, they dissolved into the air.

5.

M●●N_cicero_666 @Moon.Cicero 15s

I'm it and it is me, the weather at last.

6.

When the police called Tina to say that there had been an accident, she knew instantly that he was dead. She could feel her pulse
in her eyelids.

She called her daughter, off in Montreal doing god knows what.

"Hello?" the girl answered lazily.

"Have you seen?"

"What are you talking about?"

"It's your father. On the news, there's been an accident."

"But everything could change, Mom. You'll see. The transports
will really make everything better."

7.

Jenlena swallowed. Outside the suite, the housekeepers made their
way down the hall. It was checkout time, the liminal hour. Christopher was either alive or dead. The world was about to change or
not. They would succumb to the weather or they would outsmart it.

She walked home, through downtown, up the mountain, into
the neighborhood with the old Greeks and Hasids and young
people she knew from parties, saying goodbye.

At the apartment, Daphne asked if she was okay. "I saw the
news. Your dad worked there, didn't he?" Everybody knew she had
a stepfather who worked high up in the oil industry but it wasn't
polite to talk about it. They didn't want to make her feel bad.

"He's my stepfather," Jenlena said. "My real father left when I
was a baby."

Daphne's father had left her too. When they were new friends,
just getting to know each other, this had been something they'd

bonded over. But it was rare that girls ever had fathers, not at that age, never the fathers they felt they deserved. They both knew a lot about Monica Lewinsky and liked Joni Mitchell's paintings. They had the same middle name.

There'd been attacks in Germany too, and one in Houston. "It's the Moon Bethlehems," Daphne said. "I can't believe they actually pulled it off."

Jenlena looked at pictures of the rubble and the fire. She realized she was on her phone, scrolling. People from her high school said they were Moon Bethlehems now too. They said it wasn't pretty but if violence was the only way to make people understand then their small, petty lives didn't add up to much in the long run. So be it. *It was a wonderful feeling to realize this*, her grade's prom queen said. *A great release.*

"But it could all change," Jenlena said. "The time machine can change everything. We just have to wait."

They set up Daphne's phone against a pile of old textbooks to watch the live feed. Roderick Maeve was onstage in front of a large photograph of the time machine, a gleaming black box. He stood proud, tall with broad shoulders, like someone Jenlena couldn't fathom knowing. Maybe she still had particles of his skin underneath her fingernails, but he was a stranger. He laughed and smiled as he read prepared remarks about the past, present, and future. Reporters asked the normal questions. Nothing mattered, everyone knew that everything up until the transports was just ceremony. The physicist stood behind him in a new suit, with the British CEO there too; she wiped a tear from her cheek.

The technicians waved and smiled in their period costume. They were given a round of applause and said a big farewell to their families. The male technician told his children to be proud of him. Maybe there were some people who'd tell them that they didn't have a daddy anymore but what they ought to understand was that their daddy was all over the place. Every time they saw a solar panel they'd know it was their daddy. Their daddy was in the fridge and all the lorries.

"You couldn't ask for a more lovely day," said the correspondent, a beautiful woman with long, tousled hair. It was three o'clock in California and there was hardly weather in the sky.

"I'm so excited," said Jenlena, her eyes brimming with tears.

The technicians left the stage together, followed by Ricky and the physicist. The correspondent explained how the time machine was kept in a cement room in the basement of the laboratory to limit the spread of radiation. For now the world would have to wait. "To repeat: Roderick Maeve's time travel expedition, the first of its kind on this planet, is now underway."

"I think I can feel it," Daphne said. "Can't you?" She gripped the edge of the futon. "Oh, I'm really starting to feel it."

Im so excited, Jenlena texted Roderick Maeve. <3

8.

"I don't know. From my corner of the room people seemed mostly interested in the free champagne. We're not really taking this seriously, are we?"

—LINO NGUYEN, OAKLAND, CALIFORNIA

"I felt the hair on the back of my neck start dancing. I felt nauseous actually. It was hitting me all at once what we were doing, the audacity of it. I had to excuse myself. I couldn't see clearly. When would it happen? Was it happening already? The crowd was impossible. Everyone was sweating, looking at Roderick Maeve, the man who thought he could do anything. But time was the one thing we'd never

touched before, not like that. Someone had to do it, I sup-
pose, but in my lifetime? I braced for it. I got sick in the
bathroom. The room began to spin and surely that was it.
I was ready for the sky to collapse, the walls to crumble.
But back in the room, everything was normal. I asked a
young reporter if she knew where the exits were and how
soon it was going to happen. 'I don't want to be in the ele-
vator when it happens,' I said. She just laughed. 'Dude, it
happened five minutes ago.'"
                    —DAVID MITCHELL, MOUNTAIN VIEW, CALIFORNIA

"Me, I was just there to serve champagne. It was like any
other event to me. They send us all over, I was on Top Chef
one time. And Randy told us specifically not to watch. They
were strict about these high-profile events. We weren't
allowed to smile or wear jewelry—one girl got caught with
a tongue ring and she was fired on the spot. I tend to listen,
though. You do enough of these kinds of events and you
get really good at listening without anyone being able to
tell. And some of it got to me. All that crap about time and
second chances. Because for so long I've been feeling like
my whole life's decided, working these dead-end jobs and
making art that no one cares about. But they left the room
to start the time machine and I felt something. I'm telling
you, it was a wonderful feeling to be there even as a waiter."
                    —LUCIA CORWIN, SANTA CLARA, CALIFORNIA

9.

His collar itched in front of the crowd. Everything felt too tight
and the cameras blinded the young physicist. It wasn't normal to

be looked at like some kind of god. Everyone was so obsessed with being in public, yet almost every story of someone who lived a public life ended in tragedy. For the physicist, the only interesting things were those that occurred between numbers in private.

At Christmas, his mother called him and said there was something she needed him to know. "I'm not angry anymore," she said. "I've accepted what happened."

He was silent.

"In case you felt you were doing this for us," she said. "I just wanted you to know that I'm at peace. We don't need to go around changing things that God's decided."

He bit down on his piece of chalk and it shattered into pieces.

"Honey," she said like he was still a kid, "I just wanted you to know that I love you."

Now he was onstage in California with his version of a smile on his face. "This is it, buddy," Roderick Maeve said. He slapped his back three times. They left the stage and descended a narrow flight of stairs to the basement where the machine was in a concrete room joined by a glass wall to the control panel. The technicians began to chatter. "It's a beautiful day, isn't it?" said the female, playing with the strap of her bonnet.

"True what they say about California, then. It's been lovely since we got here," the male technician replied.

"Me, I don't mind some weather. I always liked the autumn going-back-to-school feeling and my mother used to say that there was no better excuse than a rainy day."

"Well, shall we then?" asked the male technician, gesturing limply toward the machine.

But the female technician hesitated. "Will it hurt?" she asked the two men in charge.

The physicist had taken off his tie and his jacket, undone the three buttons on his shirt. Only your body, he wanted to tell her. But that's not so much, is it? Look how silly they've made it look now with those costumes.

"It'll only pinch a little," said Roderick Maeve.

"Well, we'll be going, then," the male technician said, standing perfectly still. Roderick Maeve walked them to the door of the machine and guided them inside. "We're all grateful," he said. "You'll be remembered."

"But we won't," said the female technician. "There'll be no reason to remember us, not if everything goes well."

"So, let me write something down," said male technician. "Just let me write—"

Roderick Maeve closed the door.

He and the physicist went into the control room and from the panel the young physicist turned on the machine. It began to make noises and it got hot, fast. Somebody, either technician or both of them, began to bang on the walls and then they stopped. It was silent for five minutes or so, until the physicist stood up and walked through the door to the other side of the glass. Ricky followed him. The physicist opened the heavy steel door and they peered inside the empty box.

"So, it worked," Ricky said.

"She was right," the physicist said. "If it worked, we'll never know the difference."

10.

In the new world, Jenlena wondered, would she be happier? Would she be more or less afraid of other people? What would her hair be like and might she have a more supple body. Where are her daddies in the new world?

In the new world, he would call her. He would ask if she remembered him and she would say, "Benjamin Franklin?" and he would laugh.

"So you did it."

"Appears so," he would say, ever bashful in the new world. "Run away with me."

"Are you sure?"

And he would say, "Why yes, I've paid my debts. I'm free."

11.

Can you feel it?

Do you feel anything now?

All over the world, people were waiting.

CHAPTER FOURTEEN

Les Animaux!

1.

The endings were begun together, then unraveled upon their own accord.

2.

Once, Jenlena had been told that when people died they rejoined the earth. It was a particularly poetic friend of her mother's who said this, a woman with long, golden hair and heavy turquoise earrings. It meant that people came from the earth too, but Jenlena knew she was not made of leaves. Dirt was not a part of her; she could always wash it off. Her mother had a lot of poetic friends on the coast, all of their earrings looked like candy. Then they moved to the prairies and her mother made new friends. They talked about window treatments and how to control their dimwitted husbands.

Later, when Jenlena told people about how she had known the California billionaire Roderick Maeve, it was hard for them to believe her. But she never blamed them. She knew she wouldn't have believed her either, even if it did constitute violence to not take people at their word when it came to sexual matters.

There were many questions: Are you serious? What did you really know about the time machine? What was it like back then? What were people really expecting? Everyone wanted to know what drugs she was on and if she was brainwashed and what was his dick like. How could you like a man like that? Did you know he had a factory in China where so many workers tried to commit suicide they installed safety nets along the bottom of the towers? And have you heard about the money behind Big Pharma? He owned sixteen houses and five private jets and gave money to Republicans. Really, what was his dick like?

3.

"Can't you feel it? Just this morning I threw out my inhaler!"
—HENRY SWAIM, LONDON, ENGLAND

"The thing with me is that I've always been an optimist. I can't help it. I know it used to drive my sister crazy. I remember even when the dog got hit by a car I told her he was going to be okay. I understand now that she held that against me for a long time. I'm understanding more and more lately, since the transports. I'm thinking a lot about my sister but also all of us. Most people I know online say that it's been impossible all along and everyone's fallen for the hoax because that's just what kind of people we are. But little do they know, that's believing in something too. There is no way around it, as far as I'm concerned. I for one prefer to believe in something I actually like.

"The world has changed before. Like in this country, where the time before the white people came actually lasted longer than the time since we've been here. And I heard

recently on a podcast that the reason China's had their time machine for years is that they think in centuries instead of years. Sometimes here we think in minutes. Like I said, I'm beginning to understand a lot of things differently now."

—BONNIE CICERO, TORONTO, CANADA

"There's the same old pain in my leg, the same old throbbing migraine minute I get up. Same ol' thirteen percent taxation. Far as I'm concerned we're livin' in the same."

—TOM RHODES, JACKSON HOLE, WYOMING

4.

When Daphne woke up the morning after the transports, Jordan had already texted her, **Welcome to the new world.**

JORDAN: **HI BABY**

JORDAN: **ITS LIKE I CAN SMELL YOU**

JORDAN: **YR RIGHT HERE W ME CAN U FEEL IT?**

Yes, she said, sliding her hand under the drawstring of her sweatpants. **We can have everything we want**

JORDAN: **I'LL DO EVERYTHING 4 U**

DAPHNE: **AND ILL BE YR SLUT**

When she orgasmed she felt the new world all around her, all things oozing toward their rightful place. Nothing existed except that feeling.

DAPHNE: **I CAN ASK JEN ABOUT THE TIME MACHINE.**

WHAT MACHINE? HE REPLIED.

DAPHNE: **BACK IN TIME?**

DAPHNE: **LIKE WE TALKED ABOUT?**

JORDAN: **BUT DON'T U SEE?**

JORDAN: **I FEEL LIKE SERIOUSLY I UNDERSTAND EVERYTHING NOW. LIKE BACK TO THE 18TH CENTURY WHEN MAN WOULD DO LITERALLY ANYTHING FOR $**

JORDAN: **$ JUST TO CREATE PRODUCTS WE DIDN'T EVEN NEED AND HUMAN BEINGS BECAME THE PRODUCT TOO**

JORDAN: **SOOOOOOO MUCH VIOLENCE**

JORDAN: **WE TOOK FROM THE EARTH AND ITS PEOPLE IT TAUGHT GENERATIONS OF CHILDREN THAT OWNING WAS NATURAL AND WHEN SOMETHING WAS "OURS" WE COULD DO WHAT WE WANTED WITH IT**

JORDAN: **BUT NOW THATS GONE AND WE BUILT SOCIETY OFF OF THE SUN THERE IS MORE THAN ENOUGH TO GO AROUND AND I NEVER WOULD HAVE HIT THAT GIRL**

JORDAN: **THERE WOULD BE NO NEED TO**

JORDAN: **I CAN FEEL IT DAPH I'M FREE**

Then he sent her a picture of himself smiling with a sunbeam across his face and it was true there was something different about him. He looked younger but that wasn't it, not exactly. It was strange and she didn't like it. He could be with anyone, she thought. If he'd never done anything wrong then anyone would love him, it would be obvious. Without his past he would float far, far away from her.

Jenlena knocked on the door and asked her why she was crying. "I'm happy in the new world," she responded.

So it was true what they said about girls. They were crazy. They didn't make any sense. Driven by feeling and wild, wild mood swings.

5.

Both girls watched TV on their phones, waiting for someone to tell them if the world had really changed. Much of the evidence was compelling: snowfall for the first time all year in Manitoba; a woman in Sweden claimed to be pregnant at fifty. Men could have babies in the new world! the internet said. Women no longer had to remove their facial hair. One man in Prague could do a handstand for the first time in seventeen years. A small but decisive victory in the Middle East.

But on another site: thirty-two children drowned during a monsoon in Cambodia, new fires waged across the Australian rainforest. A woman's lover left her to become Moon Bethlehem; another realized she herself was one. She had been since childhood, yet never allowed herself to even approach her truth until now. There were Moon Bethlehems everywhere, photos of them in their drab clothes, the color of weather and dirt. At one march for the new world in Scotland, they counterprotested with posters that said, "We remember."

"We forget!" screamed a man who believed. "We've moved on and we'll forget you too!"

Jenlena checked her phone. She hated not knowing. It made her feel like she had to go to the bathroom. Only her mother had texted: **Do you feel anything?**

Roderick Maeve had been photographed leaving the laboratory after the transports and stated through his representatives that he was happy with the results. But the internet was louder. It said that the transports had failed, the science wasn't possible. It was obvious wormholes didn't work that way. The internet said that the technicians had died. It would have been like putting your head in the microwave. Or else a group of Moon Bethlehems had hijacked the time machine and gone back themselves to accelerate the world's decline even further.

The internet said they were going back in time to make everyone communist—look at your children, it's already working. China'd had a time machine for years. Roderick Maeve was a joke, anyway, everyone knew that. Now he was off on a beach somewhere. He and all his friends had gone back in time to escape the weather and now they were laughing at how gullible the world was.

Was it weather or did it just feel like weather? Jenlena hated not knowing. She wanted to crawl back inside of her mother, then back into her random father through his sperm and just get jerked off into a towel somewhere or perhaps down the shower drain and that might be nice. She'd be swimming.

"Jordan believes it," Daphne said. "He says it's obvious from Gabe's apartment."

"So maybe it hasn't gotten here yet," said Jenlena. "Because they live on the third floor. Like it starts up in the sky and travels underground slowly."

"That's an idea."

"Sure." Jenlena checked her phone. A message from her mother: **Still haven't heard from c.**

"If there were animals," Daphne said.

Jenlena turned her head. Daphne's hair was in a low braid, brassy in the dimming light.

"Then we'd know for sure if it was true. If somebody saw an animal."

Jenlena refused to look at her phone. Then and only then he would text her and he did. The device felt like fire as she read the words under her breath: **Let's not kid ourselves. We come from different worlds. If i could do it all again, I would. But would u even notice?**

She felt her throat swell. The mood was stale, like a mouth after a long night of vivid dreams. "I'm going to go to sleep," she told Daphne. "We'll know more in the morning."

6.

In the morning, Tina called and said they'd found some of Christopher's teeth in the rubble across the street from his office. When you were a baby you were loved and had done nothing wrong. Now that Christopher was dead, she hoped he'd gone back to that, that he was free from his humiliations and this tired world.

Jenlena thought about how much she'd hated him, his awful pants and the way he chewed his food. She'd felt so sick of him alone with her mother, doing things. And her mother making faces. Sounds. She'd heard them together on a trip to the mountains. She hated that he didn't hate himself. This created a rage inside her, real fire—how dare he walk around with his head held high when he watched such bad television shows! Then when they shared an interest in, say, *The Sopranos*, it was literally worse than a stranger forcing her to touch his penis on a beach in Florida.

But he was kind too. She'd hear her mother laughing. Another time in Canmore he did a funny impression. She liked the way he buttered toast. Sometimes when she was sad he'd bring her up a plate of breakfast and she'd dip her fingers into the little pools along the surface of the bread. So multiple things were true at once and it wasn't frantic. Nothing was switching rapidly back and forth, both were steady and both were very calm. She loved him and she felt nothing for him. He was her father and he was not.

"Why are you laughing?" Daphne asked her. She was lying on the futon in one of Jordan's old T-shirts.

They could hear the sounds of people marching up Saint-Laurent with pots and pans, just a block east of them. "Do you know what it's for?" Jenlena asked.

"No," said Daphne.

"Have you been up all night?"

She nodded.

"On your phone?"

"Just thinking. I feel it. I think I really might feel something."

"I don't think it's true," Jenlena said softly. She sat down beside her on the futon. "I'm sorry, but I don't."

Daphne looked up. "Did you hear from Roderick Maeve?"

Jenlena shook her head. "He's a fraud," she said. "I was crazy about him, but it was all a lie."

"You know where he is? They're saying online he must have gone into hiding."

"Wherever he went, I'm sure it's a lie. He had animals, you know. He showed me."

Daphne squinted. It was as if she didn't understand.

"Did you hear what I said?" Jenlena went to her room for the T-shirt she'd worn in California and said, "Maybe you can smell it."

Daphne kept staring at her. "Animals? Animals!"

"This whole time, just not for everybody."

"How many?"

Jenlena said she wasn't sure. "All over the world. Even here in Montreal there's a horse he keeps in a barn and she's beautiful. There are dogs in California with long beautiful fur and we had sex in a shed with all of them around us. I'd never been so happy in my life."

Daphne had a big smile. "Do you remember where, exactly?" she asked. "And the horse, could we get there?"

7.

Their Uber driver told them he believed in the new world even though his life was exactly the same as before. The only difference was that he realized how happy he was. His wife was beautiful and his daughter was really good at math. During the weekends he worked on the menu for his brother's new restaurant.

On the way there, Jenlena and Daphne worked collectively on a series of posts:

Today we live in a world where more and more women are expected to be their own fathers. From an early age, we teach ourselves how to tie our shoes, how to ride a bike, apply for a credit card, even negotiate large purchases. There are even some who cite the rising number of women in leadership roles to say mommies rule the earth, though others argue these types are simply daddies in pantsuits.

But what we might not realize is that we do have daddies, all of us. Men like Roderick Maeve.

Rich men, the powerful ones we read about on the tv, have become the daddies of our society. They make decisions on our behalf and we trust them to know what's best.

I spent some time with him over this past winter and we got to know each other quite well.

He was born 42 years ago with no daddy of his own and worked his way up to become one of the most powerful men in the world. Roderick Maeve is so powerful that no one has seen him in 7 days. Is he the only one who can tell us if the world has changed?

I am not Moon Bethlehem. I am proud of my name but I too spent many years denying the things I wanted, mistrustful of desire. I used to think that wanting things was only for chumps. Tryhards, kiss asses, teacher's pets. You have a desire and there's two possibilities: you don't get it and you're disappointed. You get it and it disappoints you.

But right now I can admit it. I, Jenlena, am a closeted wantaholic. I want to tell you about the animals Roderick Maeve and his friends have been keeping from us. I want to tell you exactly where they are.

It didn't take long after that. Jenlena was detailed about the house in California and the elevator underground. A crowd was at the gates.

8.

In Quebec, Daphne and Jenlena made their way through the woods. It wasn't always easy to see but they let themselves be guided by the smell. Deep in the dark, something was alive. It became more and more clear the closer they got.

As they approached the barn, Daphne took Jenlena's hand. The girls opened the door together. Jenlena looked at her friend. All this time, she'd been hoping someone would love her, but even when they'd pretended it had only been in the most normal ways: dull, predictable. Ricky too, in the end, was the most normal thing to have ever happened: just a boy who ended things over text. But deep down she knew that there was so much strangeness inside of her, and here at her side was someone who had such a beautiful strangeness too. It was almost too much to fathom, when thought about directly. Out of all the thousands of ways a person could be in the world, what were the chances, and they were best friends.

The weather was in the way they held their shoulders and it seeped out of their pores. All of the trees were breathing. The weather was in the sky and growing out of the soil and inside old photographs, it hung in the background of all their stories. They would have been unrecognizable without it.

Inside, the horse was thin and her eyes were bloodshot but she was alive. Daphne gasped. Jenlena pressed the button to open the wall, just as Ricky had shown her all those months before. The great mare neighed. She stomped her right foot three times and began to run.

9.

"Look!"
"Over there, do you see?"
"Is it real?"
"Yes, so beautiful!"

Acknowledgments

My deepest thanks to Kelly Joseph and Deborah Ghim. Your care and guidance with this book has meant the world to me. Thank you to the whole team at McClelland & Stewart and Astra House.

Ellen Levine and Audrey Crooks, thank you for taking a chance on me and for all the support along the way. Thank you to Arthur Flowers for setting it all in motion.

I am indebted to so many of my teachers and classmates over the years, among them Annie Trizna, Dan Peck, Erin Gravely, Vt Hung, George Saunders, Dana Spiotta, Jonathan Dee, Mary Karr, and Arthur Flowers (again!).

Thank you to the Barnet-Mitchell-Spector-Styles-Swaim family and to Steff Schimeck, my most lovely tall friend.

Nothing in life or writing would be possible without Jacob. Your tireless support and encouragement is one of my life's greatest blessings. Lastly, thank you to Henry, who slept by my side as I put the finishing touches on this book. Perhaps one day you will read it and tell me what you think.